Part 1: Princes of the Tower

Chapter 1

"He is possessed by the Devil -- you have cursed him Lord Nameless!" shouted one of the young monks, all of them crowding a few paces back from the novice whose limbs moved in convulsions, his body stiffening and shaking upon the floor, his face contorted hideously such that the youths surrounding him where struck with fear at the sight of poor Norris Veysen.

"It is the falling sickness," said an older monk, pushing past the gathered throng, "get away all of you, someone ought send for the Abbot. You," he took one of the novices by the arm and pointed him to the door while the rest continued to stare in paralysed fear.

"Lord Nameless has punished him, he did I saw it!" came a shout from the back of the room.

Someone grabbed Arthamaeus and flung him forward such that he stumbled against the epileptic boy upon the floor.

A muddle of shouting and curses erupted from the crowd.

"What is going on here!" it was the Abbot's voice, at which a hush gradually fell. By then the boys who lay on the floor had managed to pull themselves onto their feet, with Arthamaeus supporting the youth who wiped the drool from his face with his sleeve, trying to compose himself and brush the dust from his cloak.

"Again I ask -- what market fair spectacle has summoned this congregation of reprobates?"

They all lowered their faces in contrition, although a whisper here and there was half-heard by the old man who paced like a wolf about to choose his victim.

"Answer me when I speak to you," the Abbot's voice grew sharp, causing Arthamaeus to look up at him and see the cane poised.

"Yes, sir," he said in a half-audible voice.

"Speak up"

"Yes, sir"

"Yes, sir what?"

The young monks around them laughed.

"Silence!" the Abbot turned like a dragon, surveying the room. "I do not have time for your games -- get back to your duties, all of you. All except Arthamaeus and Brother Corbyn"

Slowly the chapel was emptied of idle onlookers, moving reluctantly towards the door with many glances still following the Abbot who dragged his two prisoners to his study for interrogation. It was a small dimly-lit room with light filtering through a lancet widow of stained glass above a heavy carved desk strewn with manuscripts. Since the Abbot's informers at court brought news of the monastery's pending disillusion, he and the senior monks were set to take inventory of the libraries and smuggle away the most valuable of volumes, while leaving enough not to incriminate them.

"What were you doing in the chapel Arthamaeus, have you not told me recently that you have no interest in the company of your brothers, nor in the word of God?"

Arthamaeus continued to stare mutely at the stone floor.

"Look at me when I address you," said the Abbot's voice close to his ear, as a the tip of his wooden cane raised the boy's chin to force him to see a pair of eyes -- fierce darting black eyes which he met with perilous disdain.

"Or is it there, all written there in the dust -- the secret to your salvation," he struck the youth so suddenly that Arthamaeus staggered once more.

"You keep all of my secrets, sir, I have no more of my own to strike out," said Arthamaeus.

"They are no longer mine," he laughed bitterly, strangely, like one deprived of sleep -- he paced while his fingers toyed with the cane, as if wishing he had something to tear apart, "nor yours, oh no, someone else will deal with you soon enough, an adept in such matters -- you will have a new guardian, and the time could not have come soon enough, for you have overstayed your welcome"

"Who is the man who shall take over my guardianship, if I may ask?"

"Corbyn," his eyes fell on the slouching forgotten figure who anxiously and unobtrusively eavesdropped upon the conversation. "You may leave us, at once -- you have not suffered injury from this episode, have you? And no one had provoked you -- you may speak freely"

"N-no, Father Abbot," replied the boy. "I was just --"

"Good, no need to stand there -- get back to your duties," said the Abbot with a touch of impatience, "and next time, be more discreet. I do not want a scene"

After a cursory bow, the Abbot waited for Corbyn to shut the door behind himself, then he turned his attention back to Arthamaeus.

"No -- you may not ask. You will wait, it should be no more than a fortnight before he comes to collect you"

"M-my father?" his stomach twisted with a sense of vulnerability, as if preparing for a fatal strike.

"Not your father, God preserve him from beholding such a wretch," answered the Abbot, "he would be ashamed to know what kind of son was borne to him, therefore it is well that he is in the grave"

"Or might it have been God's punishment -- how did he die?" asked Arthamaeus, unable to hold back the words, for the Abbot missed no opportunity to hold up his father as a paragon of virtue, despite having produced a child out of wedlock and kept him hidden away since birth lest it should affect his reputation.

The Abbot only glared at him, and then went on. "One that is preserved from being hanged only by the reticence which is required for the sake of this monastery and the good families who send their children here to be raised under the Lord's protection. Remember that even beyond these walls, I will make sure that just punishment comes to you -- lest you think that you may threaten mine or your father's name with dishonour. No, hanging is too good for you, you ought be burned like any base-born witch, for such must have been your mother"

"You speak thus against her, yet you know nothing of her origins," said the youth coldly, taking the liberty of sitting down in the chair across from the Abbot.

"Proud as Lucifer," the old man laughed dryly, "I know more than you think -- now tell me, have you given consideration to the annuity since our last discussion?"

"Excuse me, but I wonder that you ask of me to grant you further powers over my property, given the fine treatment I have just received at this most worthy establishment, at such a time -- well, forgive me, but I cannot see how you might expect anything but a reiteration of my firm refusal"

"Ah, so you are as much of a fool as you are rumoured to be, unable to see that favours call for favours -- it is at times of greatest need that sinners are most inclined to make generous donations," smirked the Abbot with an air of condescension. "May I make it clear -- this is your last chance"

"You overestimate my need," replied Arthamaeus, "and my generosity, and my faith in you, Father Abbot to look after my interests -- and not your own, which are two opposing poles, as I see it. As you said, I am a sinner and a witch, and may the Devil look after me, unless he has received a better offer from my guardian and therefore deserted me at the last, although you take him for my constant ally. I depend only upon myself"

"Be careful of your insolence," the Abbot said slowly in a low tone, "you will find that your new master is a less tolerant man than I -- and if you had had a proper whiff of poverty you would temper your self-assurance"

…

"What is that you are working on Lord Nameless?" Norton, a lanky boy of about sixteen, leaned to peer down at the table where scraps of parchment were scattered in disarray.

"You are not supposed to be here," a young man with disorderly blond hair and a bruise on one cheek was arranging them in neat piles, still in an ill temper from his interview with the Abbot.

"Where you fairy-taken?" the boy pressed on, ignoring the mild reprimand whilst attempting to assist him with his work -- but the youth swatted his arm away.

"Aright then, no need to be angry with me -- you go on about it," he forced a half-mocking smile. "But I mind it when you do not answer, I am your superior and you are a disobedient one by reputation, I know your tricks Arthamaeus," he imitated the voice of the Abbot, "elf-led I mean, some call it elf-led, do you understand me, were you elf-led, impstricken, bewitched?" he persisted. "I really must know before you go, you are leaving soon, are you?"

"Let me leave me in peace, please," said Arthamaeus, not looking at him.

"I know such a thing once happened to a girl of my village -- she too had fair hair, those are the type which the elf King likes. Perhaps he was your father -- do you think that may be?"

"Yes," muttered Arthamaeus. "Now please leave me in peace before I curse you"

"You are lying, you cannot do curses," Norton furrowed his brows, annoyed that the older youth should give in so easily, not taking the matter seriously. "The Abbot would have had a tail by now"

"Two," said Arthamaeus under his breath.

"Your nose is bleeding you know, I heard you got a whipping, too," he kicked at a blood-stained handkerchief on the floor, "there is still some smeared on your face. You better wash it before the Abbot sees"

Arthamaeus said nothing, picking up the handkerchief and casting it into the fire of the hearth which burned in the study. It was the one that his attacker dropped before running away -- he had no need of evidence, it made no difference, the older monks rarely got punished.

"Could have given me that," said Norton.

Arthamaeus reached into the pocket of his cloak and flung a new handkerchief towards him.

"That is too good for me, and it has your initial embroidered on it"

Arthamaeus scowled, stooping down to pick up the handkerchief and stuffing it back into his pocket.

"Do you think it will be worse here or there?"

"I probably will not see you again to tell you"

"Will you miss me?" teased Norton.

"Not particularly"

"Nor I you, but may I have some of your books, those that you are not taking with you?"

"The Abbot would not like that"

"He does not have to know," he patted him on the shoulder"

Arthamaeus sighed heavily and threw the remaining stack of papers into the fire.

"What were those for?"

"For banishing covetous pick-pockets," he answered.

"I never pick-pocketed you," he looked offended.

"And why is that?"

"I do not want the falling sickness, my grandmother once saw a boy who had it who bit his tongue so hard during his --"

"It is well that I am leaving then," said Arthamaeus. "You and everyone else here may keep their tongue and use it as they see fit. Say what you please, as you can see I too shall go about my work and am not in fear of any master"

"Then the Abbot has not beaten you hard enough," he remarked. "Have you heard about the dungeons here?"

"No," replied Arthamaeus, "what use would they be, this entire place is like a dungeon"

"You have it better than you know, he does let you get away with much more than we can," said Norton. "Not that he has any fondness for you, but if any of us spoke to him like you did we would be cast out in an instant, and he even lets you keep these books," he picked one up from the table, which Arthamaeus quickly snatched from his hands and placed it into the large travelling trunk.

"As long as I keep them out of sight," said Arthamaeus.

"Will you not leave something to remember you by, I did keep watch for you that one time when you sneaked out to examine the holy relics"

"And I kept watch for you when you raided the larder, I think we were even on that score," said Arthamaeus, "but you may have this"

He took out a bag of sugar almonds, pistachios and dates.

"Is it from your secret admirer?" Norton sniggered, reaching into the bag and taking a handful of sweets. "Imagine if he sees me with these"

"I would avoid him in a dark corridor, eat them in your chamber at night"

"What, do you think he will try to kiss me too?"

"Just get Hoffman right in the nose and run fast if it comes to that, he will leave you be then"

"Too afraid I would tell, I bet," he smirked.

"You make a fine business of telling, you already have a reputation as the Abbot's spy"

"And yet you do not mind having me around"

"It is more that I cannot get rid of you"

"I will remember you fondly Arthamaeus," he gave him an earnest look, "this has been a fond friendship of mutual interest. I will send you a bag of sweets, once we are both old men"

"I never took you to be sentimental"

"I am not, but you are an interesting sort of fellow, and everyone enjoyed seeing you and the Abbot do battle, we do not get much in the way of diversions here -- I will miss it all"

"I will leave you a book too then, in that case," he debated whether to give him a book of ethics by Aristotle or a grimoire certain to earn him a beating.

"That is mighty generous of you -- I am not awfully good at reading, I only pretend most times when I can get away with it, so may it be one that will sell decently well?"

"You are terrible Norton, you must know that"

"Oh yes, everyone is in their own way, but at least I do not put on airs like some here do, and since you are leaving I do not mind telling you all kinds of things, after all you are a decent sort of fellow -- I like that about you Arthamaeus, I can tell you are of the same blood, you do what you need to do and are ready to pay the cost of it rather than reform"

"It is not quite like that"

"How not?"

"I do not mean to provoke him, the Abbot I mean, I just could not survive here pretending all of my life that we are any closer to something sacred than the people beyond these walls -- most of us are here because our families have little need of another mouth to feed, or have themselves transgressed and sent us here to make amends"

"In a sense, yes," Norton sat down, taking another handful of sweets.

"Are you finished packing yet?" a voice came from the door. "Norton, what are you doing here? You should be at mass"

Arthamaeus was not finished packing, finding to his own surprise that the thought of leaving did not rest easy in his conscience. As he lay in bed that night, he though of the Abbot, as he had known him some years ago. The man had sought to make him his protégé and had shared with him manuscripts on music, science, mathematics and philosophy which might not be met with approval for one of his vocation.

Through these common interests which the master sought to instil in the pupil there grew a confidence between them, which was only put to strain by a further secrecy surrounding Arthamaeus's lineage.

Being of a wilful nature and aware of the preferential treatment which he received from the Abbot, the young man pressed him for further freedoms, such as to be granted leave from the monastery to travel. But the Abbot could not condone aimless wanderings, repeating to him that one so guileless, and thus sheltered from the sinfulness of the outside world, would fair poorly. Whether his guardian truly believed in these words, or was oblivious to the goings-on within the monastery walls, Arthamaeus could not be certain -- sometimes men shroud the truth from themselves when it is inconvenient to their conception of how things ought to be. In any case, he had other ambitions for the boy, entertaining hopes of sending him to Rome which were ultimately disappointed.

It was with a mixture of guilt and regret that Arthamaeus reflected upon his past transgressions, believing that his better nature had been overcome by pride for what may well be a falsehood -- that his father was a man of nobility and learning, and that one day he would be summoned to take his place as heir to a great estate.

It was not the title and wealth which drew him in and of itself, but the liberty which came with it, being of a nature which opposed the strict and monotonous routine of monastic life.

He likewise found it difficult to be in the constant company of others, perhaps a trait which he had taken from the Abbot, preferring to converse with men in their distilled form, through their writing handed down to him, forcing no reply or obligation.

Yet there were times when he longed for the closeness of a like spirit, as is described in Plato's Symposium, in Aristotle's conception of friendship in its ideal form -- this he had once projected onto the Abbot until mistrust had severed their ties.

It was too late to reproach himself for his impudence, or to blame the Abbot for what he took for greed and zealous ambition -- further disbelieving the urgent necessity for raising funds in order to exempt the monastery from dissolution under the new laws of Henry VIII.

The youth did not credit that such a thing could ever take place, that the populace would not abide such an offence to religion from their King, who style himself as a devout and righteous man, that these were temporary measures only --- thinking instead that the Abbot deceived him in order to exhort money from his rightful inheritance.

If only he had known what a pittance this was in truth, and the extent to which the comfort in which he had lived was the product of the Abbot's guilty conscience, stemming from a long-standing friendship with his father and a certain breach of good faith which he hoped the youth would keep buried.

Just when there seemed hope of reconciliation after Arthamaeus fell to calamity during a pilgrimage, news came that several monks had been poisoned and suspicion fell upon the boy. It was only years later that the Abbot would learn the truth of these events.

Chapter 2

The horses reared as a flaming torch was thrown upon the roof of the coach, two men rushing forth to get hold of the driver, stabbing a knife into his back as he turned to look about him. Cromwell got out to inspect the body of the assailant, one of whom had been slain by his guardsmen, the other by having made his escape back into shadows of the ancient woodland which flanked the uneven road.

"Shall we follow him, sir?" asked one of his men.

"No, it is late and we need not waste time," Cromwell had a notion where he had come from and where he was going.

"Indeed it is a dark night and being strangers to these parts, I am not inclined to give chase," muttered the tall man with a pointed ginger hair.

"We will take the body with us and enquire if someone at the abbey may recognize him," said his brother, who served as both solider and cook.

"That will be a nice present for the host," remarked the groom. "Aright, haul him in"

"I reckon they will see in him a familiar face, if you watch carefully for the signs of recognition"

Two strong fellows hoisted the body into the wagon which carried provisions and various manuscripts which Cromwell had sought to salvage from the desecration which had been done before he could take control of matters.

It seemed not long ago since the The Act of Suppression was passed, by which the King could add to his coffer the incomes of middling monasteries, dissolving the religious houses and, as gracefully as he could manage, sending away the monks and nuns with pensions.

But there were some who would not go easily. These had to be dealt with -- and expediently. It was to Cromwell that the King entrusted the task of doing it tactually.

It had come to the King's attention that monasteries had long ago ceased to follow the strict traditions of religious asceticism and had instead become a refuge for indolence and vice. Despite the interests and arguments in favour of doing away with these errant abbeys, Cromwell forewarned him of the difficulties which would stand in his way -- for one, the monasteries were lax landlords, avoiding disputes with their tenants so as to discourage uprisings, yet it was the King's will to increase rents for those abbeys which remained, while doing away with the feeble management which had long been the status quo.

To carry out these orders, Cromwell was to see personally to the dissolutions, a task to which he could not go to with a clear conscience, thinking to himself that despite these accusations against the abbeys, where may a vagrant traveller, ailing man or undesirable turn to but the hospitality of such places as these, whose lot it was to care for the dregs of society -- such a one he might have been if his fortunes had turned a different way.

Yet as reports reached him from his commissioners and spies, eager to find cause for contempt for which they would be well remunerated -Cromwell would ill-conceal his coldness upon greeting the superiors responsible for the downfall of their reputations through scandal and corruption.

In obedience to the King's urgent need for finances, it was not expedient to thoroughly investigate the truth of each of these claims, nor would refuting them suffice to save a monastery from its fate if its resources were called upon.

Soon the day would come when the abbots of Colchester, Glastonbury and Reading would be sentenced to death for treason.

Cromwell dwelt upon the consequences of these misdeeds, where it was uncertain how much good and how much evil had been thus struck down -- but he was willing to make himself an unpopular figure in the eyes of the multitude, taking on the risks and rewards alongside his King to whom he was beholden for his ascent to power.

He would do carry out his orders with the efficiency of a man of business -- a collector of debts owed, long overdue. Of necessity, he would limit the extent of his mercy, and yet endeavour to preserve that which was found worthy. Three new libraries would be constructed to house the monastic books which would fall into the hands of the King, saving as many as he could from destruction by those agents of his whose path was obstructed by obstinate monks who still held on to hopes beyond their ability to bribe the King's officials.

Yet many yielded easily enough, seeking instead to flee with their valuables while there was still time.

Peculiar tales were exchanged among the motley company during the long journey from court, of how Thomas Horner, the steward to Abbot Richard Whiting of Glastonbury had sent the deeds of a dozen or so manor houses hidden in a large Christmas pie. They laughed at the time, but such desperate attempts were common enough, the monks were growing evermore ingenious in their strivings to persevere something of the property which was soon to be taken from them, dispersing it near and far, drawing the line only where it might cost them their lives.

"We are nearly there," Cromwell heard a man shout from somewhere close by, rousing him from his sleep, or rather, his stupor of exhaustion. It was pitch dark when he opened his eyes, rubbing them and his neck, feeling stiff and sore.

He could see the silhouette of the abbey against the deep blue of the sky, thinking to himself how there was a fascination in the remoteness of these old stones, remembering the naive fondness with which he once imagined himself taking on the life of a hermit monk -- if only to thus shun the ambition which led him further and further from a restful mind since the sickness had carried away his wife and children. Swept onward by the transitory nature of life, he sought purpose and immortality as the King's familiar, wishing to behold for himself the inner natures of the rulers of the land when fortune brings them high and low, blurring the lines between nobility and baseness, honour and frailty, and showing them to be no more than mortal men.

While he commanded, while he felt himself in control, Cromwell felt untouched by fear for past or future, seeing merely the obstacles which must be removed, the ciphers which must be decoded as he navigated the intricacies of King Henry's court. He saw no enemies or allies, but only men and women whose motives he sought to divine and anticipate, using them to see to the end what would come of the will of his regent, who saw the world as his to command by birthright -- acting as his Mephistopheles, Cromwell would ensure that his desires and their consequences were brought into being. He would serve Henry's interests, first and foremost, and learn what kind of legacy the King of England was made for.

Even while miles were traversed to separate himself from this centre of power, the half-remembered conversations he had had in the company of the King and his fawning disciples still left their unpleasant echoes -- proud stout figures upon which one of his station was obliged to oblige, to flatter, to appease, to forget that they and he are of like flesh and blood, walking amongst them but not of them -- a necessary evil.

Upon their errands he would be sent over land and sea, in all weathers, against all odds -- they expected much and gave much, if all went in their favour.

Yet he did not envy nor admire these powers which he served, or at least not often, remembering that if he had the will to do them harm, he would manage it through the King -- he too could shape the rise and fall of lords. As for his own fate, he would lay down his cards, one by one, and see how long he could play at the royal gambling table before the day of execution. This he took for granted, as any man does who takes upon himself a dangerous trade. One cannot go into battle half-heartedly. He fastened his coat close about him and pulled on his gloves, preparing himself mentally for the confrontation which was likely to come.

There was little doubt that the monks were forewarned of his arrival, and yet, they passed through the threshold of the abbey with little in the way of a reception, either ingratiating or hostile. Unless of course the dead man they brought could be counted as an ambassador of their intentions.

A monk who had stood on duty held the door for them in silent greeting, his face a perfect semblance of sombre piety, looking furtively at the solders who accompanied Cromwell.

The sound of music, followed by the words of a sermon wafted through the abbey with the scent of incense.

From somewhere not far off, Cromwell heard the voice of a man preaching, a powerful booming echo which told of the Advent -- the forthcoming 'Day of Terror', the 'Misery of Devils', the approach of the god, when the dead were believed to rise from their graves and await judgement.

Several dozen monks were listening patiently in rows, perhaps envisioning the fiery torments of the hereafter or hungering after supper. "To be born for the sake of all mankind, at once he chose kinsmen for himself, all just as he wanted, and he decided that he would be born, exactly where he wished--," the Abbot's voice droned on with a pedagogue's clarity over the rows of bald heads. Cromwell waited until this congregations finished its business, his eyes scanning over the bored or stern looking faces of the men, young and old, in their plain wool garments.

One of them stood out in his dark blue velvet and golden chain, whose full head of sandy blonde hair was still unshorn. This youth of noble mien stood at a distance from the preaching Abbot, holding in his hands a box which he later learned contained the relics of a saint -- a fingernail or a rib, he could not recall which.

It was for him that he had come all this way, he had no doubt. The bastard son of Thomas More.

Chapter 3

A tall monk with a thick beard of grisly black hair led Cromwell through the corridors to the private study of the Abbot, who pretended not to have seen him.

Cromwell sat down in the chair before his desk, watching demurely as he dipped his quill in ink and wrote out another line in a cramped black scrawl.

"I hope that I am not disturbing you," said Cromwell, unfazed.

The Abbot set down his quill and peered at him with an assumed look of surprise. "Cromwell -- Brother Thobias informs me that you have had a long journey. To what do I owe this pleasure?" he smiled provokingly.

"Do you mean the pleasure of testing one another's patience?"

"I suppose you have come for the boy," he got up and took from an oak cabinet a half empty decanter of wine, setting it down between them alongside two small chalices engraved in silver.

"Yes," he answered. "As I have written"

"I have not received any messages but Brother Thobias has informed me of your purpose," he said, filling the chalices. "He also tells me that you have found a rouge and brought us his corpse"

"That is not quite the account I would give -- one of my men knows him to be of your monastery, he is suspected of acting upon your orders," said Cromwell.

"Ah," said the Abbot, his smile returning to him.

"What might you say to account for this man's actions, if brought to trial?" Cromwell leaned back in the chair, taking the wine offered.

"Nothing, it is too late in the night to talk of dead men," said the Abbot, his stiff smile still upon his wrinkled countenance.

"Then let us speak about the living, what can you tell me about the boy?" he asked.

"The young man is a difficult case," the Abbot answered without hesitation. "While he was still a boy, we had some hope of reforming his character, for he showed signs of a curious mind and hard-working disposition, but he as proven himself as obstinate as his father, only in the direction of heresy, showing little reverence towards his colleagues and masters. We have sought to enlist his help and yours in preserving this monastery, but it seems there is little more that can be done, unless I am mistaken master Cromwell?"

"And what form of heresy has he shown himself partial too, if I may ask?" Cromwell enquired.

"He speaks to the young monks, teaches them the dark arts which he practices in his study whenever he is left alone," the Abbot began, taking obvious relish in providing this confabulated narrative. "We have caught his servant among the lay-brothers going on errands for him to procure forbidden literature, hiding it beneath the floorboards. The man has also confessed to theft from the storerooms, taking dangerous ingredient worthy of a poisoner. After exceptional efforts had been made at persuasion, as well as making trial of all the punishments that his rank would allow for," he broke into a dry cough, "-- I can only conclude that the any progress made was found temporary and insufficient"

Cromwell attempted to interrupt him in this account but was given no heed.

"In fact," the Abbot went on with vehemence, "I reckon he relishes the torture, blaspheming that by using such means I bring the house of god into disrepute, who gave free will so that we may question all and doubt all, or words along such lines -- he thinks himself worthy to interpret the holy works and addresses his superiors with impudence," muttered the old man, shaking his head. "He is yours now, do with him what you will. I have heard that you do not vex yourself with the state of your spiritual self, and so he will go where he shall no longer be troubled. At the house of Cromwell the devil's art thrives"

"The devil's art, sir?" Cromwell echoed his look of mocking surprise.

"Here," he took from a drawer of his desk a parcel and threw it to Cromwell, who caught it by the string. Untying the wrapping paper, he found a bundle of paper scraps covered from end to end in a tiny script, as well as drawings of human figures in outlandish settings and costumes, or contraptions of dubious purpose in the company of equations, serpents or winged beasts.

"Mathematics, it seems," Cromwell, held one of the sheets up to the light of the candle. "And that other fiend, mythology"

"I confess that I had been taken by it in my time, but if these occupations are what he neglects his spiritual duties for --"

"Any other would have long been banished from these precincts as unworthy of their vocation," Cromwell interjected, nodding sympathetically.

"Yes," spat the Abbot, "surely we will be saved a fortune in the cost of parchment -- if, of course, you will oblige us by taking him and leaving this house of God unravaged, which I have little optimism to hope for," he ventured a final appeal, hoping that his speech had done good to convey a reputation for severity, piety, and economy, contradictory to the slander of a certain Brother Easton who had been brought on as a spy, or so the Abbot suspected. "I dare say one of his evil prophecies will come to pass," he pressed his palms together and gave Cromwell an expectant look, signalling his turn to speak.

"I believe that you sense by now how your efforts to placate and bribe my agents have been misplaced, and yet you deign to entertain me with young More's foibles," asked Cromwell, "let me hear then of these prophecies"

"H-he tells fortunes as well," the Abbot tried to suppress the words upon his lips, feeling that he had just swallowed something bitter. Of necessity, he went on with what he had started. "Although some have reported that it is merely in mockery at those who are superstitious, who wish to know the hour when they will be taken away from their life of toil. Needless to say, he has made himself unwelcome at this establishment. I am at my wit's end. The father is a decent man, of course, more than decent"

"More than generous," suggested Cromwell.

"Yes," muttered the Abbot reluctantly. "His family has helped support this monastery for generations, as you are aware, and the sire would be ashamed to learn of what his son has become, although his instructions were clear that he left the accountability for his education with me and I have done for him all that a mortal man could with little recompense"

"No correspondence has ever passed between them, by your knowledge?" asked Cromwell.

"None that I am aware of, although who can say what this one has contrived," he took back the papers and cast them into the fire to give Cromwell a start. "Hitherto, I had kept this as evidence, but there is more then need be and it has served its purpose -- you will find him at it at all hours of the evening, instead of at his prayers"

"Yes, you have said so already," Cromwell refilled the man's wine glass. "Although I myself do not object to some of these lines of boyish curiosity, indeed it is curious that you permit it, Father Abbot. Or was there a time when you encouraged Arthamaeus's precocious nature? It is of interest how the youth provides himself with such rare works, for I have my informants, without complicity elsewhere. *He* must have a patron"

The Abbot coughed into his handkerchief, buying himself time to consider the question, and then furrowed his brow, looking straight at Cromwell with a resolute expression. "Like I said, I have too much to look after to keep a watch on him," he raised his arms and heaved a sigh, "in the circumstances, finding him immovable in his defiance, I have no recourse but to see him not as a monk but as a boarder. How may I make this clear to you Master Secretary, I have marked him as a lost cause a year after he came of age and attempted to escape whilst accompanying the monks on pilgrimage -- nearly drowned himself, the poor fool.

In this way, there is less disturbance for the other monks and I need not waste further effort and nerves, for he will keep to himself -- as long as he does not set the Abbey on aflame, although he might have thus saved you the trouble, it is no concern of mine what he does or what happens to him.

Clearly my days are few in this realm and I will be stripped of my duties, but that is another matter. My beard has grown white by him and I am exhausted, forgive me if you think I that I have conceded his soul too soon," he sighed again, pouring himself another cup and pacing by his desk. "Perhaps you will do better by him"

"I shall endeavour to find a suitable place for him in the service of the King," said Cromwell, standing up. "Is there anything more which I must know? Now is your time to speak Father Abbot"

"You criticize me that I have granted him these exceptional privileges, I can see it in your hawkish gaze," the Abbot said suddenly, whilst slowly unfolding a handkerchief to blow his nose, wavering in his subconsciousness between grovelling and causing mild gestures of offence to one who he would prefer to strike down with his letter-knife. "Excuse me. On the pilgrimage he nearly drowned himself in the river after the last whipping inflicted by Brother Thobias," he felt obliged to add, "I do not know what induced me to take him with us, he took it as no more than tramping over the countryside.

But the other monks, well, something must have happened for they tried to set him on fire while he slept. His legs and thighs are covered in burns now so you will see he at times will walk with a limp, or at least he did when I last saw him two years ago -- I make a point not to see him -- but he is an unfortunate case, do not misunderstand me, a most unfortunate fool," he tried to read a reaction from Cromwell but was left unsatisfied. "I could not get truth of the the damnable lot of them," the Abbot went on, "each man protecting the other -- had some of of them punished under suspicion of unseemly relations, but it was too late you see"

"And what happened then, when you returned to the monastery?" asked Cromwell, suspecting that old man's rambling account was made to stall him while the monks prepared the precincts for inspection and smuggled away remaining artefacts -- a concession which he was willing to grant them. He would make his own interrogation of the youth, when the time came. "Did the others make any attempts upon his life again?"

"He took to the guidance of Saint Benedict," said the Abbot, "deaf and dumb to all, docile as a lamb, but I feared then for him more than before, when his mischief was plain for all too see -- boyish rebelliousness I knew how to deal with but then I sensed something else would come of it that would bear no good. When I was summoned from my bed in the middle of the night, it was his name on my lips. Someone had poisoned the communal meal, something slipped into the pottage most likely. Six of the monks were dead by morning and the rest could barely get up for a fortnight. I wondered if I ought to punish him but it could not be proven so what could I do. And the boy's father, what would he say? Debts had to be paid," the Abbot pronounced.

Cromwell conjured another look of sympathy as the Abbott went on, commiserating for himself as well, as he wondered what kind of obligation he had gotten himself into. As for Thomas More, the Abbot would be sorely disappointed as to the prospects of him paying out any debts, living or dead, but perhaps he had something hidden away for the youth which Cromwell had yet to uncover. He would remember to investigate this question after he left the abbey.

"I pitied him, for he is not without wits -- when he was a lad I would say to him 'you do not lack in virtues, only in the good sense to use them'," he shook his bony finger at an imaginary Arthamaeus, "and I put him to work at the copying -- a fine hand at illumination, he takes to that sort of thing," the Abbot conceded, putting away the decanter. "Who can say what ought to have been done, but I believe it is too late for reform. If you can keep him under control he may make for you a decent lawyers' clerk, for it seems to be the sort of work he will sit at when he is a man, having no sign of a spiritual vocation here. Unsociable and over-proud, you will find him, but if anyone can set him low, I believe you could"

"Thank you for this enlightening account, Father Abbot," said Cromwell. "You will be accorded the income due to you from More's estate for your troubles, I will take care of him from now on." There he sought to conclude their interview, thinking it was time to retire before the dawn came.

"A small recompense, but we are grateful all the same," the Abbot likewise stood up and made a slight bow.

…

…

Cromwell heard someone attempt the door of his chamber in the middle of the night and felt glad to have left it firmly bolted. He wondered how the others of his company had faired. Rising early on the following morning, he made no mention of the event but asked to see the Abbot after concluding the inventory and assessment of the monastery. The last matter of business which remained was to collect his ward.

"Will you care to see him now?" asked Brother Godric, his heavy eyes showing a sleepless night.

"Yes," replied Cromwell. "Please take me to master More"

"Watch your step, these stones have been scrubbed recently -- and it is best not to call him that, call him Arthamaeus," suggested the elder as he walked around the large bureau of engraved oak and took with him a ring of keys, dangling in his bony hand like the sound of a tambourine.

"It is my intention that he should know his father," replied Cromwell. The monk said nothing, leading him down a corridor and up a flight of steps.

In one of the towers of the abbey, a musty narrow staircase led to a set of chambers, most of which were storage rooms for half-decaying furniture, or so the monk said, trying one key and then another. Cromwell made a note to revisit these rooms, in the case that they had been missed by his agents.

Before he could find the right key, the door opened and a young man with an expression of alarm staggered back to let them pass.

"You have a guest, Arthamaeus," the monk announced, putting the keys back into the pocket of his robe. "This is Master Cromwell, your guardian until you complete your apprenticeship in his service. Prior to his death, your father was made aware of you fairing poorly here and therefore has chosen for you another path which he hopes will better suit you, a most painful decision. I leave it to Master Cromwell to guide you through the particulars of your station," he paused. "I wish you well Arthamaeus, may you always seek to do good in the world and be a figure of God's mercy, serving him first and foremost as your true master," his eyes resting for a moment on Cromwell with the righteous look of a martyr, "Soon we shall all be making our own ways, some as brothers, some forever parted, but may we each continue to do good works, each to his abilities. Go with my blessing and the blessing of our Lord"

Arthamaeus acknowledged the monk's words by bowing his head, feeling a bashfulness which came with the guilty knowledge that he had been a disappointment to a man who once had faith in him, wondering how much the Abbot had told him.

When he looked up he saw that Godric was descending the staircase and another man was passing by him, holding a candle, with Arthamaeus looking furtively between Cromwell and and the Abbot who had come to join them with parting words.

"We are not conspiring against you my dear boy," said the Abbot sarcastically, "your prayers have been answered and the devil of London is here to take you away. Pack your things, quick, quick" he waved his cane at the heaps of papers strewn about the floor.

Obediently, the young man went to make himself busy, as not to have to look his visitors in the eyes, something which he seemed to struggle with, Cromwell observed.

Chapter 4

A princely dinner was set in the Abbot's private rooms while the monks shared their last supper in the communal hall, bidding their adieus before final preparations and travelling arrangements were made to seek employment elsewhere, for those who could not count on a pension from the King.

Geese, roast pigeon, partridges, eels and succulent pig on a spit, oranges and dates from Catalonia, and cheeses from Sicily. Before the Abbot, Thomas Cromwell, and his ward, a choice selection of these seasonal delicacies was ushered in by the cook, perhaps the last show of ecclesiastic magnificence which the soon to be abandoned abbey would see before being allowed to fall to ruin -- the end of an era, reminding Cromwell of his days in the service of Cardinal Wolsey.

"Arthamaeus," said the Abbot, looking up at the youth and setting down his cutting knife "do not look so forlorn when there is fresh venison upon your plate and wine in your glass -- you will offend your host by such sullen looks"

"Forgive me for my distractedness, Father Abbot," said the young man, making an effort to cut into the piece of flesh upon his plate.

"Do not tell me you have lost your appetite at the thought of finally leaving this place," the Abbot said sardonically, "we know that you would have sold your soul to Beelzebub not to see these walls again. He had threatened to summon the good gentleman into our company us just last week if we did not let him out"

The Abbot swallowed down a morsel, followed by a gulp of wine.

"How is that, sir?" asked Cromwell as he carved. "I see that you make frequent reference to Master Beelzebub, but perhaps the youth would not follow him -- has the bargain been made or may it be that the gentleman wears out his hooves for nothing?"

"Arthamaeus," the Abbot turned to the young man, raising his brows and offering a strained grin which had something of an unplanned malevolent effect, "as we have discussed, you will go willingly with our Master Secretary -- you will not make a spectacle of yourself. May I presume as much from you?"

"Yes, Father Abbot, you may presume that, and anything else which extends hope that we might make a pleasing and agreeable impression upon our guest -- for I believe I have no influence over your abilities of presumption, which are as boundless as the mercy of our Saviour when it comes to discovering the transgressions of wily disobedient novices," said the youth, whose eyes darted to Cromwell for an instant before falling coolly upon his old master.

"Insolence," the Abbot hissed under his breath. "Now --- now what was it, oh yes, our little story -- there was a time when someone had locked him in his tower, I presumed, the Lord forgive me, that he did not wish to come down by his own volition, too preoccupied as always, but then I received some strange complaints and grew suspicious -- by then the shouting must have subsided. The account brought to me was that some of the young novices had taken the key to the tower and managed some mischief, locking Arthamaeus in his chamber for a prank. Our poor Arthamaeus"

"An unfortunate incident, how did you deal with it, if I may ask?" Cromwell glanced at the youth, who furrowed his brow but said nothing.

"Oh the usual, a sound whipping must have cured them of it," said the Abbot, "I do look out for the boy, ungrateful as he is"

"I am certain that you do," Cromwell lifted his wine cup.

The event happened many years ago and similar things were frequent enough among the other boys, thought Arthamaeus, but he could see what the Abbot was doing -- currying pity and contempt for him with his new master, as if he had been a poor helpless victim in need of protection. It annoyed him to be thought of as one who could not stand up for himself, but at the same time, to show himself a vengeful spirit may not be advisable either.

He could not help but feel anxious about the sort of impression he was making, furthermore wondering what role he would be obliged to play once he fell under the guardianship of this stranger, who did not strike him as a particularly amiable man as he looked at Cromwell's stern countenance. It might have once been a handsome one in a sombre way; his high cheekbones lending him an elegant dignity which he did not associate with the jocular village blacksmith. His clothing reminding him of a well-to-do banker, rather than a courtier, with the manners of one who did not suffer fools gladly while subtly taking everyone's measure.

His first impression was not completely unbiased, for this was the man who he would overhear the Abbot and other monks talk about as the origin of the monastery's calamities, whose enforcement of the King's capricious policies was sweeping across the countryside like a plague.

Still, Arthamaeus was flattered to see the man's half-veiled smirk at a proficient imitation of the Abbot's pretentious sonorous voice.

"I wonder what sort of place you are sending me to once you are done here," asked the Abbot, with a forced casual air, believing that the time had come to discuss his own situation. "I dare say the ecclesiastic community will not be pleased by these doings, although I am glad enough to hand over the management of these prodigal sons to another better suited to the work of a schoolmaster"

"Is it not what you expected of your vocation?" asked Cromwell, sparing him his answer.

"My father had been a schoolmaster and I swore to give that path a wide berth, but here we are," sighed the Abbot, taking a miniature chalice of pistachio cream and placing it on his dish.

"There is no escaping one's ancestry"

"You have managed it," he smirked, "were you not a blacksmith's son?"

"Now I am the anvil"

The Abbot returned his thin smile, pondering over his plate for a moment before looking up.

"That is very much how I feel, that someone is constantly striking away at my soul while I try to make something of brittle substances -- Arthamaeus, tell our guest here of all the progress you have made"

"In what domain, sir?" the youth made a polite half-smile.

"Purgatory, if we are optimistic," said the Abbot, his hands unknowingly fidgeting with his napkin.

"If the angels are lenient they would allow me to remain on earth as a disembodied spirit," said Arthamaeus.

"What strange things you say, only to be shocking," muttered the Abbot. "Instead of reciting what we had practised," again he smiled weakly at Cromwell for reassurance. "Do you think the birds need know their songs for their melodies to be like a balm to the soul? Perhaps you would like to hear Arthamaeus sing in Latin, he was one of our best choir boys, but alas such art is of a fleeting nature. It was for his voice that I first invested my time in him, hoping to raise him as learned gentleman like his father, but with a deeper appreciation for beauty -- cultivating his natural talents by the influence of the Italian masters. I dare say I overestimated my protégé -- but I will let you judge for yourself, Master Secretary. You, who have travelled far, understand these things better than I"

"You are most poetic, sir," said Arthamaeus. "Perhaps you will grace us with your singing instead, if music is like wine and grows more refined with time"

The Abbot swallowed hard, not intending for a repartee with the youth in front of Cromwell, who took in the scene with a bemused expression.

"I am certain that the cawing of the rooks is no sound for the supper table of a gentleman, as you will soon be a gentleman Arthamaeus, under Master Cromwell's tutelage -- so behave like one"

The Abbot then stood up and raised his glass for another toast to Cromwell, who was by then wearied by these efforts of false civility which seemed to be the universal mood at table.

"Flattery does not suit you, Father Abbot," he said after the man finished his oration, "alas, no cloying words will make amends for defying the King's orders, but may we part as gentlemen and there conclude this bountiful feast," Cromwell raised his glass,thinking of preparations which had to be made before he could depart.

"Oh but you have not sampled the pudding yet," suggested the Abbot.

"I am entirely satisfied with the cold shoulder of roast and cannot have a morsel more, you may leave the rest with your people"

Arthamaeus felt the precarious tension between the two men and wondered what he ought to say, if anything at all. He did not know the customs proper at table, and had likely already broken them by returning blow for blow the insult done to him by the Abbot -- a part of him still undecided whether his old guardian was with him or against him, holding onto old grudges and unsubstantiated crimes.

"Master Cromwell, what does it mean to be a gentleman?" Arthamaeus summoned his courage to address the King's minister. "Is it true that you had been born a blacksmith?"

"It is true," replied Cromwell.

"Then what advice would you give one who wishes to rise in the world but is without the advantages of wealth and noble birth?" he asked, a question which the Abbot found over-brazen, by the look of his strained ingratiating smile.

"That which Daedalus gave to Icarus"

"What are the signs that one approaches too close to the Sun, our King?"

"When wax melts," he replied, filling the youth's wine cup.

Arthamaeus looked between him and the Abbot, wondering if this was a rebuff of his question, the latter looked likewise at a loss, and an uncomfortable silence fell between them for a moment.

"When your wings begin to melt -- when you begin to fall," spoke the Abbot at last, "do you recall the allegory Arthamaeus? Icarus's wings of feathers and wax -- he means it allegorically you see"

"I mean it figuratively, actually," said Cromwell, "when you begin to fall, it is often too late. When one receives news that letters are being intercepted and opened by the King's agents, that is the sign that suspicion has fallen upon a courtier and he risks royal disfavour by proceeding further upon the enterprise which had aroused these fears of disloyalty"

"And do your messages arrive safety Master Cromwell, or is it difficult to know?" the Abbot enquired, feeling sick to his stomach and wondering if he had been poisoned, or merely sampled too much of the wine in effort to settle his nerves. His mind slipped to the words of the Brother Harding, who had claimed that his amethyst preserves one from drunkenness, always wearing it for a night of revels -- like the toad-stone which gypsies claim to be a remedy against poison. He had no need for such trifles, he assured himself, trying to refocus his attentions.

"Take my advice Father Abbot, always send a fool to deliver your epistles -- they are under the Lord's protection and beyond suspicion"

"You are an extraordinary man, to be sure," said the Abbot. "For both our earthly and heavenly Lord protects you from much harm -- any other statesman might have been torn apart after thus transgressing against the Church"

Arthamaeus set aside the wine jug before the Abbot could get hold of it, pretending to refill his own cup.

"You are mistaken Father Abbot," said Cromwell, "I am a completely commonplace man surrounded by commonplace people, would you not say that there is no scandal at court which has not already been done?"

"I would say it, though it be treasonous -- you will get at me one way or another, I suspect the roof is crumbling around me as we dine," the Abbot laughed darkly. "But the question I ponder, is it otherwise elsewhere? I believe that human nature has changed little through the centuries, and yet we must pray for the coming of a more enlightened age"

"It is the holy men and saints who are truly extraordinary," Cromwell observed, "for few others are able to conjure miracles and see into the future. I believe you are well acquainted with one Elizabeth Barton -- she speaks to angels and foresees that King Henry shall lose his kingdom soon after his second marriage. Does that align with your astrological calculation, Master Arthamaeus?" he gave the youth a conspiratorial look.

"Miracles and divination should be used with an eye to moderation," answered the Abbot, "although some say that there is very little that saints cannot do these days, those who are sensible are so often inclined to idleness that imposters are allowed to take their place. I will say no more of it. Now how is your son, Gregory?"

"His tutor has taken him to Cambridge and writes me the most amusing letters of his progress," said Cromwell, "not long ago he has sold all of the furniture to pay his gambling debts, claiming that it were lost in an accident -- of course pressing me to pay damages. Gregory unfortunately has taken ill"

"I am sorry to hear that," the Abbot commiserated, "I shall pray for his recovery so that he may soon resume his studies"

"Thank you, Father Abbot," Cromwell inclined his head. "Indeed I am paying dearly for him to be able to forget such a great many learned things, nervelessness, Chekyng asserts that he has been so badly taught that he could hardly conjugate three verbs when committed to his care. In your opinion, ought I to blame the tutor, or the pupil?"

"Always the pupil, for they yet have time to improve themselves," answered the Abbot. "As one grows old he has the experience to see things more clearly, but often forgets his spectacles," he confided. "I am set in my ways you see, and if I ought to know better, I would rather be buried than take the Oath of Supremacy -- you may say so to the King, if you please"

"No man can see things as they are, is it not so?" spoke Arthamaeus, feeling himself uneasy for the Abbot's sake, fearing lest he should soon repent of his words.

"Indeed," Cromwell looked at the youth, whose company they had for a time neglected. The three of them felt tired and were glad when the half-eaten remnants of the dinner were carried away.

The Abbot sensed that the conversation had certainly gone far enough, having some measure of his own intoxicated state -- the consequence of a long abstinence from wine. All the while treading upon perilous ground, it was Arthamaeus who he mistrusted to be sensible around their guest, uncertain of the youth's morals and allegiances.

He stood up and addressed the youth, clearing his throat loudly. "I am grateful that your father has been generous in his benefice, for which you have been spared much suffering, were you to be cast into the streets as an illegitimate son, but you must remember that this is the end of indolence -- no longer shall you be spared knowledge of the world. Now you are Cromwell's creature, so give him a taste of your singing, that you can surely do, unless maidenly modesty prevents you"

Arthamaeus hesitated, wondering if the Abbot was mocking him or speaking in earnest. At last, amid the silence and uncertain gazes, he got up from his seat, attempting an Italian sonnet.

Chapter 5

The fair-haired youth sat across from Cromwell in the horse-drawn coach which moved slowly onward past the windblown hillside flanking the road. Rain continued to pour down, making difficult work for the driver, who many a time had to get out to push the wheels from a hole half-filled with rainwater, cursing that in no time at all their path would be a river. There was nowhere to stop nearby, however, and so they had little choice but to proceed onward.

Arthamaeus pulled his cloak tightly about himself, holding onto a bundle which contained provisions from the monastery, what was left since the larder was raided.

Alongside the road they would at times pass by monks whom he recognized, they must have started their journey at dawn, having anticipated the outcome of Cromwell's arrival. He wanted to ask them where they were going to, wondering if it was a better place than where he would soon find himself.

Some still wore their wool habits, others had already changed their monastic garments for layman's clothing, having made arrangements as farmers, apprentices and guilds-men.

Not all had been this fortunate, Arthamaeus had no doubt, and would be obliged to walk on as vagabonds until they reached the larger towns.

Meanwhile Cromwell regarded the youth's pensive face, for their conversation had waned since he had received the answer to his most pressing enquiry, the identity of his parents.

Cromwell had known Thomas More, although he could not claim a friendship existed between them, rather, a kind of begrudging respect despite a difference in morality. As Master Secretary, knew that More had turned to him out of necessity, as there was no one better placed and more willing to take Arthamaeus into his household.

He, at least, had the favour of the King during these time of uncertainty, and would know how to find a place for him. Cromwell reflected that Arthamaeus would soon have need of black robes, those of a man in mourning, for such was proper to son who had lost his father.

His eyes lingered upon the waifish face of his ward, obscured by fair hair cascading past the youth's shoulders as he gazed out the window, reminding the statesman of a portrait he had seen of 'The Princes in the Tower', both the deposed King Edward V of England and Richard of Shrewsbury, who bore a similar expression -- an embarrassed look of dread or foreboding, as if one ought not to show their fear and dislike, but could not help it.

Indeed there are times when courage and force are of will are of little use against a powerful opponent, when stratagem and appeals to pity would serve one better -- such is the refuge of women and children.

But was Arthamaeus to be regarded as a child, or would he progress better as a man -- Cromwell had yet to assess what sort of upbringing the youth had received, and how long it would take to make of Arthamaeus a self-sufficient figure at court.

The Abbot seemed to intimate that he was one who has seen little of the world -- if that was the chief concern, he would have time enough to learn, having seen enough of by way of the monastic microcosm.

In a year's time, this unwilling ecclesiastic would come into possession of More's much-depleted estate, thought Cromwell, resolving to add to it lest it should disappoint.

Although his gray eyes seemed fixed upon the dreariness of the landscape, Cromwell had no doubt that his new apprentice would recall little of the passing moorlands and dilapidated villages -- it was surely his own precarious future which occupied him in that moment. Then, as if jolted back to the present by a particularly rough turn in the road, his eyes passed swiftly over the man across from him, with the sheepishness of a newly-wed bride, followed by the remembrance of what had been done to his father, to whom he still owed a degree of filial loyalty. Cromwell observed how the expression of silent defiance rarely failed to visit the pale face when their eyes met for too long.

He had More's aristocratic air -- a degree of pride unsuitable to one whose fortunes have taken such a steep decline, having never been particularly high to begin with.

It surprised him still to imagine a man like More taking his liberties with a kitchen-maid and then resuming his posture as a haughty pillar of Popish piety. Nevertheless, he would make sure that young Arthamaeus was well taken care of -- he could not say what had become of the woman, perhaps she had died in childbirth.

Or was this boy the outcome of a liaison with a revered patroness of the ecclesiastic profession, who for the sake of decency was not further spoken of by the Abbot. Nor did Cromwell seek to know more than was necessary in that regard, save for in casual speculation.

...

As the long journey progressed and the sun began to set, Arthamaeus resigned himself to sitting sulkily in the seat shared with one who may have well been his executioner. So this was the illegitimate son of Thomas More, he imagined Cromwell thinking to himself as he glanced up from his papers.

It was during his last days that the wayward father had sought Cromwell's favour in protecting this young man, entrusting his future to one who would have the power to keep him from his enemies, despite the ill-will which marred the days before Thomas More's death.

Cromwell had been busied with the work of surveying the monasteries and identifying further opportunities to reduce the toll which they took upon the royal coffer. It was upon this pretence that he came to collect Arthamaeus, having learnt that the man was not without some education and may do for an assistant.

He would carry out his promise to Thomas More with goodwill, it being one which was little in conflict with his own ends, being in need of a son or someone he could trust to make himself useful, uncertain if Gregory would return to him from his illness and the opposing force of the boy's disinterest to follow his father's profession.

Of course it was too soon to tell how malleable Arthamaeus would prove to be, and what kind of notions he held of the King's and his father's position. In any case, Cromwell was not the King, but only his instrument, he hoped that the boy was wise enough to realize that.

"That is a fine locket," Cromwell spoke to break the silence, "whose portrait is inside, or is it a religious reliquary?"

The young man reached out to touch the trinket, his pale hand wrapping around it as if it might be taken from him. It bore the symbol of the cross surrounded by minute writing which could not be read at a distance.

"Is is an image of my mother," he told him reluctantly. "The Abbot gave it to me when I grew from an infant"

"May I see it?" he asked, intrigued by this sudden revelation.

Arthamaeus hesitated for a moment but then opened the locket, displaying a miniature of woman with fair hair and a willowy figure, her large gray eyes staring out at him from her nun's habit with the same expectant look as the boy. It made Cromwell think of his wife, wishing that he had had her portrait made before she had passed away, but she had excused herself, whether from a kind of modesty or the sense that she had too much to do to sit still, and so they always put it off.

He had seen these portraits of Saint Gertrude sold by the dozen by street peddlers, but he did not say so to Arthamaeus, wondering only whether the youth had begun by deceiving Cromwell or himself.

"Is she still alive?" he leaned back in his seat.

"No," Arthamaeus replied simply.

"Do you know your lineage, from her side?" asked Cromwell.

"Perhaps I come from a distinguished line of bakers, I could not tell you -- if *he* did not," replied Arthamaeus, closing the locket, "as a child, I liked to think that she was well known for her almond cakes, back in her village"

"How quaint,"said Cromwell, "will it satisfy you if I presume that it was by the means of these cakes that she charmed the distinguished Thomas More?"

"I believe she had other charms beside these, although I only laid eyes on her a few years ago," said Arthamaeus, "it was while going on an errand to collect a certain manuscript from the copiers, the man who usually did it was away on other business and the Abbot let me do it, a rare occasion and I made the most of it. I was going to speak to her but relented at the last moment -- perhaps it was not her, if it was, she must have known where to find me, if she had wanted to, they could not have denied her.

Of course it must have all been make-believe, I was eight or thereabouts, but I thought there was a resemblance, an uncanny resemblance," he said almost apologetically, he had hoped to amuse Cromwell with this childish tale, but the man only looked at him with obvious discomfort, maybe even reproach -- or perhaps it was the Master Secretary's misfortune to have a cruelty in his expression which did not suit him whilst he listened.

"I had to be disposed of fairly quickly, when I was first born, and I acknowledge it is likely for the best," Arthamaeus went on, "as not to cause more problems than need be. It could have been worse, certainly. Most likely she is dead now, the plague took her -- it is still bad now, even in these parts, or so I have heard" he gestured beyond the window. Although the sun had long ago drifted past the horizon the familiar silhouette of a steeple marked the way for Arthamaeus.

"What were you told of your father?" asked Cromwell.

"Most recently, that he is dead, and not much prior to that -- perhaps the secrecy made me think more of him than I ought to have," the young man replied with an alacrity which would have appeared sardonic were it not for the obvious impression of timorousness about him.

He continued to fidget with the locket of Saint Gertrude, or with the loose thread of his travelling cloak, at the same time trying to appear like more than a man of twenty.

Cromwell recollected his records showing the boy's age as twenty one, but if he had to guess, he would have taken off five or six years. He wanted to ask if the monks fed had him properly there, or if he did not much care for that particular pleasure of the flesh.

"What else were you told?" Cromwell hoped that the son took the best of what was in the mother's and father's blood, in spirit as well as in body, for he could easily admire the classical features of the youth, were it not for the look of haggard sleeplessness which lingered about him. His youthful face had an effervescent delicacy about it that suggested to Cromwell that he too would soon follow in his parents' footsteps, if exposed too soon to the harsh realities which his forebodings promised.

"That I ought not to know much else, or even that," Arthamaeus said after a pause.

"And you never had a desire to know him, until now?" Cromwell pressed on.

"If his will was to sever our bond then it is not my place to seek him, and yet I did seek him, in his writing," Arthamaeus admitted, believing perhaps that some manner of confession was needed before the other would release him from interrogation.

"I see," Cromwell looked at him thoughtfully, "and what did you make of his writing?"

"That likely it was not meant for me, nor did it do me the good which it did others," he replied. " I searched long for meaning in dust-covered monastic manuscript, as a dutiful son would, but I felt like one of the alchemist in search of their gold -- do you think that some really found it, hiding their secrets beneath allegories and symbols, or were they all charlatans?"

"It would be bad for trade, if making gold was quite that simple," answered Cromwell, "and men are only men. Those in possession of genius or luck are bound to be boastful, and if such mysteries existed, they would with time have come to light -- some immoderate apprentice would have long ago flooded the market, or so I believe"

Arthamaeus knew what he was referring to, pausing as if recollecting something.

"But they hide their secrets behind archaic dialects and runes -- what is it all for then, if they have nothing to hide? Do you think they are merely taking advantage of other men's weakness?" he drew one such figure upon the glass, "it is the same with religion, they do not want it to be simple. It would devalue the market for souls, would it not?"

"The market for souls?" he laughed dryly. "What words"

"Forgive me, sir," he looked abashed, recollecting that he ought not to have made such easy speech with the stranger, and at the same time, longed to unburden his mind of that which could find no vent in a monastery, surrounded by those who had to keep up appearances for the boy whose father paid for their feasts.

"There is nothing to forgive," said Cromwell, "it is the silent ones that I am on my guard against"

"Then what does it mean to you, to live a virtuous life?" asked Arthamaeus. "The dividing line between good and evil is not drawn so firmly, I know, but I have heard much spoken against you, if I may speak candidly, and so I wonder what rules of honour you take as your own"

"You are quite right, I have a reputation for being an incorrigible sinner, and therefore bother no more about it," he said with a levity which displeased the young man. "It is like that, when there is something that one can do, there is no need to be ill at ease, and if there is nothing one can do, then, too, the conscience is untroubled. There are times in every man's life when he finds himself backed against a wall, and must choose whether this cause is the pyre upon which he would like to die, or preserve himself for another, more worthy end. If it is the latter, then he must bow to a force greater than his own, and be spared. Such things are understood at court, but must be done with discretion"

"They say that no one is beyond redemption, while he lives and can still repent, I suppose that you make ample use of this principle," said Arthamaeus.

"It is not yet a convenient time for me to become penitent," Cromwell replied. "Although my minor principles must bend to preserve myself and others for acts of greater good, it is not to a point when I must lose respect for myself. And yet, there are many who think that true belief comes in the form of boastfully striking quarrels with the opposition and parading oneself as a martyr -- take this lesson from your father, who was sent to the Tower for refusing to bow to the King's wife"

"Am I to bow to you then, to avoid a similar fate?" he said this matter of factly, without sign of anger, but Cromwell could not doubt that something of the sort was there beneath the amicable surface.

It was not that the young man was attempting to provoke or deceive, rather, he did not know how to conduct himself with one upon whom his life depended, and who had wronged him through his father.

It was true, Cromwell had sacrificed and made an example of Thomas More as part of the means of furthering the King's ends. A wound and a gift were given him from the same source, and Arthamaeus had yet to make up his mind where to set Cromwell down -- as a friend or as a foe.

"Not a servant per say, but as my right hand man, if I find you capable," he tried to flatter Arthamaeus, "it is the least I can do"

"Will you train me to be a statesman and to serve the King, and to honour his lawful Queen?" he asked, this time his bitterness could not be masked.

"If you wish to live," said Cromwell, returning his papers carefully to his satchel, the hour having grown too late to read over the accounts, nor was he in the mood, his mind diverted with other thoughts and other company.

"That really depends on what kind of life you have drafted for me, Master Cromwell," he answered.

"I suggest that you give up your imperiousness Master More, as much as it suits you, nor to exchange it with melancholy, as is the case of many thwarted egos," he advised. "There are enough tragedies at court, a surplus of tragic actors. It is useful and amusing men that the King favours"

"My ambitions do not stretch so far as winning the King's favour, of that I am certain," Arthamaeus retorted.

"That is unfortunate. Would you say then that you find the King's favour beneath you?" Cromwell suggested.

"I would not say that," he answered, with tone of challenge, losing something of what may have been mistaken for childishness candour. In truth, Arthamaeus did not take kindly to such snares as had caught more world-wise men than himself. Even within the monastery walls, he had heard something of Thomas Cromwell and his methods of eliciting treason.

He was told of the proceedings of his father's trial, having especially sought out what information he could. When he first learned of it, the death of Thomas More, and much that surrounded it, was by then common knowledge.

Only to the bastard son did it come as something of a shock, the monks had debated amongst themselves about how long they could keep the news from him. But they bore him no malice, seeing him as little more than a reclusive unsociable lad whose chief rebelliousness came out in his choice of literature, some of which made the Abbot most uneasy during a particularly avid period of book burning.

"Good," said Cromwell, "although it is the proclivity of all young people to be thought provoking, if I am to be your guardian, I would like to be able to trust in your good sense -- do you think you have enough of it?"

"I would not know, sir," he answered. "Although it surprises me that I should be in need of a guardian, being already of age"

"Do not be ungrateful Arthamaeus," said Cromwell without malice, "your father had begged through his teeth that I should look after you, and I suppose he had good reason to think that you would have need of me, would you not agree"

"I would not know, sir," he repeated, looking away. Somewhere in his conscience, it equally annoyed and pleased him to imagine his father grovelling before this man, for to both he was bound in a state of ambivalence. Both had made him fatherless, both had sought to look after him, in their own way.

"Now then, there is in no need for you to curl back within yourself -- it is my intention that the debts on each side be equitably settled," Cromwell attempted to reassure him. "May I count upon your honour that we shall begin our acquaintance with a clean slate?"

"Forgive me, but that is hardly possible," he said gravely whilst looking down at his feet, as if delivering unpleasant news to a distant relative, "despite your good intentions, the past cannot be fully erased"

"I have seen it done," said Cromwell.

"I will attempt to control my emotions better in the future," he promise, by way of compromise, "as I see that they have gotten reign of me and you have seen through my efforts to keep my composure. I confess, for it seems I have grown accustomed to making you my confessor, having no other who will entertain my madman's notions, that I have need of you and will serve you to the best of my abilities, but I cannot promise you my goodwill or my loyalty, once we reach the end of my education. I will place my trust in you for as far as that goes, Master Cromwell"

"What makes me worthy of your trust, but not of your loyalty?" he asked.

"Because I think you are a man of your word -- which you interpret as it suits you. You would not lie to me, but you would let me believe what I chose, if you thought it for your -- for my good," Arthamaeus looked up, looking at him expectantly, as if in need of reassurance.

"I am glad that what you have heard of me is not entirely to my discredit, although it be not praise"

"Djinn are also known to keep their word to the letter, if not to the spirit of it," he said, remembering a tale he had once heard from a Persian merchant.

Cromwell smiled dryly.

"Is it the same with you, sir?" the Arthamaeus's gray eyes were fixed upon Cromwell's amber ones. There had been times past when it seemed to his imagination that the statesman could exert an unnatural influence over the court, recalling the monks' tales when they discussed King Henry, his enemies and his followers, his intrigues and his lovers in hushed tones before retiring to the dormitory.

"I will leave it for other men to judge," said Cromwell.

"They already do," answered Arthamaeus. "And then there are those like Plato who believe that one must firstly know his own character, rather than leaving it to the esteem of others, who may be less fit judges of conscience and character"

"Is my ward a pagan then, or merely fond the ancient Greeks?"

"I may be," said Arthamaeus.

"Whatever shall I do with you?" he smiled.

"You can leave me at the crossroads, if you find me ill-suited to your work," the young man told him, thinking to himself that this was just as he had found him, with his faith astray and the future a blur of unfathomable choices, having few whom he could call an ally.

It oppressed him to be so long before the Master Secretary's scrutiny, for he could not tell what there was in those amber eyes.

If he could have read the other's thoughts, he would have found that during their dinner together with the Abbot, Cromwell was wary of such distractions -- lest his admiration for the youth would cause a lapse in judgement -- cautious of the possibility that by some word or gaze or action he would reveal a vulnerability which would discredit him in front of a man who would be glad to have power over him.

He was aware that being alone with Arthamaeus made it tempting to let down his guard, half convincing himself that he was one who could coldly admire beauty in all of its forms. It was long since he found himself tempted, lust not being one of his besetting sins. Yet he saw in Arthamaeus that singular combination of beauty which he had admired in the art of the old masters -- a conception which he did not imagine would be find moulded in the flesh and presented to him as a burden upon his generosity.

He had not had to struggle to possess custody of the unexpected benefice of beholding Arthamaeus, where he would have given much to recollect him in a delirious dream.

It made him uneasy to be the guardian of such a dependant, as if he had stolen the opal from the altar of a pagan god, finding himself undeserving and inept to sacrifice to the King's court a treasure which ought to exist among the immortals -- which would surely perish if settled in a London street, or paraded before the serpents of aristocracy. He had no right to love him, nor desire him. He did not know he would do with Arthamaeus.

"I think not -- I will send you instead to Henry Sadler," he told him, the words coming to him through the haze of self-interest, a part of him still snatching with its claws to drag them back.

"I thought that I was to become apprenticed to you," Arthamaeus said with no small amount of surprise, wondering if he had gone too far.

"You will be known as Ralph Sadler, his son, and will stay with his family for a time -- it will all been arranged once we reach London. When I have settled some matters of diplomacy and have leisure enough to play tutor, I will make sure that you learn something of statecraft," he promised Arthamaeus. "Sadler will give me a full account of you, I hope that it will be a favourable one"

"Who is Henry Sadler?" asked Arthamaeus, feeling uncertain about how he felt regarding this change of expectations.

"A dependable respectable man of middling rank, exactly suited for the position of masquerading as father to the unknown son of Thomas More and teaching him the precepts of the Law"

"Does he have children of his own?" Arthamaeus felt unconvinced that this was a favourable turn, surmising him to be a minor official or clerk of some sort who Cromwell must have bribed to be saddled with More's bastard son -- another mouth to feed.

"One Ralph Sadler," he smiled at him and the young man looked annoyed at this evasion.

"I had agreed to take Ralph on as an apprentice at the age of seven, but the boy had succumbed to sickness during his journey from home," Cromwell explained. "His family had gone abroad and my agents were delayed in informing them of the dire news -- he had to be buried in a small parish on the way to Windsor castle. I had received summons from the King and expediency called for an unmarked grave for the boy whose life had so quickly been cut short. Nevertheless, his name may still be of service to us"

"Am I to impersonate this Ralph Salder then, after all the years that passed?" he looked incredulous.

"That would be convenient, if it would suit you," he suggested. "Or if it would please you better, we can lightly tarnish your father's legacy of his saintly martyrdom and bestowing upon yourself the name and associations of a traitor -- which may make future introductions to the King rather difficult. The choice is yours"

"Would it matter a great deal, if Thomas More had an illegitimate son? The King himself is not innocent of that fault," he observed, crossing his arms and leaning back in his seat.

"It would matter to some," answered Cromwell. "What will signify more is his position in defiance to the King's authority. It will be presumed that you share in his views and are furthermore hostile regarding your father's execution"

"I understand, then you advise against it?" Arthamaeus felt uneasy. "But you have at times made yourself unpopular at court and with the people, has it really gone so poorly with you?"

"Public opinion is a capricious beast, but it is more difficult to shed one skin for another when your family has made a stand, you would need to plead mercy from the King and reassure him of your allegiance," he explained. "Even then, he may remain wary of you, and it places me in an uncomfortable position"

"You do not wish to be associated as an ally of Thomas More," said Arthamaeus, feeling that all was plain to him now. "It would not serve your interests to shelter *his* son"

"Nor would it serve yours, Arthamaeus -- I would rather you not enter into society at a disadvantage," Cromwell replied.

"I am not a débutante. And I have no intention of revenging myself, if that is what you are afraid of. What good will it do me, to further dishonour both myself and my father," said Arthamaeus after a pause of silence between them, which by the shortness of their acquaintance was a heavy one. Cromwell could tell that there was a desire in the other to be liked, and he would not withhold what was sought, despite its dangers.

He remembered the proud holy airs of Thomas More, and the striking resemblance which his son bore to the man during his youth, as he recalled him while still a boy. There was still something of that disdain, although sensibly taken down a few notches. He wondered how much of the young More's animosity towards religion was due to the monks, and how much for his father's sake, who forsook him all these years only to die for his faith without ever having known him.

"I hope that I have not been too brazen or made a fool of myself," he went on as Cromwell made no answer, only looking at him patiently as his hand toyed with the clasp of the satchel in which is documents were laid.

"I take it you are not a fool, although you are over-easy to trust in strangers," he answered at last, "some think those two qualities are one and the same, but I do not believe so. I find it a refreshing characteristic, coming from my line of work -- much mishap could have been avoided if the words, thoughts and actions of men were in accord"

"I-I should be grateful to you," said Arthamaeus, a downcast softness crossing his features.

"Give it time," said Cromwell, "I understand that this must not be easy for you"

Arthamaeus said nothing, hesitating. Slowly he reached out his hand and rested it on that of Cromwell, whose expression also seemed to change.

"I am sorry," Arthamaeus murmured, hardly audibly, "I will trust in your judgement, as I have promised"

Cromwell wished to comfort him by saying that he would not forsake or turn against him if he were to choose a path contrary to what he advised, but thought better of these words, which may seem cloying or unnecessary after the young man's oath.

He pressed the other's hand, looking into his eyes for a long while, such that he felt reminded of someone who had once reached into his heart, a hand cold from the grave whose reproaches he still heard whispered in the night. But that memory had never been more than a faint dream which he was too ashamed to acknowledge.

"You have not eaten since morning, I suppose," spoke Cromwell, withdrawing his hand.

"I had skipped breakfast," he accepted a pie and some apples from their store of provision. "Thank you," he said shyly, something of his initial embarrassment returning. Cromwell presumed that, like himself, the youth was not one who liked to accept favours from others, great or small.

"So how did you spend your time at the monastery?" he asked once Arthamaeus had finished his repast, brushing the crumbs from his lap.

"I used to have various tutors, while the Abbot took an interest in me -- mainly for music," he sought for where to begin upon his answer, "but since my voice changed, he decided I ought to take to the sciences. I would help him make copies from esoteric texts, for his interests leant in that direction -- he and some other men he had met in Italy thought themselves alchemists, the Abbot would send them money sometimes.

It was always a little more, and a little more -- until the mystery could be unravelled. Once he realized he was being taken advantage of, the Abbot quarrelled and cut ties with them, holding a grudge ever since.

He gave their books to me and on occasion would ask if I had learned anything, I tried to make sense of them -- thinking it would please him, but I did not get far. Then I started inventing things, making drawings in the style of the alchemists and leaving them for him in unmarked letters -- I do not know why I did it, I suppose I missed our time together.

He had grown bitter and melancholy, and would see almost no one, feeling that all of his plans would come to naught.

The Abbot was furious when he found out and treated me like a fiend ever since, it was childish of me to feel that I ought to give him a reason to despise me. We both knew one another's weaknesses and how to use them to effect.

I suppose I ought not to speak of it all, but seeing that he will be leaving the country I do not think it will make a difference now. Since I had fallen out of favour, I would make myself my own tutor and find occupation where my interests would lead me.

I enjoy making codexes, it was a kind of game a few of the monks and I would play -- writing secret messages, although most of the others soon grew tired of it. When I finished my regular studies, memorizing or copying scriptures, that is what I would do -- here is one, I think," he began searching through his travelling bag and finally found a bundle of folded parchment wrapped in cloth. He handed it sheepishly to Cromwell, who took it and began looking it over; it contained peculiar diagrams with letters and symbols arranged in winding patterns, reminding him of the engravings of an astrolabe.

"I see that you learned something of secrecy from the alchemists," he held one of the codexes closer to the lantern for light.

The young man began to talk about the origin of various ancient codexes used during the times of the ancient Romans to carry messages, and other more modern inventions, some of his derivative attempts, although he had yet to fully test how well they worked to keep their contents hidden, having only tested them with a less than enthusiastic companion.

Cromwell promised that he would send him an answer within a month if he could, and encouraged him to write as well, on this and other matters, if he was ever in need.

Arthamaeus thanked him, embarrassed by how pleased he felt that Cromwell had not disapproved.

"You ought to rest now, as the journey is far from over and you will not have an easy time of it otherwise," Cromwell suggested when the youth put away his travelling bag.

They tried to make themselves comfortable in the small compartment of the carriage, leaning against the cushions. Cromwell put a blanket over the other's knees, remembering that there was one in the trunk at his feet.

Arthamaeus himself had brought little, thinking that most of the worldly possessions that he had would be more of a burden to carry so many miles than what they were worth, with the exception of a few rare manuscripts which he was not given permission to take with him, being told that they were the property of the monastery -- or however was soon to be owner.

He wanted to ask Cromwell about the libraries but did not wish to bring up a subject which might renew the strained ambiance between them which the faint touch of familiarity had melted, like a token of some sentiment which could not find itself in words alone.

He had sensed that there was something different in the way that Cromwell looked at people, with a scrutiny which seemed to elevate one's sense of importance, but perhaps this too was something he imagined. There are people who have delicate features or sensitive eyes, but do not share in these qualities. Arthamaeus knew that the man's cruelty, as his kindness, would reach deeply into his heart.

His thoughts turned to the monastery and what he had been parted from. The King, he reckoned, was not in need of further pretences for disbanding their congregation, and yet he did not want the illicit manuscripts to fall in to the wrong hands, he chose to destroy some them himself, giving them a dignified funeral and acting as their chief mourner, rather than imagining them set aflame upon a heap of commonplace hearsay.

He wondered if he had made a mistake, if he could have made Cromwell understand, to take his side.

Arthamaeus wondered if he could ever be made into a proper dignitary of statecraft, or if his head was filled with too many daydreams and fantasies, things which he had not yet learned to abandon, being his chief source of amusement and comfort -- having outcasted himself from his peers by a reserve of manner which was taken for pride and aloofness.

In truth, he resented to have been made their prisoner, for it was the monks and their Abbot who had forbidden him his freedom, fearing that it would compromise his father's goodwill towards their establishment. He did not believe that this was the motive, for the Abbot had others of his own.

That he was allowed to know Thomas More's views, they had always believed an act of imprudence, but perhaps in his way the man still hoped to preserve a family tie, always sending him copies of his works during holidays, never sullied by earthly common-places or so much as a letter.

. . .

Cromwell wondered how he could have fallen asleep, imagining that it was the sheer exhaustion of past sleepless nights that accounted for it. Outside the window, he could see the inn at which they intended to stop, breaking up the journey to restock their provisions for the long road ahead.

Cromwell alighted, offering his hand to the young man, whose stature made disembarking something of leap.

Two small girls of about twelve approached them carrying a wooden box, one of whom found the burden too much, for it teetered dangerously as they made their way towards the strangers. Cromwell had seen contraptions of the sort before, containing tableaux of finely-dressed dolls representing Jesus and the Virgin Mary, at times moving upon intricate wooden joints.

"How quaint," the Master Secretary stepped closer to take a good look at an effigy of himself being pulled at by manticores and fish with sharp teeth and human legs. "What excellent craftsmanship. Did you make this?," he asked, offering one of the young ladies a coin, which she took gladly -- testing it with her teeth before slipping it under the Virgin Mary's dress.

"Our brother did," her sister lisped out.

He seemed to consider this fact for a moment but said nothing, nor did the son of Thomas More, who had been watching their exchange.

"This is for him too, having gone further in his wassailing than pouring cider over the apple trees," the coach driver took a coin from his belt and held it out to the the second girl, who scampering away with it while her sister set down the heavy box on an old tree stump, looking after her with some annoyance. "I think it is time for a drink Master Cromwell," he said after the girls had gone. "I will make sure we get some fresh horses for the morning"

At the inn, they saw a large group of twenty or so men of the village singing raucously and passing around a large bowl of cider, blended with spices, honey and eggs. On the table was a heartily carved turkey stuffed with herbs and surrounded by partridge.

"Are you tired from the road or would you like to partake in the festivities?" Cromwell asked Arthamaeus.

"I think that I could use some rest," replied the youth, not feeling himself fit for a merry company, even on a good day.

"Would you like food brought up to your room?"

"May I eat with you?" he asked, desiring to continue their conversation in private.

"If you wish," Cromwell replied, sending a servant to make arrangements and confirm that their rooms were ready.

...

They took their supper at a small table laid with two bowls of leek soup and rye bread. Neither had felt particularly hungry for heavy fair. "Do you regret what you must do, is it only in obedience to the King that you must disband the monasteries?" asked Arthamaeus. "Forgive me if I cause offence by my questioning, it is only that I have heard much talk at the abbey about the King's intentions, and wonder where is truth and where is the presumption"

"I imagine that the the monks take an interest in the men who must rob them of their livelihood, do you still see yourself as one of their number -- a defender of their faith and way of life?" asked Cromwell, setting down his spoon.

"Naturally they do," answered Arthamaeus. "As for myself, it would depend on the monastery, some have strayed I suppose, but I think there are good honest men to be found even in such places. Our Abbot, despite his shortcomings, is well regarded in the villages -- he has taken decent care of the lands and in caring for the sick, some are sent to the abbey from miles around. I have heard rumour that the plague is making its way"

"Naturally," Cromwell repeated, amused to see that the youth had not yet been satisfied with interrogating him -- wondering if it was because they would soon be parting and again he would be cast into dependence upon another stranger. "Do you pity them then? You need not, for the King plans to rebuild the monasteries to a higher standard, improving the rigour of their administration. Your Abbot may have a place for himself still, although I cannot give guarantees at this point"

"The King has been known to change his mind, when financial concerns are pressing," Arthamaeus answered, "or so I have been told. No, I do not pity them -- it is to them that I owe my loss of faith in all that is set down by men and taken for religion. I believe you understand, otherwise I would not tell you this"

Cromwell nodded vaguely, thinking that there must be some deeper bitterness beneath these words than he had hitherto seen. Perhaps some act of indecency or vileness which sufficed to turn the man to smile upon the ill fate of his fellow ecclesiastics, if the Abbot did not exaggerate.

"I think the monasteries are a source of good in concept, but not always in practice, if I had to clarify my feelings about it," added Arthamaeus. "But I cannot help but see that there is a conflict of interest, if the King is the one who takes up the work of reform in this heavy-handed manner -- that it is not merely raiding and robbery"

"Of course, I see your concern," said Cromwell, not having a suitable answer, for his own suspicions were the same. "Not all of these monks will end badly, or are deserving of punishment -- most would be accommodated elsewhere," he felt obliged to repeat, "although more modestly than what some had grown accustomed to"

Arthamaeus turned his attention back to his soup, debating whether to press Cromwell further on this matter, being one who enjoyed debate and relished the opportunity to talk to someone who seemed to take him seriously. Languidly lifting the spoon to his mouth, he considered where the line was at which he might offend his host or appear quarrelsome, ever self-concious and yet yearning to interact with those who have lived beyond the abbey walls.

Even servants and merchants who passed by were a source of fascination to him and he would often seek opportunities to slip away and ask them out the news in the village and elsewhere, glad to meet a person who had travelled far.

"I have made up my mind," said Arthamaeus, drawing Cromwell from his own speculations, "I would rather be known as Ralph Sadler than as Arthamaeus More. Although both have a sense of the imposter, it is not for me to walk in my father's footsteps. But perhaps, just amongst ourselves, I may be known as Arthamaeus, so I need not completely forget myself. I will be discreet, of course"

"Very well," said Cromwell, "I am pleased with your choice, Arthamaeus, it will make our path together a great deal easier"

Chapter 6

"You do not look well," said Lord Norfolk as he passed by Cromwell, handing him a message sealed with wax. "Where have you been -- have you brought the plague back with you?"

"No, just a boy, your Grace," he replied, dismissing the prior question. Indeed he sensed a certain faintness, wondering if he was beginning to feel feverish, but saw no use in troubling this man with his health -- needing it to be nothing more than weariness from the long journey.

"A boy you say?" he set down his papers, surprised.

"Yes, a fair creature, I saw him in the King's chapel carved in marble, he had bathed in the rivers of Florence -- King Henry, he will know -- " he spoke not to Norfolk, but to Anne Bolyne, into whom her uncle had morphed in the light of a stained-glass pane.

She smiled at him enigmatically, flashing her white teeth, as if she might almost pity him or laugh.

He could hear another voice calling him, hands shaking him into wakefulness from a feverish sleep.

They had not yet left the inn -- Arthamaeus was standing by his bed, looking down at him like a bird from a tree.

Chapter 7

"What are you doing?" Cromwell entered his bedchamber to find the young man crouching on the ground.

"I am putting lavender sprigs under your bed," replied Arthamaeus, getting up from the floor.

"Why?"

"It is said to keep nightmares away," he answered, somewhat embarrassed.

"You are like a child," said Cromwell, smiling at him slightly.

"I-I heard you last night and thought it might help," he went on.

Cromwell took a letter from the small desk by the window, not knowing how to answer him.

"It is alright, I often have curious dreams myself," said the young man. "I do not think most of them mean anything"

...

...

The bodies were piled in a corpselium where they would be burned to keep at bay the spread of the infection, but to little avail. Three days had passed at the inn and letters were arriving from the court enquiring about the cause of delay.

Cromwell lay upon the bed, his brow drenched with sweat as a servant washed his face with a cloth soaked in rosemary water. He wished the man would go away, but leave the cloth. It was almost unbearably hot and he tried to move away the blanket but the physician had pinned it down with his knee and was forcing his mouth open with his thumb and tilting his head to pour some vile liquid down his throat, sending him into a fit of coughing.

At this they all backed away, wary of infection, and he could hear faint murmurings of the shadowy figures which surrounded his bedside.

The room was pungent with strong-smelling herbs, only made bearable by the draft from an open window, which was to carry out the odour of sickness in the air, brining in that of the spring orchard beyond.

Why could they not all leave him be, he thought, the sickness making him irritable and impatient, having little faith that a travelling apothecary's concoctions could offer him a cure, knowing that his own body would need to fight off the illness by force of will, or else succumb to the miasma. He craved for rest, for silence.

"I ask you again, Master Cromwell, have you made your peace with God or may now be the proper time?" the priest hovered over his bedside.

"Not yet," Cromwell replied wearily, thinking that he had already dismissed the man. "I believe I will live awhile longer, to do a little more of what is harmful to the soul -- for of what is middling good and passably evil I have done a great deal, and am left feeling unsatisfied. I am humble before God and make no great pretence to virtue -- it is inconvenient to one of my position"

"Do not blaspheme so, sir," said one of the servants, looking askance between him and the priest. "We must all make confession before our time comes"

"I would expunge these wicked deeds from my conscience, but I fear what would remain might not be sufficient to make a mortal man," replied Cromwell. "Please leave the porridge"

The old woman swallowed whatever she was about to say and set down the bowl with nervous trembling hands, leaving the room, soon after followed by the priest whose pace was one of offended briskness.

"What news?" he asked of Arthamaeus, who was going through the post which had just arrived.

"A Virgin's holy girdle had been stolen from a chapel, I think they have someone who they want you to interrogate, but I cannot quite make out the florid writing -- is that a euphemism? The letter is from a Bishop Curwen," he replied, trying to keep a straight face. "Oh and a parcel has come for you"

"Is this what they will weigh me down with when they drown me?" he nearly dropped it onto the floor.

Carefully, Cromwell opened the engraved cast-iron box, finding within a skilful carving of waxen images from Florence by Benitendi Fallimagine -- it was the King and his dearest companions done in miniature.

"Now I need not miss them," drawled Cromwell.

"Should I place them on the mantel, Master Cromwell?" asked the servant who had come to take away the dishes, lingering by the door and looking at the gift admiringly from a distance.

"Throw them into the fire, I have company enough"

"Really? It is rather well done," Arthamaeus examined them closely, as did the servant girl.

"Put them back in the box, find a safe place," he said, "and now if I may get some rest, that would be much appreciated. It seems that there is little care for catching illness in this house"

He did not know when he had at last drifted into sleep, and when he had returned from it, such a thing occurring in intervals several times during the night.

It seemed that someone had poured water onto the mattress all along his back, but it must have been sweat from the fever. He opened his eyes faintly and looked around the room at the disarray of drying rags, bottles, mortars and a wax candle, now extinguished.

In a chair by the bed slumped a young man with dishevelled blonde hair falling past his shoulders.

"Arthamaeus," he spoke his name, Cromwell's voice feeling hoarse.

Arthamaeus was awake, having had little luck in making himself comfortable, but not wishing to depart from his post.

"Y-yes," he rubbed his eyes and got up, smiling lightly before kneeling close to the bed, looking over Cromwell in the manner of a sepulchral angel, and then as the apothecary -- searching for some sign of sickness or health, but feeling reassured of neither. He felt himself begin to drift off again.

"Are you listening Master Cromwell? The King's physician arrived a few hours ago," Arthamaeus explained, "he sent me to another inn with his assistant but I ran away you see -- no one answered my messages and I thought something was wrong. I got tired of waiting there so they let me keep watch in case you need anything -- do you?"

"I-I will make arrangements to transfer your inheritance to you, it was meant to be done when you reach the age of five and twenty, but as I --"

He broke into a cough and he reached for the cup of tea which had grown cold long ago. Arthamaeus helped him sit up to drink and then to lower him back against the pillow.

Cromwell was displeased with the idea that this was the impression he would leave Arthamaeus before their parting, to appear to him like a sick old man. His ward looked at him with a troubled pitying expression, telling him to speak no more about the will or the inheritance, he had not come for that. There would be time enough, and he thought of the pile of letters which came in almost daily, most of them on state affairs calling for urgent attention.

These too would have to wait, albeit less patiently.

"It is better if you leave soon, I will make arrangements in the morning and you will finish the journey without me, will you do this?"Cromwell allowed himself to sink back against the pillow and close his eyes, listening to the hooting of an owl somewhere in the forest outside. But perhaps this too was a phantasm. "Please, can you close the window for me?" he asked, feeling that the cold night air would not do him good.

The young man got up hurriedly and closed it, returning to his chair and looking between Cromwell and the night-stand.

"Should I boil the kettle perhaps?" he offered, wishing to make himself useful.

"You have not answered my question," said Cromwell.

"I had come to become your apprentice, as you had promised me," said Arthamaeus, "I think that I may serve you well and learn more than what would be taught at Sadler House"

"If I survive this"

"I will be here, if you need me," he said, pressing the other's shoulder.

Arthamaeus shaded the candle light.

"I want to tell you something, in case we do not speak again soon -- if you have to go back to the King or the physician calls me off, I mean," the youth sat down on the rug next to the bed. "Do you remember, there was a boy in Florence, who you found half-drowned by the river?"

Cromwell opened his eyes again, feeling a tension in his limbs as he searched for the others face in the shadows, preparing himself.

"That was me -- surely you knew"

Cromwell did not speak.

"They shaved my head and I had grown a lot taller since then," Arthamaeus went on.

He had suspected, but it seemed too uncanny.

"You would not tell me your name, or why you had done it," Cromwell turned onto his side towards him.

"I did not want to involve you then, or anyone, but I am grateful for what you did," he said. "I confess that it has made me question myself, that our paths should cross again, although we are still little more than strangers"

"You should not cling to me, you do not know yet which way it will go," said Cromwell.

"If fate had brought us together, then maybe there is --
"

"Fate, or chance," said Cromwell, "you are perhaps still young enough to search for meaning where you can find it, but romanticizing the past rarely brings forth wise choices"

"You think I am inexperienced and naive, and likely you are correct, but it does not matter -- if one's life is what he chooses to make of it, I would like to follow through with our bargain. I do not want to be passed between houses like an unwanted waif"

Cromwell took another drink of cold tea.

"We will go to the countryside, when you recover -- there we will be safe from the plague and you will feel better in spirit too," said Arthamaeus decisively, such that even in his delirious state Cromwell wondered at the other's authority.

"I cannot do that," he replied, already feeling a twisting in his stomach at the severing of his words and his desires.

"Maybe that is not true," Arthamaeus felt disappointed, but had not yet lost hope. "Maybe you are afraid to leave, like I was -- the King will let you go, he will understand it"

"You do not know the King"

"He is a man who places his private desires above the good of his people, he must understand if his subordinates choose to do the same," said Arthamaeus.

"You may tell him so when you are at court," answered Cromwell. "Have any letters come from Austin Friars?"

"Yes, two -- would you like me to read them to you?" Arthamaeus offered.

"Please"

The young man told him afterwards that much of his household had gone on, setting down a paper with the address -- their distract was being evacuated by those still in health, fleeing like rats from the spreading pestilence.

"And Gregory?" murmured Cromwell.

"I am sorry," Arthamaeus had hoped he would not ask.

Cromwell closed his eyes again and the young man knew better than to speak then, wondering if he ought to have kept the news from him.

Arthamaeus saw his lip tremble and his brow crease, but no other signs of the anguish which he imagined. After some time passed, Cromwell was able to collect himself from this blow, opening his eyes and looking up at the fair-haired youth, whose face had a strange ethereal glow in the moonlight which filtered from the window, making him think of those cold pale angels carved in marble which he remembered from his dream, gazing down upon one with a knowing serenity, only Arthamaeus's face was fixed with worry.

Cromwell could tell that he feared being sent away, he made no secret of it -- he felt his resolve wavering to banish an unnatural sentimentality, an excess of ill-placed affection which felt almost adulterous, yet Cromwell did not think he had the power to, in his present state, to enforce such an order even if he knew it to be proper.

The young man did not hold tightly onto life, and oddly this gave him a conviction that he would be spared. Cromwell himself was of the same disposition, although at times he feared for his recovery, when he felt a sharp pain somewhere between his heart and his lungs.

Arthamaeus continued to sit by his bed, at times slouched in an uncomfortable chair, at others peering over Cromwell's letters and helping him in answering them according to his dictations.

"You have received complaints from Queen Catherine on the treatment she has received, and another from the Emperor addressed to the King," said Arthamaeus as he sorted through the stack, giving them to Cromwell who held out his hand for them.

"The day when I stop receiving complaints is when I am assumed dead," Cromwell said dryly, opening the seal of the letter.

"The Earl of Hertford has written for you a prayer to stop the flow of blood," said Arthamaeus.

"What else?"

"He sends along an unguent for bruises and a nostrum to bring back lost youth, which you may have need of upon your recovery -- as it comes at a bargain price if one purchases both from Richard Babham, whose address is written for you if you require another dose," he held up a dripping package, which must have been damaged in transit.

"No," Cromwell closed his eyes, "what other messages have arrived?"

Arthamaeus smirked and opened the next letter, then set it down again.

"Would you like me to read something else to you, something less taxing -- it might help you sleep," he suggested, taking an old leather-bound volume of folktales which Brother Linacre had collected from the neighbouring villages, a parting gift. Pulling his chair closer to the bed, the youth carefully set down the candle-holder to give him light enough to read.

"It has been a long time since anyone has read nursery tales to me," Cromwell remarked, resigning himself to it.

"Then you are in for an experience," said Arthamaeus. "Here is the page -- the Minstrel, translated and abridged from the vernacular of one Bertha Grahame, scullery maid, of Greenburough lane: a tale about a youth who was walking through a mountain valley and paused to rest --

playing music by a lake where the old melody his father passed down to him was heard by a water nymph, who sang to accompany him in the ethereal voice of her kind. When the hour grew late and he was obliged to return to his home, he wondered if it was a mirage or a vision he had seen and sought to find the lake again but could not, only hearing about it in legends. Years pass by and he travels much as a wandering minstrel, having left his village long ago -- but one day, remembering the ancient song and remembering the strange memory from his youth, he returns in old age and finds the lake again, playing the same melody as the water nymph sings, her voice and beauty unchanged"

Arthamaeus paused and looked at Cromwell. "Would you like to hear another?"

"I doubt that I can sleep, but do not let me keep you from it," he replied. The difficulty in breathing made it hard to find rest, and every time he swallowed it was as though he were swallowing crushed glass.

"I do not mind," he said gently, setting down the book and placing his hand over Cromwell's eyes and brow, to whom it felt cold and oddly soothing. "You still have a fever, is there anything that I can do for you -- should I send for the physician again? Or some water?"

"Water," Cromwell nodded slightly and Arthamaeus went to refill the glass from the pitcher, finding it empty. He had to leave him for some time, going outside to the well and fetching a bucket full, then setting the large kettle over the fire to boil it as the cook had taught him.

His patient took a reluctant sip, rather hoping for something less hot, and sick of the taste and smell of rosemary all about him, but Arthamaeus told him that Hippocrates recommends it so, and was in no spirit for debate. Cromwell himself had only a slight interest in medicine, not trusting himself to distinguish the charlatans from the true professionals -- who had failed his wife and his children, therefore leaving his own body to face the miasma alone if it were not for the presence of Arthamaeus.

Cromwell agreed to listen to a book of poetry which had belonged to Elizabeth before she passed away, he had given it to her as a gift on their wedding day. It was a surprise to see it again, previously he had thought it had been lost or buried in storage somewhere. There it had been at the bottom of his satchel.

It had also been amongst the books which he imagined he would read if he ever retired from his worldly affairs. But as the years passed by, it seemed more difficult to imagine a life of leisure.

He would attempt it now, thought Cromwell, if only for an interval, sickly with plague. Listening to Arthamaeus's soft clear voice he could feel his eyes growing heavy, the words and their images half distracting him from the pain of his illness.

At times he would look up at the other with half-lidded eyes, thinking to himself that something of the resemblance between More and his son was vanishing, and again he saw in his mind's eye the portrait of the two murdered princes of the tower, imagining that this was one of them, come reincarnate to lead him to the hereafter.

Cromwell remembered this feeling of loneliness, so long ago when he was hardly more than a child himself -- believing that he would meet with such a figure of beauty in the ancient woods beyond the lake -- as the elf king he would lead him, or one of the knights of King Arthur, who would take him away to another realm where he would remain immortal, or else crumble to dust once returning to visit his old father and the family, taking for them a wallet of elven gold out of a sense of guilt or filial piety -- that he could be allowed to be so happy without paying for it, thinking of what had once been, not knowing which was the real and which the illusionary.

It was all illusion now, Cromwell dwelt upon the thought as the candle flickered, little more than a stub -- soon it would go out and the entire room would fall into darkness again, and no longer could he look at Arthamaeus between his lashes, stained with sweat and tears of suppressed death pangs, or so he thought them, not knowing what to pray for.

It was almost for Arthamaeus's sake alone that he forbore. It seemed hardly shameful not to endure, not to struggle with Death, when one is alone -- it is to fall into sleep, into heaven or hell, being too tired to do any more for the earthly.

Arthamaeus closed his book and felt Cromwell's brow again and then combed his fingers gently through the man's hair, light brown intermingled with strands of grey.

As he slept, or seemed to sleep, Arthamaeus had the opportunity to look at him more closely, his was a clean-shaven face beginning to show signs of age, a gentle careworn expression possessing a subtle melancholy which seeped into his voice when they were alone, at times cruel and sardonic, at others, wavering into a sympathetic softness which embraced him as he made to his confessions.

Their eyes met and Cromwell felt the clinging emotion of fear, fear that he should bring the youth down with him before his time, fear that he would die alone in the dark room, where perhaps days or weeks later his decaying corpse would be found by a stranger, maybe a neighbour or town official returning from the country, or a man coming on matters of business, or a thief looking to see if there is something left to take, or a vagrant in search of some abandoned place to stay the night.

All of these ghostly figures marched before him and, as if sensing this distributed thought, Arthamaeus pressed his hand and said, "Do not think now, rest, just rest". His voice was firm and pleading, as if speaking to a child. It was he who was the child, Cromwell thought, still remembering their first meeting.

The way Arthamaeus smiled at him -- faintly, sadly, as if he too feared the same things but was too kind to say them. Not even the physician had said them, although he could read it well enough in his face, that he was unlikely to survive the night.

…

...

That night Cromwell dreamt strange delirious dreams
from which he did not think he would awaken, doubting
that he would outlive even the Cardinal, whose days
seemed long numbered. He had forgotten that Wolsey was
already dead, the past and present blurring into itself. Pale

figures walked along a bridge which he could not cross, there too was Arthamaeus, lingering behind -- waiting for him, but two black dragons or devils pulled him onward like kites tied to his arms. Cromwell could see the youth calling out but it were as if he had no tongue to speak -- soon the bridge began to drift away, or was it himself who was being swallowed by the mist.

He was following a golden sphere which rolled along the winding paths of a garden labyrinth, it moved quickly and he struggled not to lose sight of it, knowing by intuition that if he did, he would never make it out of the maze of towering hedges.

The wind billowed and the branches shook about him with a kind of fury that made him rush forth, eager to be out of their shadows.

As he continued to run, the golden ball became a skull, he did not know when exactly this transformation took place, only that it made him wonder if it had always been as he saw it then -- its grinning mouth mocking him.

Still he followed it, believing that there was nowhere else that he could go but in obedience to the forces which led him in this vision of phantasms.

A green lawn stretched out before him when at last he made it out, the earth opened up for the skull and it fell within, swallowed up as by the maw of a devil. He did not know where to go then, waiting for a sign, then it came -- a black stag which gazed at him with eloquent eyes, so that he could not doubt its sentience and its call. He found himself surrounded by others, in merciless pursuit of the stag. On horseback he rode after it through the brambles, the arms of outstretched branches scratching at his face and tearing his cloak. The King and other men were with him, all seeking to be foremost in the chase.

They went deeper and deeper into the woods and still the stag eluded them.

Suddenly, they were forced to stop before a precipice, although not all were able to halt their steeds in time. No earthly steeds were these, for they did not grow weary despite the hard riding for what felt like many hours. He had no notion of time; although the sun was a fiery blaze, he could not tell in which direction it was setting. When he looked again at the faces of the men about him they had the grim features of purified flesh, long in the grave.

There was the Cardinal, he saw, knowing him by his signet ring and the voice which called him from a distance -- he had his horse but stayed back form the chase.

Wolsey pointed towards a cavern and there he saw the dark form of the stag.

The others of the wild hunt stood fixed in place, as if turned to stone, while he set out alone to follow in the direction where the Cardinal summoned him. The stag waited for him, unflinching as he touched its flank, its black eyes watching him as he reached for the golden chain about its neck from which hung a miniature locket.

Decisively he pulled it off, almost wincing in preparation for what would come, but the awaited punishment did not materialize, instead there lay a large heap of furs tied with red cords. He tried to untie them with his frost-bitten hands, for something moved inside, something alive.

Pulling back the black hides, casting them aside one after the other until they seemed unending, he revealed at last the curled up figure of Arthamaeus.

He knelt beside him, reaching out to touch the pale burning skin of the other, wondering if he was alive, and what he was.

The young man's eyes opened, but they were not the gray he had known them to be, they were amber like his own.

Arthamaeus reached out for him as he held his breath, keeping him from staggering back, in fear or in wonder as the long stems of feathers began to grow from his skin.

Although his face remained human, his legs contorted into the shape of a hawk's, his feet sharp talons of bone.

The being shook its great wings, rising onto its haunches, giving no time to run to a man dazed by its influence, a hypnotic power which made him weak and submissive to the will of the realm of wonders, trusting in it to carry him to where he need be, having struggled too long against that which he could no longer deny.

It picked him up by the shoulders and carried him over mountain landscapes, their icy pinnacles ending in the towers of cathedrals, decorated with crosses and the figures of saints, sometimes with gargoyles or windmills.

Phantom hosts of monks flew in great processions, like a lost army circling about, like vultures around carrion.

Suddenly he felt himself falling through the air, the harpy that was Arthamaeus descending with him, falling like an arrow pointed towards the earth from a god's bowstring.

His feathers were falling from his back and his arms like leaves from a wind-blown tree. Cromwell took the other's arm, bringing them closer so that they fell together into the sea.

The waters were still as a mirror's surface and they sank through the darkness to the depths of sky -- stars or crystal floating around them amid the echoing howl of something that seemed not to be human, reminding him of a thousand voices singing together in a celestial choir. He felt a burning in his chest and again the pain of glass moving down his throat, he struggled to breathe, clinging to the frail form of Arthamaeus, who had wrapped his arms around him, burying his face against the his neck.

When at last Cromwell awoke from the vision in a cold sweat, it was morning again. The sun filtered through the diaphanous fabric of the curtains, which moved with the slight breeze from outside.

He tried to sit up and saw that the young man was still with him, laying on the floor on top of Cromwell's fur-lined coat, using it for a mattress.

He decided not to disturb him, but he had heard him getting up, a creaking floorboard rousing the youth from a shallow sleep.

Groggily, Arthamaeus propped himself up on his shoulder and was about to speak when Cromwell said first, "It is fine, I told you to rest -- I will be back"

"How are you feeling? Better?" Arthamaeus asked him.

"Than last night, yes," he replied, trying to get out of bed.

Reluctantly, Arthamaeus obeyed, and Cromwell went to wash himself and change his clothes, splashing cold water over his face to bring him back into the present.

He wanted to bring himself back to a presentable state, to feel less like an invalid, as far as that was possible. It would take some time for the water to warm but once he got back to the bedchamber he asked Arthamaeus for this favour. The young man went at once and made them both a bowl of porridge from what remained in the kitchen, thinking that food would also help restore him.

Cromwell did not wish to see his reflection, whist shaving he could feel that his face had become gaunt, but if the fever had subsided, perhaps there was hope of recovery.

He worried more for those who had attended him, feeling that it was foolish of Arthamaeus to have come, and yet in his heart he could not fully say that he wished otherwise. Likewise, he hoped that those of his relations that remained were somewhere safe, glad that at least they were willing to obey his orders, while he still had the strength to give them. They would not expect to see him again, having left them with his will and the conviction that he would not rise again from his bed.

…

Their horses had been stolen and even mules were in short supply, they were wise to go away when they did, before the roads were closed. He had never seen a plague wreck so much devastation, so that there was little room to be ceremonious.

Cromwell did not make his confession to the priest; he would not have known where to begin, and to trace the source of regret would lead him upon strange paths and unfamiliar destinies, further and further from what made him the man he was.

No, he would face alone whatever it was that awaited him on the other side, if it called him to account.

But as he lay in the warm bath, it felt that it would not call then, maybe not for some time, that he might have the misfortune of reaching old age or outgrowing his usefulness.

He tried to focus upon the present moment, to a peaceful sense of washing away sickness and horror.

Chapter 8

When he again opened his eyes, it was still night. Upon the mattress beside him lay a hunched figure huddled under the blanket. The fire had gone out and a deep autumn chill filled the room. Arthamaeus shuddered slightly as Cromwell's hand pressed his shoulder.

"You should not be so close to me," said Cromwell, seeing that the youth's eyes were beginning to open, groggily sitting up and turning towards him, adjusting the blanket over the both of them.

"I do not care if I get sick," murmured Arthamaeus.

"Do you feel sick?" asked Cromwell.

"It is hard to tell, it feels as though I have not slept in days," he replied.

"You ought to try -- where is the physician, or the innkeeper's servants?"

"I cannot, my mind just keeps going and going," he told him. "The inn was to be marked with the plague cross and *'Lord, have mercy upon us'*, they left not long ago taking what is left in the larder. I think soon we must go likewise or else starve here. I am uncertain also about the well, speaking with one of the grooms --"

"Yes -- I have heard, do not go to the well. Soon we too must leave here," said Cromwell. "Bring me a quill and paper and find one who may deliver a message. Then we will pack our belongings"

"How do you feel?" asked Arthamaeus.

"I think the worst of it has passed," answered Cromwell.

"I hope you are right," Arthamaeus brought him a book to write against. "I will find a messenger if I can"

"Thank you Arthamaeus," he returned the man's nod as he left their chamber.

Chapter 9

When morning came, Arthamaeus took inventory of what supplies they had left in the house. There had once been preserves and dried fruit, as well as cured meat, butter, and cheeses in the larder to last them through the winter -- these were all gone now, he would have to tell Cromwell. They were out of firewood too and he decided he would see what could be found before his master awoke.

There were few people out on the streets and some of the shops were boarded up. He walked down a few blocks while a stray dog barked at him, following at his heels and making him uneasy.

At last it gave up on him, seeing that he had nothing to offer it nor posed a threat to its territory.

It took him longer than he had hoped to find what he was looking for, along with a few other articles that would come in useful from the apothecary, who was doing brisk business, although his supplies were running low.

Arthamaeus purchased some black tea and ginger, vaguely remembering them as suitable things to offer during illness, for not much was left for the asking.

The stairs creaked and a draft closed the door heavily behind him as the young man made his way upstairs, leaving his heavy burden in the hall.

"I found an old cart abandoned in the street and broke it down for firewood, do you think anyone would mind?" asked Arthamaeus, "I got some nasty splinters hauling in the decaying contraption"

"At least you have yet to use the furniture for timber," Cromwell remarked, watching the other carefully examining his hand. "I wonder if the innkeeper will come back"

"I think he has abandoned this sinking ship, otherwise he will not be pleased when he sees the carpet," he confessed peremptorily. "There is a hole in the thatch, it is an old place -- I wonder that it is still standing"

"It has history and location, well -- the latter is not what it should be, not until the plague passes on. Shall I not come downstairs then?"

"Better not, at least until your bath is ready," said Arthamaeus, trying to cheer him.

"That is good of you -- I do not regret taking you from the monastery, unless you might have been safer there"

"I think I would rather be here," the young man admitted. "I think a change of scenery was long overdue. Since you seem to be somewhat better this morning I though it was about time we made ourselves and this place decent, who knows when we might find a horse," said Arthamaeus. "The kettle is boiling too, I am going to make you drink some awful potion. I know you hate the taste of ginger root -- and do not worry, there is a different on the other side of the river"

Cromwell wondered how long Arthamaeus was imagining they would stay there. "I will not forget your consideration, you always mix my bitter potions with honey"

"I want you to get better, where would I be if you died?" he said ingeniously. "You must get your strength back. Have you any appetite?"

"Not much," said Cromwell. "I will do my best not to leave you with the business of carrying out my corpse, it would be most ungrateful of me after all the trouble you have gone through"

"It is no trouble," said Arthamaeus. "I think we get along well, you never ask anything unreasonable of me -- if I bring you some bread and cheese, will you eat it?" he asked, "I will try making some soup later, although I do not know how well it will turn out"

"Anything will do, throw it in the pot if it is not yet spoiled," he nodded.

"You doze for a bit then and I will bring you down when the bath is ready"

…

Arthamaeus led him to the wash-tub which he had rolled with some difficulty to its place by the hearth, warming the water in large pans over the fire and pouring them over several trips, followed by a bundle of forget-me-nots -- plucking the flowers into the bath water.

"Why the flowers?" asked Cromwell, returning his quizzical smile.

"I thought that you might like it -- I hope it is not odd of me, but I thought they looked beautiful like this. I once saw flowers floating in a pond, one of the farmer's children had been throwing them to bring good luck to their sister who was getting married," his voice drew on in embarrassment. "She was taken to her bridegroom by boat along the river, the boat was full of wildflowers"

"I am certain that your wife will find such rituals most romantic on her nuptial night," said Cromwell, slowly removing his robe and lowering himself into the water with an unusual self-conciousness, wondering why the young man had not left. "T-thank you Arthamaeus, I have never had such a fine baptism, and I am sorry that you have to see so much of me"

"I have seen everything at the communal baths at the monastery," he replied awkwardly.

Cromwell sat down in the bath, his knees close to his chest, feeling like small child while Arthamaeus massaged his hair into a bird's nest.

"Is this what you and the monks would do?"

"Not really, I was not really familiar with anyone," he told him, his face burning, "some people are though, the Abbot would say it is for lack of women. Some would be scolded for sleeping in the same bed"

"Did you miss the company of women?"

"I am too afraid of them -- their reaction, to know them in an intimate way"

"Why is that?" asked Cromwell, surprised by the other's modesty.

Arthamaeus paused, debating how much he ought to say, if it was perhaps too soon.

"Well…I…I guess because they would know that there is something wrong with me, if I grew too close," he answered. "Of course, there was never much opportunity, although some managed if they really wanted to"

"What do you believe is wrong with you, if you do not mind me asking?"

"I was born with a kind of deformity," he began, turning away and folding and unfolding the towels, "or more truthfully, I was made to have a deformity," Arthamaeus admitted reluctantly. "When I was young, it was intended by the Abbot that I sing in the Italian choirs, I was going to be sent as a servant to the Pope, in addition to sacred reliquaries and illuminated manuscripts.

A year passed while preparations were being made, my voice began to change, as I got older. The Abbot had learned many things while visiting his friends in Italy, they introduced him to the practices of the *castrati* and a renowned surgeon was persuaded to accompany him on the way back to England.

He went reluctantly and for a generous fee, some time before the operation I recall their argument in half-hushed voices, how I was too old for the usual methods to be used, but the Abbot did not lose hope.

I remember the agonies of the procedure and the days which followed it, grateful for those hours when I had passed out from the pain. I feared that there had been a mistake with the surgery because I had struggled, that I would die from the wounds, as such things did happen often enough.

I did not know any others who had something of the kind done to them and was ashamed to speak of it with the other monks, who were led to believe that I had taken ill"

Cromwell listened in silence, realizing that the young man he saw before him was a eunuch. He had heard of such things from his time in Rome, but was not aware that these Italian practices had been taken on in England. It must have been another of the Abbot's eccentricities, for which his ward had paid the price.

"In the end, the surgery took place too late for it to salvage my voice, to the Abbot's discerning ear," Arthamaeus continued. "Nor could he risk sending me to the Pope, seeing the change it had affected in my character. The Pope had only to look at me for him to believe that I had been possessed by the Devil, those were my guardian's words. For some time after I would not take food or let anyone come near me.

Well, to put it concisely, I am neither a man nor a woman now, in the ordinary way -- yet even before this surgery, I think I was born with something wrong with me and that may be part of why my father sent me away to the monastery.

I try not to dwell on it much these days, it was over a decade ago when it happened, but sometimes it bothers me, when I think of the life I could have had.

But then, maybe even if my body was just as it ought to be, my soul would not be -- I could never just do as I am told, I guess you could call it a sort of restlessness of the soul. I did not mean to give them a difficult time, I just wanted to get out. Sorry, I will stop talking," Arthamaeus breathed heavily, setting down the brush with which he had been combing Cromwell's hair. He had not intended to make such a full confession, but it came out of him -- for a long time he had wanted to tell someone, someone who he thought did not believe in the same god as the Abbot did.

"It is okay, you need not make a fuss about me," he took the comb gently from Arthamaeus, setting it down. "It is difficult to believe, what you are telling me, but I do not see what motive you would have to deceive me -- it makes no difference, in either case; what you were born as, or what you were made into, you are still young and may make yourself what you wish within the bounds of your capacities"

"Thank you," said Arthamaeus, almost inaudibility.

"Do not thank me"

...

Cromwell put on clean robes, walking back to the bed where he sat down on the edge of the mattress, looking at the young man and wondering what difficulties may lay ahead for him. He did not know how to help him or what was needful, but he would do his best for Arthamaeus.

"I-I should go, I am sorry," the young man held the door ajar but seemed to hesitate, as if he had neglected something. "Is there anything that I should bring you, if you --"

"There is no need to be my nurse anymore, I assure you," said Cromwell, "I am feeling well enough to look after myself. Tell me -- is there anything that I can do for you?"

"No, I am fine," a sudden overwhelming feeling pressed him to depart, as if remorseful of having said too much in a faltering moment.

He had felt frightened for a while; of the surrounding calamity, of himself and of his guardian, of the uncertainty which clouded the future like a mist.

He wanted to relieve himself of some of his burdens, for he had collected too many new ones since he had left the abbey; he would have to relieve himself of the burdens of the past to make room for those of the future, feeling an intense anxiety about what would be expected of him, cloaked in a fear of failure, of disappointing his master.

If Cromwell should reject him, he would rather that it happen sooner than later -- he would get the pain of it out of the way. He did not know what he had expected, but what he received left both his inner loneliness and secret masochism unsatisfied, leaving undeserving unquenched desires for comfort and loathing.

He did not trust himself to remain in his guardian's presence until he had gotten a hold of the crippling, terrifying, and deep-rooted things which he had long kept locked somewhere in the dark, permitting him to go unassumingly about his work.

. . .

Cromwell was surprised to find that Arthamaeus was still up, and more so to find him kneeling by an icon of Saint Gertrude which he had propped up against a book, nearby a red wax candle which burned faintly in the gloom of the bedchamber.

He was murmuring something which he could not hear.

The words stopped and Arthamaeus turned, having heard a movement and faint footsteps behind him, startling him out of his reverie.

"You are awake still," he got up slowly, brushing the dust from his night robe.

"Were you praying?" asked Cromwell, approaching the improvised alter.

"Y-yes," he said, "I do not do it often, but then, I felt that I needed to speak with someone"

"Someone who would not answer back?"

"There is a comfort in that, in a way," said Arthamaeus, "but during certain moments, it is enough to believe that there is a being beyond the stars who listens"

"What do you pray for?"

"For you, for us," he told him, avoiding Cromwell's gaze.

"You need not, I will take care of you and myself, now that the illness has passed," he told him.

"I know," said Arthamaeus.

"What is she like, your saint?"

"She is the patron saint of travellers, of madmen, and of gardeners," he tried to find the words, seeking them in the dark, "but mostly she is the soul of my mother and something else I cannot explain really. My gods have no rules -- no desires, no expectations, no miracles or curses; they only are"

"Then what good are they to you, if they can do nothing for you?"

"I do not know," murmured Arthamaeus, "it is just a feeling"

"Saint Gertrude," Cromwell approached the icon, looking closer at the miniature. The painting was of the type that was mass produced in batches and sold on market days alongside girdle-cakes and rustic rosaries, yet something about it in that moment seemed to imbue the artwork with an aura beyond itself.

"This is the mother of the motherless," pronounced Cromwell.

He stepped closer to him and reached inside the pocket of his cloak where, alongside some folded letters and documents, was a silver lily which had been given to the guests departing from Queen Anne's table, infused with perfume at its waxen heart. Something of its aroma still lingered as he set it down beside the icon.

Cromwell's hand trembled as he ran his fingers through Arthamaeus hair.

The young man looked fixedly into his eyes, an earnest questioning expression within them, a thing unspoken.

Chapter 10

From the door he could see the other standing by the glass, looking at his reflection as if for the first time, a strange expression on his face of sorrow intermingled with resentment.

Cromwell did not mean to intrude into the room, yet what he saw left him paralysed, beholding the deep scars across the young man's back and the strange deformities hidden beneath his linen robes, which lay discarded upon the floor in a small heap.

He felt ashamed to have lingered so long at the threshold of the door.

"I know that you are there, I heard you going up the staircase," the other's voice had a defeated tone of resignation. "I wanted you to understand, you would have found out -- sooner or later, and it is better that you get over the shock now. Do you see what I am, do you know what sort of creature god made me to be?"

"How much of it is the work of god and how much of man?" spoke Cromwell, stepping closer to him, feeling a lump in his throat.

"It is the work of both," replied Arthamaeus, "how much do you think it matters, that I am an abomination, if I were never to marry?"

"How else has know of your secret?"

"The Abbot, but I have kept it from most of the monks," he answered. "It was my duty to scrub the floors and the washbasins, so I would bathe alone afterwards. Once I was caught, but I told the Abbot and the monk was apprehended and sent away. A scandal was circulated, involving the cook's daughter -- he was a layman; an invention of course, the monk never met the man's daughter. Even after his plans with the Pope had failed , the Abbot tried to keep me safe, in his own way. I was given my own chambers partially for this reason"

"I see," said Cromwell, taking in these revelations in their resurfaced form. "It is well to keep this to the few

who you can trust. Do not give into these fits and passions -
- these are old scars, I can see that they are," he tried to
instruct the youth, not knowing what words of comfort
would suffice.

"T-there was once a girl who would carry the milk
bottles from the village to the abbey and one of the monks
who had duties in the kitchen fell to desiring her," he began,
catching his breath, "he laid with her and told his comrade
who stood guard for him that she had a strange mark upon
her, like a claw in shape.

He and the friend quarrelled and the latter informed
one of the superiors of what had come to be. He who had
forced the girl had said that he had stripped her only to
know if the rumours were true that she was marked with
the hand of the the Evil One, and was a witch -- it was she
who made the baker's wife to miscarry. They burned her
on the day of Saint George"

"This is pathetic superstition which wicked men had
used to further their ends, but I will not let it come to that
for you," said Cromwell, "you need not fear it"

"How can you prevent that which looms in the
future?" he asked with despondency. "What reason have
you to take in such a wretch as I?"

"That is enough," said Cromwell, pulling him closer
as Arthamaeus staggered into his arms, a shiver running
through his body at their proximity; crying quietly into the
fabric of Cromwell's night robe; Arthamaeus felt warmth
and shame entangled in his heart and knew not how to
escape from it -- desiring that it should engulf him, possess
him like a spectre of starved desire projected onto one
being.

"You are too old for snivelling over what may or may
not be," Cromwell's voice reached him, pulling him away
from the momentary embrace of illicit feelings which in
that instant had transgressed into the realm of reality, in

that flicker of knowledge which seemed to have passed between them -- then swiftly vanishing back into the darkness where it had long laid dormant. "Dress now, there is no need to display further what brings you horror, nor do I advise you to put others to the trial"

Arthamaeus looked at him, unmoving, startling Cromwell with a premature awareness of something which ought not to have been brought to the light, yet despite himself, it drew nearer and nearer as he breathed in Arthamaeus's intoxicating closeness -- his pressing vulnerability, stirring his desires amid the thought that this vision would soon vanish like the phantoms of an opium dream.

"I-I am sorry," Arthamaeus sank to the ground, wiping his tear-stained face with his arm.

Cromwell picked up his clothes from the floor and helped him to dress, clumsily pulling on his night gown, adjusting the sleeves.

"There -- you are cold," he murmured, "take something to drink. I will find you --"

"You are not disgusted, you do not think that I am --"

"Do not berate yourself," said Cromwell, "speak no more of it now. Understand that I am not easily shocked, having lived long and seen all manner of inner and outer deformity. Have no fear that I would shun you Arthamaeus for the wrongs done to you by others, it is I who ought to suffer at your feet and not the reverse. My regard for you has not changed and that is my burden, that is why I must send you away"

"I do not understand," Arthamaeus felt his heart beating in his chest.

"It is well that you do not, it is I who must ask your forgiveness"

Cromwell pressed his lips to the other's brow before releasing him.

He turned to leave, cursing himself for his ill-spoken words.

"Please, what I have done -- I am sorry," the youth clung to him, not allowing him to depart.

"Arthamaeus --"

Chapter 11

When their horses stopped at the third inn, the last stage of their journey together, Sadler's agent was already waiting inside, impatient to get going. Cromwell debated whether to wake Arthamaeus or carry him inside the other's coach, deciding upon the latter -- feeling ill at ease about a prolonged parting ceremony. He realized then that the youth had taken a sleeping draught, for the glass bottle lay empty.

Their acquaintance had indeed been brief and yet he could feel that he had known Arthamaeus for some years, in the semblance of his deceased father. Not only his face and figure, but even his mannerisms and way of speaking.

He asked himself if it was his conscience vexing him regarding his role in Thomas More's death, or a different force which made him wish to delay their separation, which seemed to Cromwell all the more necessary with the possibility that his distorted feelings were requited.

It was easier to deceive himself before, to make pragmatic excuses for his motives -- he did not think that he could manage with the hindrance of having Arthamaeus about during this critical time in his career, nor could he rightly neglect his duties to the King -- but since the prior night, he was obliged to face a side of himself which forced him to recoil.

Therefore it was well that he had delegated his guardianship of Arthamaeus to a man better suited for the job, whose relationship would not be marred by inappropriate attachments which would cloud rational judgement and bring further pain and confusion to a young man who had already endured much.

When the passing of time allowed these strange passions to subside and fade into memory, he would return to take him from Sadler and make good his promise -- hopefully better learned in the practical arts and sciences of his profession than what he had likely been taught at the monastery.

As Cromwell made the final arrangement and paid the necessary fees, he still felt the painful aching of treachery -- both against himself and his ward.

If there was a devil perched upon his shoulder, it would suggest to Cromwell whether it was not too late to go back upon the exchange. He knew that he would not act upon this temptation, but neither could he ignore it -- he would dwell upon it in the years to come, after the dead body of the coach driver was found by the roadside on the following day, but not that of the youth -- wondering if the coach had always been empty, were it not for the letters, statements and accounts which assured him that there once existed an Arthamaeus More and a Ralph Sadler, and that they were both dead and not dead.

He would send his agents to search for the ghost of a young man, and like the princes of the Tower, he would one day resign himself to the enduring mystery of the disappearance.

The myths of the ancient Greeks are full of such beautiful beings who the gods do not long permit to remain amongst mortal men, instead they carry them back to Olympus where their fair limbs of flesh and blood are transformed into a more enduring substance -- and should they decay upon the earth, the blood which falls from their ambrosial veins transforms itself into wildflowers as was fated for the fair Hyacinthus, beloved of Apollo.

But these events had yet to pass.

In the interval of ignorance, on the day of parting, Cromwell could give himself a day to repent -- a day to sift through his pangs of uncertainty, believing that what is done can be undone -- watching the silhouette of the carriage receded away into the distance.

When at last it disappeared from view, Cromwell vowed that he would return for Arthamaeus when he freed his conscience from the deformity hidden in his nature, while in the meantime he would serve his old master, King Henry, who was ill pleased by the prolonged absence of the Master Secretary.

…

"Promise that you will write to me when you arrive," Cromwell had said, shaking hands with the young man, who nodded his assent in bashful politeness, still groggy from the effects of the sleeping draught.

In a daze, Arthamaeus remembered picking up his bundle of provisions from the inn and checked that he had not forgotten the money and travelling papers which Cromwell had given him, dropping them to scatter on the floor of the coach. Then both he and the papers were lifted and arranged in their proper place.

He remembered how Cromwell's eyes had followed him with a lingering gaze, wondering how long it had been since he had felt the stirring of affection towards a stranger, all the while aware that the warmth of this fatal attraction was illusionary -- knowing little of the Master Secretary's heart. Cromwell had once told Arthamaeus whist he lay sick that he had a comely face, like that of an elven princeling, a face long engraved upon his memory. He had read much into these words and repented of his false hope, yet it had already taken root inside his heart. There too was the memory of their prior night, the anguish and relief of having made a full confession, lacking only the profession of his feelings, which he dared not speak of.

The coach driver made signal that the horses were ready and that it was time to leave, one of the two black steeds pawing at the ground in obvious restlessness.

The remainder of Arthamaeus's meagre luggage was loaded after him and the driver manoeuvred the horses onto the cobblestone road under Cromwell's sombre gaze.

Arthamaeus watched him from the window of the coach, a part of him still hoping that the journey would be stopped -- but Cromwell had been firm with him, that he wished him away from the regions struck by the plague, hoping that the house of his improvised father would prove a suitable refuge from London, where he was headed. Arthamaeus did not ask further questions, seeing that it was decided. He took a small vial from his pocket and drank it down, not wanting to think or to see, not wishing to be awake until he reached his destination.

Chapter 12

"No -- he is breathing"

"Are you certain?"

"Well give him a shake"

"Let him sleep, what does it matter"

"This is the one?"

"Cannot you not tell"

"Be quiet"

"What is that there?"

"You had your own"

"Look, he is moving --"

Arthamaeus slowly opened his eyes, his head still aching.

"Do you speak any Greek?" a gentleman with a trim white beard asked Arthamaeus, offering him some cherries from a wicker basket placed between them.

He and others had joined him in the coach part-way through the journey. Arthamaeus wondered who they were, and if this was part of Cromwell's arrangements, but reserve and exhaustion kept him silent. Finally the effects of the sleeping draught were subsiding and he felt himself roused by hunger.

"Not well, I can read…a bit," he replied, seeing the man look at him with a kindly interest, like a visiting uncle.

He imagined that the gentleman would soon introduce himself, but he did not.

"Go on, take some cherries"

Arthamaeus took a handful, thanking the fellow.

"Can you read this?" he gave him a piece of parchment.

Arthamaeus looked down on it -- it seemed to be some kind of story, about a boy whose village had been attacked by soldiers, he and his sisters were taken prisoner. But then the Persian King, the King of Rubies, had saved them and taken him to his palace to serve him. The King of Rubies called himself so because that is how he made his fortune -- from the mines.

"Can you read it out loud?" the man asked after a pause. "I will give you this, if you can," he held out a gold coin, scratching his whiskers and then grinning broadly with a twinkling in his eyes. "Let us see how well they taught you at the monastery -- I know you had been a special pupil and had a fine voice"

"Excuse me sir, but have we met before?" Arthamaeus looked at him closely but without recognition. This effort seemed to amuse the man further.

"I am a personal friend of the Abbot," he explained, "he had told me much about you"

Arthamaeus laughed nervously, trying to overcome his reticence, as if wishing to contradict any negative impression the Abbot's words might have made upon this stranger, imagining that any reference he might have gotten from his old guardian could not have been in his favour. And yet, the gentleman took a visible interest in him, this could not be by coincidence. Gathering spirit, he began his narration in a clumsy stammering Greek which the stranger was weighing like a schoolmaster.

"Not so good as I had hoped, but it may do, it may do," he rubbed his beard like a stage actor while looking aside. "What do you think William?"

The stocky man across from them shrugged and made a strange gesture at Arthamaeus.

"Certainly, certainly," the older gentleman nodded, then turning to Arthamaeus. "Are you willing to rehearse a little bit? For a proper fee, of course"

"Excuse me, with all due respect, I do not wish to join a theatre troupe," said Arthamaeus.

"That is not what we had in mind for you, young man, you are going where you shall be appreciated by a more discerning audience," he explained.

"Sadler House?"

"Oh no, somewhere further than that, most certainly -- you would like to do a bit of travelling, is that not so?"

"I-I am not so sure," stammered Arthamaeus.

"Your father meant it as a bit of a surprise you see, an adventure -- be at ease now, it will not be long before we reach the port," the gentleman reassured him, ruffling his hair in an over-familiar manner.

"What about Master Cromwell?"

"What about him? He will be waiting for you when you arrive -- do not worry lad"

Arthamaeus pushed the hand away and tried to grasp the door handle of the coach, but the large man across from him made a lunge to restrain the youth, forcing him to sit between himself and his fellow guardsman. Arthamaeus had no doubt that something was wrong, when he saw the the coach nearing a bustling port and seaside he doubled his efforts at escape.

"Sit down you sissy," muttered the older gentleman, cursing under his breath. "Do not bruise him, better that you tie up his hands now than later so he does no harm to himself, God knows we will not soon find such a eunuch"

Chapter 13

 Cromwell observed the passing of time, wondering when the message from Sadler, or Arthamaeus himself, would come, a sense of duty to Thomas More weighing upon him, lest he had discharged it without his usual due diligence.

It had been his intention to accompany Arthamaeus to his destination, but a subconscious wariness towards his own intentions made him renounce this obligation, which meant more to him than it ought. He was obliged to admit to himself that he had been transfixed by the young man's beauty, which appeared to him frequently in times of distraction, evoked by the adornments of King Henry's palace -- paintings and engravings, even the figures of pages who would pass by him before he could behold their faces.

When he went with the King to his private chapel, there were the marble statues of the twin angels, kneeling with their faces turned towards heaven. He wondered if Arthamaeus still prayed, or if like Cromwell, he believed that God helped he who helped himself.

There was no sin in admiring his noble countenance, confessing to the loveliness of a form, the perfect mean -- a strange androgyny of the masculine and the feminine, strength and softness, submission and defiance. It was the being of flesh and blood which he feared to approach, and not the vision, lest he should contemplate it as more than an ideal of his dormant desires.

Hitherto he had never felt such admiration of the male form. It is not love that he feels, but a mode of worship towards an unknown -- for what can weave itself between two men who had know each other by sight and presence alone by the banks of a Florentine river, drifting along separate paths until being again united by obligations and by plague. He pondered this strange romance and its possible conclusions.

Each has his assumptions and the unspoken rules of society to restrain him against impropriety, as well as the likes of conscience and timidity in all of its forms. This delicate balance of etiquette would leave little room for intimacy of thought and feeling -- not before the public eye, which would soon suspect their sin. All that remained was intimacy of the body, whereby he could remain in the presence of the object of his admiration, enjoying the subtle pleasure of familiarity and the subtle pain of longing for something which he would not grasp, were fate to offer it to him.

These were the thoughts which moved within Thomas Cromwell as he conjured the already distorted images of the young man whose guardian he was to be.

What vices, what virtues lay beneath the fair lacerated skin of Arthamaeus, he would never know except in the pangs of sickness -- allowing him to be painted in the mind's eye with a shroud of shadow and light, growing dimmer with the passing of each day, like an old painting left to decay.

Perhaps, with the passing of years, he would discover it again, much changed, and repent that he had not admired it, while the fresh colours of youth still graced the surface of this creation of god. Not the god of the ascetic, who flagellated the human form, bleeding out its wickedness, but of the pagans, who worshipped it and lay upon it its wreathes of laurel, oak, and myrtle.

In the months that followed, he did not permit himself time to dwell upon these futile thoughts, immersing himself within the usual balm for anything which resembled loneliness or unrest within his soul.

He worked through the long hours of the night, until his body told him that he was weary enough to sleep, and not before. To lay within his bed while his faculties were still alert would mean that he would be visited by phantoms -- their pale arms pulling him nearer and nearer to the abyss of longing, a Hades where he could not follow them, these ghosts of the fair Arthamaeus, these ghosts of his wife, his father and mother, those whose lives had been prematurely concluded by means of his ministrations.

He did not know what roles gods, fates, kings, and men took, and that creature -- the servant of man. Cromwell wavered in the degree of accountability which he allowed himself to take within the recesses of his conscience, a cerebral chamber which he found distasteful to visit often, for it would interfere with being able to effectively carry out his duties. He tried to balance his scales each morning -- if with one hand he had tried to punish or condemn, with the other he tried to save, to forewarn, to advise one in such a way that they may still save themselves, if they acted decisively, if they trusted in him.

Sometimes they manage to elude the hand of the King, of which he was an extension, and it pleased him to see it so, for even devils are bound by the terms of a contract, limiting their powers to do evil -- but their nature, and the purpose to which they were born, prevented them to approach too closely the sphere of the blessed and the good.

Then, to think of dichotomies of good and evil -- it is the way of children. All men bear these contrary ties within them, internal and external forces rocking them to and fro, so that one can never be certain of that thing referred to as character.

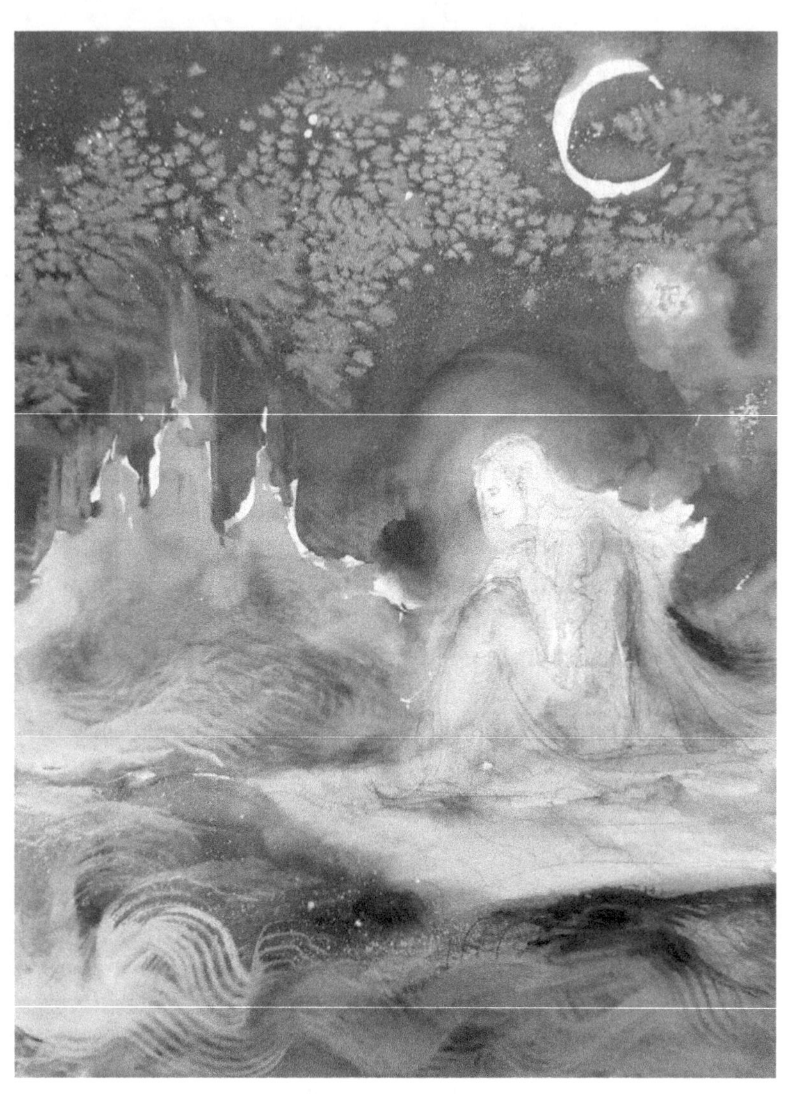

Part 2: The Memoirs of Arthamaeus

Chapter 14

I was taken aboard a ship along with an eclectic collection of books, furniture, instruments of alchemy, preserved specimens of plants and animals, and various other curios which I later learned were bound for Persia. The surgery which made of me the being I am now took place aboard the cargo vessel, done by a barber who specialized in such work, and two men of the crew who held me down, warning me that it was in my best interests to lay still. At first I thrashed and tried to free my limbs from their hold but as the barber approached with his instrument I did as I was advised, my eyes and my jaw clenched tight.

Their motives for hurrying the procedure, as I understood from my fellow prisoners, was that if I were to die from the complete gelding, then expense would be saved in disposing of me early on in the journey. I suppose they did their best to be careful, seeing that I was an unusual specimen -- half of the desired procedure had been completed years ago, I had lived; there was reason to be hopeful. For several days thereafter, I was subdued with opium and kept under a close watch until they felt I was out of danger. For the remainder of the sea voyage, I was to lodge with the rest of the human cargo.

Cabin space was scarce in the musty chamber which was shared between myself and a dozen or so other slaves of various capacities, sorted by occupation -- some intended as labourers, house-servants, and courtesans.

Some had come willingly, hoping to find better opportunities abroad, a few were criminals fleeing from the executioner's block, the rest were foolish figures like myself who had come unwittingly to their demise. Among us was a taxidermy bear which could not be found a home elsewhere and like myself, kept his own council, meeting anyone who approached with a look of impotent ferocity -- the object of crude banter.

For some days I lay prone in a corner, I could not touch food and would barely get up to take care of nature, which was as a torture to me for a while after the surgery.

Sometimes I could not help it and would sob in the night from the pain; I was certain that the wound had festered and I would be left to die somewhere like the scraps from a butcher's shop, not knowing whether it was good or dire fortune by which I had managed to conquer this illness.

As the days passed, I grew acquainted with some of my shipmates, these were mostly street urchins and low courtesans, chosen for their looks rather than their temperament. Some were sullen and spoke little, others were prone to quarrelling and venting their spleen upon one another, and at times upon the man who was sent down to check upon us and bring us our dollop of gruel.

The sea sickness and stench aboard the ship seemed unending. I spent as much time as I could by small port window over which there was much brawling for precedence, the same was the case for straw mattresses. At first I did not think myself up to the challenge but thought better of it after a few days passed in this way.

We stopped by several ports which I had no way of recognizing, having travelled little around England and the continent. Occasionally I caught fragments of bastardized tongues being shouted as cargo was loaded and unloaded.

This sometimes meant fresh provisions and occasionally we were given fruit such as I had never tasted at the abbey.

I prayed earnestly when we were given the command to disembark, wondering whether the worst was soon to be ending or only beginning.

The fever which had taken hold of me around the time of my arrival had only half subsided when they thought it best to prepare me for the market, while there was still a chance that I might not die. A touch of heat, that is all, they would say as the buyers examined my sickly countenance.

The first, second, and even the fourth day at the stalls did little good for the slave vendor's pocket, in fact, I think I had a negative effect on the rest of his merchandise, especially when I collapsed from the makeshift pedestal he put me on. The price which he asked for me was too high, given the risks that were taken, and it took some time to haggle it downward.

It really was the heat then -- I guess I was not used to standing outside in the scorching sun, although they gave me water. I think they thought it would help get rid of the fever, which in a way I suppose it would.

I was too much lacking in courage to attempt to run away, not knowing where I was or where I could run to for safety. The city seemed to be a large and crowded one and I was to stand out like a target for ransom in any multitude, with the heavy irons paced around my ankles. Perhaps I could have twisted out of them, but something told me it was best not to attempt it, not yet. I had not reached the point of desperation, foolishly I thought that a better opportunity of escape would present itself once I was sold -- once I gained their trust, if they were cruel masters, I would let them think that I am meek and submissive, waiting until they sent me on an errand, and then I would make for the docks, hire myself out to scrub the decks or work as a scullery cook. This was how I imagined it worked. They could not keep me from fantasizing, dreams which alternated between the morbid and the wondrous. Anything that would get me away.

By the fifth day, the slave dealer's old woman scrubbed my skin raw, muttering something under her breath while I tried to stand still, I am ashamed to say that I felt like crying, not for this strange treatment but out of feeble self pity and waning hope. I had turned twenty two that day and was thinking about how it did not matter anymore, putting on a strong face, pretending that I would make something of myself once I became a man.

I was the white crow in the flock, only with large brown birthmarks like splatters of mud upon my back. It was these that she was trying so desperately to wash off, unwilling to admit that my market value would be less than what she anticipated. She felt deceived by the vendor, but it was too late to bring down the price. They feared the buyer for whom I was intended had changed his mind -- only his agents were late in coming.

The man who I mistook for my new master was far from being an illustrious personage, a swarthy garrulous figure who sold large quantities of silk and dried figs across land and sea, slave dealing was but one of his secondary lines of business. These figs I ate so often that I was quite sick of them after a few weeks, although the recipes which I learned I carried with me -- the cook was always in search of something to delight the King's harem women.

The matter of my education to be received into the Ruby Court was delegated to one more suited to the job, the son of this merchant, who had been sent to study under a Greek tutor who had fallen upon hard times. To supplement his income for teaching stoic philosophy and Aristotelian ethics, he taught court etiquette and other such refinements which met the needs of the burgeoning merchant class. After my morning lessons, I would assist my master with assorted clerical duties and at times by helping the other slaves carry parcels to and from the storehouse, or upon errands as a messenger.

The climate was often hot and stifling and it took me time to get used to it. During the summer a poultice of aloe would have to be applied to my sun-burnt skin before I went to sleep, usually in the morning most of the pain would subside, and I soon learn my lesson to wear long sleeves against the midday sun.

The lady of the house had two daughter who kept a lizard as a pet, this creature had the remarkable property of changing colours and we would amuse ourselves in hiding and searching for it in turns.

I would not have despaired quite so much if I had known at the beginning that this would be my fate, a fig merchant's scribe and errand boy. But I was mistaken, for there I did not remain long.

What followed could have gone one of two ways, either the King liked oddities, novelties and curious creatures -- or he did not. It was not him that would make the choice, of course, I was already spoken for by the man who sought out potential servants. I suppose he knew the King's tastes, or maybe this was a new venture, something to brighten his monotony. My face was a fine one, the crone's husband said for me, holding me firmly by the shoulders as he smiled with in ingratiating but impatient manner, annoyed that he had still do to some persuading. I was too thin and bruised for the commissioner's liking.

They talked some more and I waited in the shade in line with the courtesans and their masters.

I overheard that this man had once been in the carpet business, but had recently branched out to slaves. I had been a bargain, his brother had brought me in, having served the army and taken many from my village prisoner. I think he was lying, but it did not matter to me. I was asked to write down my name.

I picked up the quill and wrote *Ralph Sadler.*

It would be a crime to set down the name of my family, knowing the station which I would occupy, coupled with my god-cursed form, I could bring nothing but further dishonour. Besides, a name meant nothing here.

The King had wanted a Greek. I spoke and wrote in Greek passably well. The bargain was made.

They gave me a Greek name, *Ganymede,* which I thought was in poor taste, like naming an old crone Aphrodite, or a small dog Hercules.

They could call me what they liked, I just wanted to lay down, feeling my sickness returning. I do not know if it was nervousness or the heat again, or something that I had eaten.

The King's delegate took me to a room with sparse but well-made furniture of an oriental fashion -- a desk, a chair, two heavy wooden storage chests. He then asked me about my past.

I knew better than to contradict the merchant's account, which would perhaps lead me back to the slave's row.

I summoned my fragmented knowledge of the Greeks and began my tale, intending to stir the man's empathy if I could, although his hard lip and furrowed brow did not make me hopeful. I did not like to deceive, but neither did I wish to die. How naive I was then.

I had not been raised for battle, I told him stammeringly, my father had been killed thus and left me to my aged uncle. I could not defend my mother nor my sisters, or even myself. We tried to run for the forest, each taking what was about the house that would make due as a weapon, and hoped desperately for the best. Perhaps they prayed, but as for me, I could only hope, not trusting in the gods. I did not understand them, neither the ones who stood proudly in white marble temples, nor in dark musty caverns, with their crude faces etched in wood.

We scattered between the trees, thinking that would improve our chances. One of the solders went after me while I sprinted at the top of my speed, my side hurting and my throat parched. I recall how the sun penetrated through the canopy of trees, making shapes and crossing lines of shadow on the ground. I ran until I reached the river, then I knew that it was too late. This part was true, based on my first attempt to run away, when the ship took anchor at a trading port. Needless to say, I did not get far, most of us who made this attempt were beaten and kept on a close watch. The slave who killed the guard got the worst of it, I did not see him again.

Continuing with my narrative, I described how I turned around and thought that death might come quickly from the soldier. That is what happens to men with only a broom to defend themselves with, I felt ridiculous, standing there staring at him. He too was still as a statue, except for his strained breathing. We were both trying to catch our breath from our race. I could tell that he was looking me over, wondering what I was. Maybe he never saw such a thing as I before, a eunuch, maybe he mistook me for a woman or a djinn. Not knowing what fury compelled me, I suddenly lunged towards him, imagining that I could grapple his sword from him.

Then I returned to the lie that was not quite a lie, an altered memory from the abbey -- at home I had been raised as a potter's apprentice, until my father could save enough to send me to be a scribe at one of the noble houses or even for the court, or perhaps make a priest of me if I had shown any inclination in that direction. In the evenings, my sisters and I would gather at the family table to copy out letters and accounts in the fair methodical script which our father had taught us. When business was good, even my mother would be asked to take part and we would all work together by the candlelight late into the night. Our house had earned something of a reputation for our trade, or rather, my father did -- not correcting the belief that he could do the work of four men in an evening.

I could only wonder where he and the rest my family was, whether they were alive or dead. The soldier grasped my wrist in his strong arm, gripping it tightly and then flinging me backward, knocking the air out of me. He knocked me over the head I think, or maybe it was a punch to the nose -- likely it was both, whether by him or by another, in any case I awoke in a kind of closet aboard a ship which smelled of urine and decay.

The journey was several days and sometimes a boy would come to bring me some food. I tried to talk to him but we could not communicate well. I tried various fragments of different languages that I had picked up during my market-going days, but he either did not understand or did not want to make any sign that he did. I guessed that he wanted to stay out of trouble.

I ate the stale bread ravenously, grateful for anything to feed the gnawing feeling in my stomach. Sometimes the seasickness would get to me and I would add to the stench of the tiny chamber. It was a loathsome journey and yet I felt ashamed to be glad when I had finally reached my destination, I did not know then where I was headed, being too foolish of the ways of the world to still cling onto hope.

We stopped at several ports, but I could not tell where, having had little experience of travel, and in any case, there was little to be seen through the small begrimed windows. Still, I listened to the shouting of the men outside, the crashing waves of the sea, and the call of the gulls -- anything to give my mind material for thought besides dread or anxiety for the future. Perhaps I would get another chance to fight for my life, perhaps not.

I imagined various scenarios and how I would respond
if I were again faced by some of the soldiers who raided
my village, and how I might have helped my family get
away if I had my wits about me, cursing the paralysing
horror which took over me when I first heard the screams
and beheld the flames engulfing the lower floor of the
house. The room where my father's sword was kept was
too far out of reach -- anyone would have been scorched to
death if he tried to get it, and so I hoped that it was in his
hands before the fire took over. These were all useless
thoughts now, I said to myself, repeating like a mantra that
I must not look back. There was nothing left of it, surely.

This is the story that I told the world-wise man who
set down my account in short-hand for the King's master
eunuch to inspect -- a hodgepodge of truth and lies which I
hoped would suffice for these men to suffer me to live. I
felt ashamed of what I had become, as even to deceive a
stranger who did not see me a fellow man seemed to me
baseness. In my position, an honourable person would have
spoken words of truth and scorn, been prepared to die
rather than to beg such people in order to live as a slave.
Yet in that moment, in which heroic figures of a bygone
age were summoned within my conscience, I saw little
relation between their world and mine, where the rewards
of goodness and the punishment of evil in the hereafter
seemed less certain than the right of might, the reality of
the present, the poignancy of bodily pain. I was still
feverish and weak from the journey, I hardly knew where I
was and felt as one without allies either in this strange land
or in the place which I ought to call home. I was not
prepared to die, nor to live. Therefore, I obeyed, as this
seemed to me the path of least resistance. Almost
unthinkingly, I wished to please the one who inflicts pain,
like a dog or an old mule who fears the whip. There was
still a hope in me that the master would be just, if not kind,
if I did what was wanted.

And if I in some way erred, or was not such a marketable specimen of my kind, then my wish was that the pain would not last long. They say that God does not give one more hardship than his soul is able to bear. Looking back upon these thoughts in hindsight, I could see the spirit of youth still in me, which sees himself still in an important dramatic role, where each act and its consequences holds meaning, believing in profound motives rather than impulses -- feeling joy and sorrow acutely, like an taunt strings of a lyre being pulled for the first time.

At a distance, devoid of these existential tribulations, I would have seen something like this: I stood before the imposing desk as a schoolboy summoned to recite his Latin for an examination, trying to stand straight and not fidget, while managing some garbled pronunciation of what would have to pass for Greek.

"You will not see your old village again, nor can I say that it ought to lingers strongly in your memory after all of these years, for I am told that you have long been under the tutelage of the scholar, Agapetus," spoke the man behind the desk.

He had a thick black bearded and a muscular build, and looked at me with an unnerving unwavering kind of scrutiny which made me turn my eyes back to the ground.

This, I presume, he took for modesty.

I should mention that contrary to instruction in delivering my narrative, I had neglected to mention my descent from Alexander the Great of Macedon, which I believe was for the best, stretching credulity rather thinly.

"You will became a šarēši, a eunuch of the royal court", the man went on. "Unlike many, I was not severed at a young age such that the memories of my home are like a mist-shrouded dream, half-remembered and half-imagined. You are the property of the King now"

With these words he dismissed me, summoning an attendant to escort me to the unmarked palanquin which waited outside.

I pondered over his parting remark, whether it had been a subtle acknowledgement of my feeble attempt at corroborating the merchant's false tale, or a kind of confession, at times made of a sudden by world-weary men to strangers who they will never see again.

I too had my memories of a gradually receding land, buried for those intervals when I wondered what was out there beyond the palace walls of the Ruby Court. Although I had little love for them then, I desired for them more fervently when they felt leagues out of my reach.

Perhaps this is best, not to remember the past too fondly, when it had not been fond; it does no good to desire what is far from one's grasp, much less, what has always been a spirit of the night air, not made for the grasping hands of men, but for children who still know how to dream.

It was long overdue for me to become a man.

From arching windows I would I behold the outer world, as the birds do from the treetops. Upon perfumed branches and bountiful fruits many strange creatures perch, learning to be content with the surreal realm of the royal court.

To the outsider who knows not the ways of palaces, I can say that Susa is indeed like a wondrous vision -- I still recall my first impression of the imposing gates and tall ceilings, the mosaics and lush gardens, what could very well be imagined as the seat of a god.

But this is an earthly place, that cannot be doubted, with the passing of years I had seen much of the kaleidoscopic nature of men and the foibles of kings, being but a shadow or adornment for these majestic walls, although while I faded and decayed, the latter departed to heaven, carried upon horses of fire and ash.

Some say it is grand to depart from the dust of the earth while still possessing the strength, beauty, and unquenched faith of youth, but it is the pleasure of old men to watch the interesting things which pass them by in the streets, to hear news of those who they once knew, or observe the changes which sweep away kingdoms.

As Herodetus writes, it was believed by the Persians that we šarēši are to be prized for our honestly and loyalty, that like gelded horses and dogs, mankind also becomes docile, obedient and subservient.

My experience serving at the inner court of king Xerxes has shown me otherwise, having witnessed enough plots and violent intrigues to discredit this assertion. This is but one of his eccentricities, that our wealthy master styles himself with the name of an ancient King -- none dare to speak his true name or speculate upon his royal lineage -- not publicly, not with servants and dependants such as myself. The further one is from the court, the easier it is to doubt and to disbelief, the reverse is true as one nears the centre and beholds the theatre of opulence, in which we are each the master's carefully selected actors.

I had been born in Greece, they called me Ganymede, but my home in Pedasa is little more than a name to me now, I repeated to the master eunuch, who had the sole of my left foot branded with the royal insignia -- reminding me of a wax seal in the shape of a winged lion. This was to be renewed on certain ceremonial days, when I would be required to repeat my oath of loyalty and make obeisance before the royal throne.

It was expected of me that I forget these relics of my past, which was easy to do, for I knew little of Ganymede, and not much of Arthamaeus, who had been left at a cross-road, first by the Abbot, then by Cromwell.

Therefore, when the other servants asked me where I came from, sometimes I would weave tales for them that I had been the son of a magi, whose dealings with demons had led to him to sell my blood or my soul -- I showed them my back where the demon's claws grasped me, thus accounting for my strange appearance. I could tell that such things entertained them and it gave me pleasure to amuse them in this way. They each had tales of their own, equally fantastical, growing more so as they were passed on in rumour.

But when I was in no mood for tales, I would merely say that I had been captured while still a youth and sold to the slave-dealer, Panionius who had by then earned himself a reputation for trading in such commodities. His prized customers were the Persian nobility, who sought to replicate the ways of the court in microcosm within their own satrapies.

I do not believe that it had been Cromwell's intention to be parted from me in this way, for this was too base a deception, although I cannot be certain -- still, it is to Thomas Cromwell that I dedicate my memoirs of the Ruby Court, for I believe he is a man who would understand them -- the strange ways of powerful men, their capricious and insatiable desires, their intricate rituals and the subjugation in which they hold their disciples.

Chapter 15

At first they thought it best to put a dark pleated wig and gold circlet over my thin white hair and dye my barely visible eyebrows, outlining my eyes in khol -- not wishing for me to stand out from the other young men, who seemed to have a uniformity of appearance, standing at the ready like soldiers, except instead of weapons they held palm leaves, wine jugs, and platters of appetizers and sweet ices.

Or perhaps they were saving this surprise for the King, so he would be the first to know what a prize was in store from him. Perhaps I flatter myself, but when my various disguises were removed, I caused quite a stir. Not even the black and white striped horse was so gaped at, so closely scrutinized. I was the first of the King's eunuchs to be fully castrated.

For the most part, I kept my eyes averted from the royal gaze as I was told, glad not to have to speak or so much as give a sign of anything I might be feeling, which was predominantly a profound embarrassment for myself and these people who I hoped would have better occupation than to gawk at my mutilated genitals, of which the court physician was giving a detailed account.

I admit that at the time what I also felt was loathing, both for myself and for everyone about me.

Then, there was something else too, a curiosity which I was only beginning to admit to myself. I was going to be a member of the royal household, no matter how menial. I wanted to know what these people were like and in those early days, I still imagined that I would see England again -- thinking with each passing day what kind of report I would bring back, in the style of great explorers such as Marco Polo and Sir John Mandeville.

I would hold inner monologues of conversations, summoned before the Master Secretary and King Henry VIII, before scholars or half-drunk tavern-goers who would lend an ear to a traveller's tale, almost seeing their absorbed faces and eager questions. It was all make-believe of course, and it saw me through the days until my duties were enough to distract me, and worse, during the nights when I could not sleep.

The King of the Ruby Court admired Greek scholarship and philosophy, and hoped that I would impart some of my knowledge to his own descendants. The master eunuch put in a good word for me, seeing that I was able to read and write, and so I was granted the honour of tutoring the children of the royal hareem in alternation with five other masters of various arts.

At first they were wary of me, never having seen such a one as I and expecting I knew not what, but we soon grew used to one another and got on well enough. The chief difficulty was managing them when they felt no patience for these sedentary occupations which required a degree of focus which young fiery tempers would not forebear.

It was only by arousing their curiosity in a particular text that I could keep them still. These I would select from the royal library, containing many a scroll which had not seen the light of day in generations, or so it seemed to me, being of a nature that could only interest the most erudite of scholars.

Among them were the old account books of past kings and their noble subordinates, which gave me something of an idea of the lavishness of the ancient courts, which seemed to have only increased with the passing of time, or so I was eager to believe, captivated by the realm of this Xerxes reincarnate.

Indeed, the palace at Susa is a wondrous place to behold, and I have included detailed drawings of the architecture, ornaments and pottery in my memoir, which would serve you better than my words. But as for those who seek an intimate account of this reigning royal personage, they must search elsewhere, for my station was not one so elevated as to bring me often into the royal presence, not since my display as a novelty of the medical sciences.

Except for on grand occasions, where one may perhaps be fortunate enough to find a good vantage point from the balconies to take in a procession or the festivities of a banquet, only a select few eunuch and courtesans were summoned to wait upon the king -- a tall imposing man with a thick black beard, sensual lips, and a fondness for heavy golden jewellery in the form of mythic beings.

Once I had been called upon to fetch a bowl of rosewater for a foreign diplomat to wash his hands in. Although I did not know it then, it was this man who I would grow to know better than my master. His name was Ardashir, an advisor to the King who acted as his agent abroad. He was not of Persian descent, but was kept for his knowledge of statecraft and a renowned wile which made him a dangerous enemy, although he rarely altered his loyalties.

Whenever I had the chance to eavesdrop at these dinners, which I did not scruple to do, given that this was the currency of the realm and the occupation of us caged beings, I had grown used to the men who spoke a thousand tongues, masking one word with another like an ever-spinning codex.

Those who had served the court longer where more adept at deciphering these dialogues, knowing that the

King rewarded useful knowledge handsomely, while scolding those who greedily brought him little more than trite gossip. If someone brought a real gem of an intrigue, whether from the dining hall or elsewhere, he may see a bright and perilous future for himself.

That is why there was a sizeable faction whose position it was to keep a vow of silence and bashful ignorance, certainly these would outlive the rest in comfortable tedium.

I was not of their sort, however, and often marvelled how much was said in the open, if one only knew how to listen. Yet at the time, I had but one thing which I wanted to learn from this man -- I knew him merely as the recipient of a letter, a letter written in the hand of Thomas Cromwell, enquiring after a large shipment of fine silk requested by the Queen.

From the moment that I snatched the fragments of parchment from the burning embers of the fire, I became consumed by the mission of finding some pretext for speaking to this ambassador of the King.

This was less easy than I thought, given the careful watch that I felt over me, as did the other servants during an important banquet, lest anything should go amiss -- as it often did when too many men where gathered in one place who had prices on their heads and scores to settle with one another, all hidden behind amicable smiles, polite laughter, and ever-flowing praise of the King.

As I waited for the signal to bring in the plates, I looked about the room, and again my eyes returned to Ardashir, deciding that I would accost him the next time he signalled for his wine glass to be refilled -- something which taught me that he only feigned to drink, for his cup remained half full throughout the dinner. I suppose he wanted to keep his wits about him, or else had experience with a poisoner.

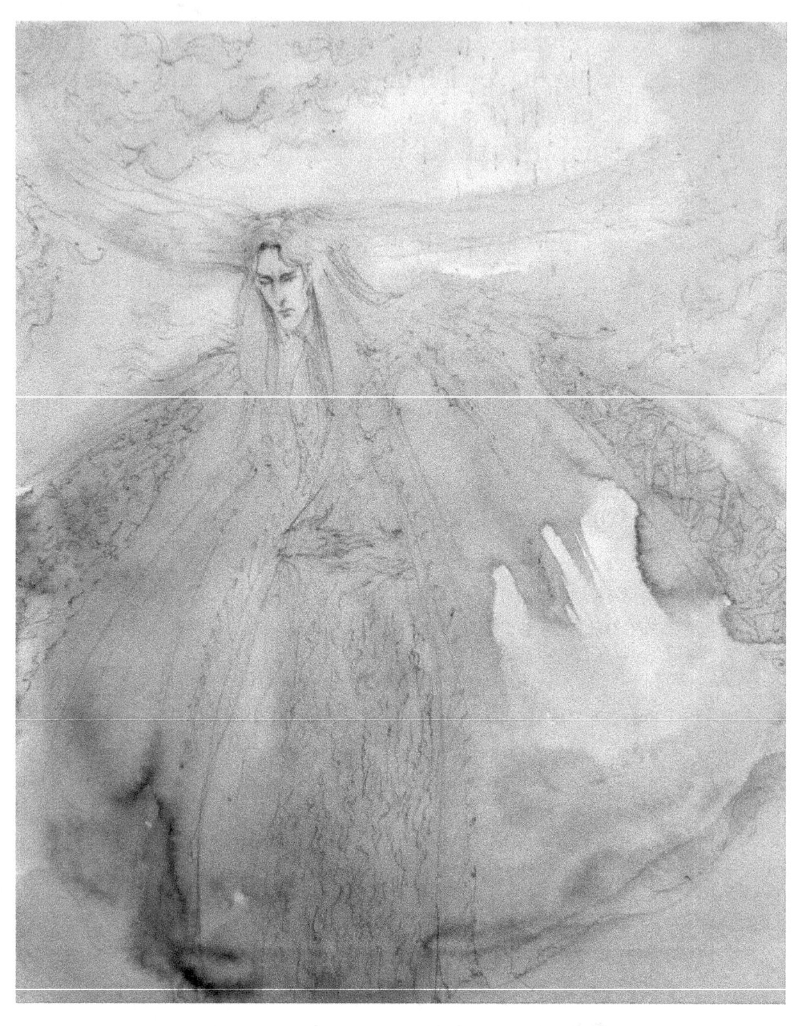

Chapter 16

Most of my time was spent running errands for middling court officials, carrying ink pots and tattered account books between this or that office, or copying out ponderous manuscripts of transitory value. I suppose this suited me well enough most of the time, giving me time to think and sufficient leisure to amble out, but I could not help but feel a creeping dissatisfaction, as is the lot of even the most blessed of men.

It is not that I had a high estimation of my abilities, or felt myself entitled to more than what I was fortunate to receive -- I could only describe it as a restlessness towards the monotony of my day to day life, and a discontent with the mistrust which made a wall between most of the other servants and myself.

I do not know why this was, that even with the passing of years I had failed to form any close friendships except those by which one saw me as a useful instrument to their ends. I suspected it had something to do with the impermanence of some of our positions, which depended so highly on staying in favour with both the King and the women of the hareem.

To be kept on indeterminately, once ones looks began to fade, a servant had to prove himself, something which was difficult to do within the narrow scope of our responsibilities.

Sometimes moving beyond duty was well received, at other times, a eunuch took a great risk upon his life -- carrying clandestine messages between one nobleman and a certain lady of the hareem, by bearing gifts to such and such an ambassador, or purchasing some unknown packet from a back-alley merchant.

The King did not like such business going about, unless it was his own, but it could not be helped. He did not like to be severe with us and sow distrust -- like most Kings, he wished to be loved and admired, rather than give signs of paranoia or cowardice.

And so, most of us believed that while a few of our number may be made examples of during instances of grave transgressions, this underground system of communication would go on as it had before. We understood these women, many of whom were captives much like ourselves, for whom the time moved slowly, gravitating towards inertia unless we reached out beyond the palace walls, even at the peril of this world of ancient customs and make-believe. The King's love was a fleeting thing and this was understood.

...

. . . .

As an established member of the royal household, there have been a few instances when I feared for my life. One of them started innocently enough, or I should say, foolishly,carelessly -- as such things often do.

The Lady Anahita had led me to the King's disused wardrobe, where he placed garments which no longer suited his tastes or the modes of the season, although many of them were lavish with golden thread and jewelled buttons, such that she felt it a pity that none should wear them.

143

As a game between her and some of the maidservants, she had us all dress up in men's clothing. I was to wear her dress.

This I had little objection to, it was only when she proposed that we go out to the King's banquet that I grew concerned. Her large black eyes glittered with mischief and taunting, daring me to go forth with this silly scheme, pulling at my sleeve and laughing at my inhibition to be beheaded.

That a lady of the King's family should be shown so brazenly in public was unheard of and I could only expect the worst to come of it. At the same time, I knew that I would not succeed in dissuading Lady Anahita, the most troublesome of my charges. Like a despotic queen, she would have her way.

I could only say that I was relieved that she did not venture to seat herself among the men, if only because most of the cushions were already occupied. We lingered at some distance by the great pillars, where the lady peered at her father and the master eunuch, while I prayed that neither would catch her eye.

I noticed that some of the maids had cautiously slipped away, leaving me to look after my lady while they summoned someone with greater influence over her to take her back to the hareem.

"You will go sit yourself there," she pointed to one of the cushions.

"Forgive me madam, but I do not think I should intrude upon --"

"It is no matter, you will merely have some wine and talk to that man there," she gestured to a comely youth who I did not recognize. I understood then the reason for this escapade. I tried to propose some less defiant way of making his acquaintance, such as carrying him a message.

This I would do as well, and a gift too, she insisted, taking a miniature box of aloe-wood from the fold of her dress.

After some further disputing, which was drawing the eye of the royal guard, I was given a push in the right direction, nearly stumbling over someone's embroidered slippers.

My presence was noted by one or two guests, but fortunately the King's attention was engrossed in conversation with the his generals and I was able to slip into the dining hall and seat myself upon the empty cushion.

I felt my face burn with embarrassment at my own audacity, questioning how I could have been bullied into this errand. But I believed then that the Lady would have me replaced, on one pretence or another, and where would I be then I could not presume to know. The monotony of my tutoring and scribe duties would grow in appeal to me at times such as these.

The youth had offered me a cup of wine and I must have murmured something half comprehensible, I do not recall, only that he asked me to repeat myself.

It was then that I sought to get the business over with.

I leaned closer to him and whispered that I brought a message from the Lady Anahita, slipping it into his hand as subtly as I could.

When I looked at his face there was an amused smirk upon it, something between incredulity and bravado. He took my gifts and slipped them into the small satchel-belt at his side, patting me on the shoulder in a familiar way, for it was too obvious that I was a man.

After that, he expected me to say something else, but I found my throat had grown hoarse with anxiety, fearing lest the master eunuch should have perceived this intrusion and breach of etiquette, and the slew of other offences against propriety which I embodied by existing in the dining hall without a platter of candied pistachios or a golden wine hug in my hands.

Suddenly, the noble youth asked me of my background. I took a long sip from my wine glass to give me time for invention, basing my narrative upon an account which reached my ears some years ago while visiting the market for turquoise beads and incense.

At last I told him that my family had rejected an old vizier's proposal for my sister's hand while he had yet to ascend to his lofty rank. This was a slight which he would not soon forgive. Then all scandal broke loose when it was discovered that my sister ran away with her beloved when she learned of the vizier's intentions, but was captured and returned to our family home. Her beloved was punished and she lost a part of herself since that event, having never been the same since. After a few years she died of sorrow and the vizier grieved that such a flower of beauty was crushed in the early stages of its bloom by the force of his own desire.

The youth listened attentively, his smiling widening as I went on. Once I had finished, he nodded gravely, took a drink from his wine cup, and burst into laughter -- turning the eyes of the assembly and of course, the King. I bowed my head low, pretending to adjust my sandal, grateful for the elaborate headpiece which partially hid my face. I hoped that the King would not remember it, for it looked some centuries old and had that particular scent that I recall whenever I visit the homes of the elderly with the monks to deliver jars of honey.

I thanked the gods that in that looming moment of mortification, an entourage of flute players and acrobats were ushered in to perform. The King was obliged to welcome them and acknowledge the guest to whom we owed these entertainments.

I quickly sprang to my feet and made a bow, overturning a bowl of olives and gracefully striding to where the Lady Anahita had stood. Of course she was not to be found, and I doubted it would do much good to look about, I was left to hope that someone of the household had taken her back to safety or that she had returned of her own accord.

In any case, I did not wish to be made responsible for one over whom I had no power and so I retraced our steps to the storage room where our game had begun and returned the eccentric garments to their proper place to gather cobwebs.

In the days that followed, the appearance of a strange gentleman was much talked of, rumoured to be the ghost of the King's various ancestors -- due to the mismatch of garments, the period of whose illustrious reign could not be fully ascertained.

Those lacking in superstitious predilections thought that it was a court fool, or one of the entertainers, who had gone too far in his antics, to mock at the ever-changing fashions of the court, perhaps making a jeer at the King himself and his royal pretences.

If the ladies had said anything, they were kind enough to spare my name, and so I considered myself fortunate.

We agreed thereafter not to use the secret passageway which they had discovered, hidden beneath a tile near the courtyard fountain of the hareem. Nor, I think, would we have had much of a chance to use it given that the number of guards had been increased. Whether this was due to some rumour reaching the King about our escapade, or because of the recent assassination of one of his generals, I could not say. His Excellency lavishly supported a private army of loyal friends and old veterans from the oft referred to glory years, for he liked military showmanship and equestrian parades, but sometimes when the mercenaries were not paid on time, things went amiss.

There was much talk about it for several weeks, until other matters began to occupy the King's thoughts, the threat of war and this or that suspected betrayal. As for myself, I tried to distance myself from such dangerous spider's webs, only going about the errands of those who sought freedom, love, or amusement -- things that might have a chance of being forgiven, or which, at least to me, had little malice in them.

My motives were to make the life of caged beings easier to bear, as I fear there is a certain kind of madness that comes with over-much confinement. It goes against human nature, to obey in all things, to hide oneself, to entertain no ambition but to please one who thinks little of us. Such a life is no life at all -- it is to fade away.

Therefore, I obliged my companions, or so I sometimes thought of them, even if I was little more than a servant to the ladies of the hareem. It is to them that I owe some of my greatest treasures, rare manuscripts which admirers would procure in the name of their beloved, wondrous histories and tales which they also delighted in when I would read them out loud over mint tea and dessert.

I kept a pet bird, or rather, the second wife of the king did, but had grown bored of the creature and so its care fell to me. It had bright orange-green plumage and its name was 'Mango'. It made a raucous each morning, as if making a point of rousing the household with the rising of the sun, but this I did not mind, liking to be up early.

Sometimes I would attempt to write poems and riddles, hiding them between the cushions or dropping them into empty flower vases for others to find, on some occasions I would have the fortune of seeing them be discovered and watching the reaction of however should find them.

It just so happened that one such parchment fell into the hands of the King. The ladies made no secret of who had written it and I was summoned into the royal presence. I admit I was nervous, scared even, as I had not been called upon in this way since I first arrived at court. Even then, the meeting had been brief, merely so that the King could examine me, dismissing me with the raising of a hand, neither one of us speaking.

This time, I believed that I would have to make some account of my actions. Perhaps I had displeased him, I thought, as I followed the page down the hall to the King's chamber.

The room was dimly lit by glowing candles, set within silver lanterns hanging from the ceiling. The King was drinking fragrant coffee, while small dishes of fruit, nuts and ices were laid out on a platter before his cushion. The servant beckoned for me to be seated, and hesitatingly I sat myself down upon the low cushion before the King, who was looking at me with unmasked interest.

"I have discovered a secret in the hareem," he spoke after the servant had left, unfolding a scarp of parchment and laying it out before me. I at once recognized it as my own. "Have you written any others?"

"Forgive me sir, I only meant to--"

"There is no need to ask forgiveness," he said, seeing that I had grown flustered, "my intention is to see you occupy your time with work more suitable to your nature, now that the children have grown older"

He explained to me that the keeper of the royal archives has need of an assistant, and there I would be placed. In my leisure hours, I was to transcribe the poetry of the court, adding something of my own verses for review by the council of adepts in this art. He asked me afterwards where I had learned to write, and I explained to him my father's trade, remembering fondly the books from which I had been taught at the monastery, and upon which I would draw my inspiration in the years to come.

The King is old, cruel and languid in his ways, so he had been described to me by one of the eunuchs Miresi, who was less reticent than the rest about our master, and so from his impression I had made my own before I had the opportunity to meet the King in person. I cannot say that I had ever truly grown to know him, but the kindness which he had shown me that evening I was grateful for, and therefore could not help but feel an increase of goodwill towards him.

It was some weeks later that I learned that his praise of my poetry was not entirely disinterested, finding myself summoned again into the royal presence after the King returned from his missions of diplomacy, bringing gifts for the ladies of the hareem, and a silver quill and ink pot for myself, engraved with fighting lions.

There was a message, too, and I felt ashamed not to have understood which of the ladies I was meant to give it to, for none of their symbolic names were referred to.

I considered asking one of the elder eunuchs, but while I was debating which way would lead me to make more of a fool of myself, one of the King's pages summoned me with impatience.

I had been planning to retire to bed, for it was quite late by then, and was certain that it was because I had failed to deliver the message that he was calling upon me. It was a poem, in praise of beauty, or so I had understood it. Perhaps it held a secret meaning to the Lady Urfaya, who had recently quarrelled with the King.

All that I knew of love, I had learned second-hand, feeling that my time had come and gone to seek such blessings. It was therefore a shock to me when I found myself alone with the King in his bedchamber.

Chapter 17

In England, one would dip a thief's hand in berry-dye; the dye would soak into the skin and stain the hand for several weeks and as such, serve as an act of public humiliation -- marking one as a thief and a criminal. Here this is the mark of one who had been bedded by the King and might soon be blessed with conceiving a prince. I wondered if distinction was extended to eunuchs.

He called upon me to approach, examining my figure and my frightened expression, which likely ill-suited one past the spring of youth. I did not know what I feared most, the act itself, or that I would disappoint him. With every passing moment it became more difficult to convince myself that I had misunderstood the King's interest, that this was merely a ritual which would soon pass. He told me not to tremble so, that he would show me gentleness, as he ran his hand over my cheek.

His face was quite close to me and his scent was that of overpowering musk and perfume, I struggled not to draw away and thereby cause offence.

When the King let go of me and seemed to fall into sleep, by the sound of his snoring, I thought that it might be safe to depart, although uncertain of the custom. As I walked past the guard, who must have heard what took place or had some notion of it, I wanted the ground to swallow me.

I bowed my head low, not wishing for the soldier to see my tear-stained face, feeling again like the overgrown child who could do nothing for his family's honour but submit in cowardice, fearing a noble death more than the absence of free will to one who chooses the devils he knows over those in the hereafter.

Yes, even after this I would cling to life, I confessed to myself, thinking of all of the suffering that I had seen and heard of beyond the palace walls. Here there was no war, no poverty, no sickness, no sorrow, no treachery -- all of these things must be hidden or exterminated, such that they seemed almost not to exist. This shame I must hide from all who ventured to know me.

When I was able to return to my chamber, I called for a bath to be drawn. Although I ought to have felt tired, it being long past midnight, I knew that I would not sleep at all. I felt a disgust in myself, and likewise, in the King, although I never dared to speak of it to anyone. Such things were treasonous, surely. I consoled myself to think that it could have been much worse, if I had been sold as a slave to a house of ill repute, this would have been my life each day.

The King did not call upon me again for some weeks and I wondered if it was because he could sense the repulsion I had felt, or if I had otherwise fallen short of his hopes. In either case, I was glad not to go back and tried to banish all memories of that night. Banishing memories was something that I had grown good at during my time at court.

Chapter 18

It was the first morning of spring. After the burning of myrrh and ambergris, the household and I were busy arranging platters for the dinner guests that would be joining the King, grateful that I would not have to serve in the hall itself.

Suddenly, I felt a touch upon my shoulder and in my surprise I let the glass fall, sending it shattering to the floor.

It was only the eunuch, Davani, who I later learned had come to tell me that a servant had come back with more citrons. I must not have heard him, so enthralled in my own thoughts. It was often enough that I was scolded for daydreaming.

The master eunuch, who had seen all this, said nothing, although he gave a tight little smile which spoke enough.

Signalling subtly to a servant, he led me out of the room while others attended to the broken glass.

I was grateful to be dismissed from serving that evening, and I wondered if the master eunuch knew something of what had taken place during the prior night, although he was not one to show signs of pity. I do not think I would be glad if he knew, remembering that he too had once been so favoured by the King, or so it had been said.

The master eunuch was a man past his fifties, I ventured to guess, or else the cares of his station had turned his hair grey prematurely. His face was like that of the priests, who could tell the most fateful of oracles without sign of emotion, while all around them might gasp or tear their hair in distress.

I went to bed early that night, hoping that by sheer exhaustion I would slip into the comfort of dreams. A fire was lit in the burner and I laid down under my blanket, pulling it over my ear. I murmured a prayer the monks had taught me, for the protection of the home against demons.

It felt strange when morning came, as if catching me by surprise, for it seemed that I had only recently closed my eyes.

It was still early, and as I stretched my limbs, ambling languidly to open the window and looking out over the distant mountains beyond the walls which surrounded the court.

Sometimes, from the balcony, I would watch as the rose petals were harvested before the sunrise, spread on sheets to dry under the hot sun. Rosewater was harvested through distillation, flavouring sweets and ices, or sprinkled over soups and blended with spice. I felt then how my stomach rumbled with hunger, as I had eaten nothing before going to bed the prior night.

As I went to make my bed, I noticed a message scroll rolled inside of a ring of sapphire and gold.

On the following night, the master eunuch went to escort me to the King's bedchamber, asking me before we entered that I take a draft from a golden chalice.

Chapter 19

I struck out against him, pushing him away as if struggling with a highwayman for my life in some shadowy street, a place where no one would come to defend me, but rather, to aid my assailant.

I feared that the King would call for his guards, but this he did not do, perhaps the indignity of being unable to subdue me kept him from it. When at last he backed away, both of us stared at one another with panting breath and hatred mirrored in one another's eyes.

I knew that my actions would not go unpunished, but I would rather die the death of insubordination to a master which I do not recognize, than that of a man whose will has been broken, who is a slave to a madman's passions.

I would not submit to him again -- I would play his game of King's Court, but not here, not in his bedchamber -- not being raised to be a courtesan.

Love for me was still a cherished thought and the body with its longings instilled in me both fear and abhorrence, so I had been raised to believe and so I felt by instinct when this man's hands sought to undress me, his brutish body forcing itself upon mine, pressing down upon me with his weight as he tried to manoeuvre himself on top.

I remembered the pain and disgust of the act, his heedlessness of my revulsion. I could still recall the scent of his sweat and his perfume, heavy with musk. His desire was to possess and subjugate, mine was to repel him with what strength I had in me.

We did not grapple long, for it seemed that never had he met with one who opposed him so earnestly, rather than see it as an honour.

So it felt to me, that if I were to give into him again, knowing what I knew, I would lose respect for myself, I would be his willing victim. The judgement of my father would glower down upon my, of my mother who surely repented of a like weakness, of my guardian, who I believed was invulnerable to these temptations, whose cold eyes still gazed upon me with contempt and pity. I thought of the Master Secretary's letter to Ardashir and the man's evasiveness when I asked him if he had heard news from England -- leaving me impatient to find reason for hope.

I wished to be worthy of their respect and their love, for too long I had submitted to all that had been done to me, claiming powerlessness and ignorance as my scapegoats, if I did not fight this false King now, I would establish him as my master.

I watched this man dress, myself sitting on the floor like a cornered dog, half-choked tears streaming down my eyes, his look of loathing never leaving me. I told myself that I was not afraid of him, but this was not true. I only allowed myself to exhale deeply once he had left the room, a tiger's march showing the offended pride of a one who thought himself too high above that creature which had denied him, leaving me to attend to my bruises.

I waited for someone to come to collect me, to lead me out of these accursed rooms and labyrinthine halls, but I was left alone for the night. The door was bolted, although I tried with all of my might to jar it free.

...

…

When morning came, I was summoned by one of the eunuchs, his wordless reproof throwing daggers into me.

I need not feel guilt before these men, I told myself, they cared little of what became of me, so long as they did not lose face before their master -- his laws and his justice was not my own, I owed him no loyalty -- I was like the wild beasts or birds who are trapped only for as long as their cage remains locked.

I repeated these words in my thoughts to give me strength as we walked on.

I was brought before the master eunuch, who made me no greeting but informed me that I was banished from the royal bedchamber.

To this I bowed my head, returning his grave look and waiting if he might say more.

He asked me if I would serve in the palace hall, listing the ceremonial duties with which I was well enough acquainted. I gave my assent, to which he replied with warning that should I disappoint in this role, I would be sold on the slave markets on the day of bidding when the brothel owners got first pickings. The King did not need any more feral decorative creatures.

Furthermore, I was to receive twenty lashes and bear the black mark of dishonour on my brow for all to see until the next full moon.

Thus were matters decided and I endeavoured to make myself obscure in the coming months while planning my escape to the merchants' quarter where I hoped to find a correspondent with connections to England, realizing that it was of no use to wait upon Lord Ardashir.

Meanwhile I focused on following the orders the King's staff obediently as errand-boy and house-servant.

Again I could feel complacency and monotony diluting my anger and resolve to leave this place, when I thought of the risk and uncertainty which is the lot of a runaway slave.

I did not know what would happen if I were caught, but I did not doubt that the consequences would be most severe and that the King would afford me no further mercy.

My idle hours soon grew less numerous, as my superiors took a particular pleasure in being able to give ceaseless scullery work to one who had scorned the King's service, punishing what they took for a haughty and rebellious nature.

Word spread quickly, despite the King's efforts to suppress the gossip which circled around his strained relations with the unwilling Greek eunuch, Ganymede.

I was glad of this name then, for it helped me to distance myself from past events -- if Zeus or Xerxes chose to punish him, or reward him for his submission, that was no concern of mine -- all that might happen to this body need not touch my soul unless I willed it.

Sometimes I could still imagine myself as the reclusive monk in the high tower, the son of Thomas More, ward to the Master Secretary.

Chapter 20

The gifts of the king were never an equal exchange -- indeed, the court system stood upon a foundation of unequal exchanges in various coinages, whether it be promotions, secrets, and other favours, debts and deeds, courtiers and noblemen circling like months around one oil lamp.

Lord Ardashir was one of the King's close companions, an honour and rare privilege bestowed upon revered persons who the King favoured to sit at this table. He had come far from his satrapy to serve at court and it appeared that the King was gladdened by the reunion, although Ardashir seemed rather more reserved.

I saw other men who came as far away as Egypt, Bactria, and Armenia. Or so they were announced to the King -- I no longer sought to distinguish what was truth and what was fiction in this effervescent play which was staged daily for the King's pleasure.

Profits from the mines were flowing steadily into his coffer and the capable merchants under his reign diversified this income with other forms of trade, operating under pseudonyms and administering royal estates.

These snatches of commerces overheard in corridors and banqueting halls reminded me of dusty mule-paths, trade caravans, and vast stretches of land and sea, stirring in me the longing to set out as a wanderer, until again I was summoned by the senior eunuchs to deliver a message or clean the chamber pots.

It was some time before I was again permitted to interact with the ladies of the hareem, whose station was an elevated one from those servants who only waited at the King's formal dinners and receptions. I was told that his

Majesty wished to display me with the others -- that it was a special occasion during which my past transgressions would temporarily be set aside.

They were disappointed to see that I was immune to this show of favour, I gave my assent and nothing more.

Small dishes were brought forward, rose water and petals decorating and adding fragrance. Saffron and tamarind, walnut stuffed dates, roast chicken stuffed with apricots, prunes and orange. We finished the meal with orange and cinnamon sorbet. These were set between myself and an old shaman with long pleated hair, and were allowed to depart untouched -- for this man ate nothing and it was against custom for the younger to eat before the senior guest.

Following the dinner, the Magi priests of the warrior goddess Anahita approached the royal presence and brought news that the temple had been set aflame by a madman, whose punishment had been promptly executed.

This was taken as an omen, further affecting the King's mood. There seemed to be nothing but bad news for weeks, with cargo being attacked by bandits along the road and the growing rumours of invasions, as well as the usual infighting between the tribes along the border regions.

It was during times like these that the King's position felt loathsome to him, preferring instead to be an obscure and independent figure, high enough in rank and wealth to still have his way without such a precarious sword hanging over his head at all times, having surrounded himself with so many dependants.

There, too, where occasions where he longed for solitude, but could have none due to the onset of petitioners, giving him no rest from the duties of an expansive bureaucracy.

It seemed as if the King was ageing quickly, although I could never be certain of how close to the grave he was. It seemed both a thing to fear and also a relief to imagine what it would be like to have a new master, or else, that thing called freedom if it is ever to be found amongst men.

What was it that I hoped to find I did not know, I suppose it was an escape from my restlessness. After much pleading before the master eunuch, I was granted a special privilege on my twenty-third birthday.

I wandered through the markets accompanied by the royal guards, disguised with my wig of dark hair and khol for my brows, having grown proficient enough in this art to make myself less of an albino among the people. Whether this anxiety was an illusion of my own importance or that few people paid much heed to plainly dressed strangers, too busy with their own errands, I could not say. The isolation of the Ruby Palace changed me in some ways, making me nervous to go outside.

I was thankful that the guards followed at some distance and hoped that overall we would not be particularly conspicuous.

Such excursions were repeated several times until the rainstorms became frequent -- each visit to the market came at the cost of taking on the worst of the palace drudgery, but I was glad of the bargain. There was always something going on amid the stalls and bustling crowds, I would often walk by the carpets arrayed with wares from foreign lands -- gemstones, teas and spices, fine perfumes, brass work and clay pottery, it seemed like the wonders of the world were gathered there, until one grows used to novelty and it becomes something else. I had yet to find my correspondent from England and feared to arouse suspicion.

It was there that I saw Lord Ardashir again, wondering if he was not sweating beneath the morning sun in his dark robes, surrounded by the sailors and tradesmen. I would have assumed that they were haggling but their conversation was so free-flowing that I doubt they could have been setting terms.

Our eyes met and after a moment I turned to see him walking after me.

"You are one of the King's eunuchs, is that correct?" he asked, by way of an introduction. It had been a long time since we had seen each other.

I addressed him with the respect due to his rank, making a slight bow. He gestured for me to shrug off formalities and as I raised my head, Lord Ardashir discreetly gave me a message.

"What business brings you here?" he asked with a causal air.

"No urgency or King's errand calls me to this place, I should not be here I admit, but they are used to me going here and there like a stray dog," I smiled sheepishly. "Please, sir --"

"I will not tell," he smiled at me, amused. "You are quick to make your confessions"

"I have no enemies here that I must fear," I answered.

"You are like an acrobat, with your candour, be careful that you do not fall on the wrong side of the King's temper," he chided me. "I have heard things about you"

"The King has grown tired of me," I told him, "I do not worry as much as I used to"

"Then be careful not to pique his interests again," he smirked. "Are you happy where you are, serving the King?"

"There is no other place which I might call home than the King's palace," I answered tactfully.

"Spoken like a true courtier," he remarked. "Where are you headed?"

"To see the temple, I have heard much progress has been made in its rebuilding," I replied.

"What do you ask for, in your prayers?" asked the man.

"It is presumption to make demands upon God, I should hope the almighty knows his business"

"May you walk with His blessing," the man gave the sign of parting and I watched him as he left, merging into the crowd.

Chapter 21

We watched the shadow play, performed by an Egyptian occultist, Rythicaph, a friend of the King. Lord Ardashir was there among the audience, although I could tell from his expression that his thoughts were elsewhere than upon the daintily painted puppets and lute players.

I would see him often enough at court, his proud bearing and aloofness distinguishing from the fawning ways of the other courtiers.

He did not seem to me a man who would have a taste for puppet plays, nerveless, he and others stayed and waited upon the King who was grateful for such interruptions to the state of having all eyes constantly upon him.

Perhaps to some being the centre of a court came naturally, only recluses like myself preferred lingering at a distance, where I could watch without being seen, knowing that there was nothing that I much desired for myself, only that I might keep out of harms way by being little more than the furniture. For some time my hopes of returning to England had waned, given how fruitless my efforts had been both in the market and at court -- as if all conspired to deny the existence of other lands beyond the Ruby King's domains.

That night I felt a familiar visitor laying down beside me in my bed, placing a shroud of coldness and aching over my shoulders which kept me from sleep.

There are times when solitude is a beautiful thing, indeed it is the only time when one feels acutely the reverberations of the self, breathing in more deeply of the external world but passing it through one's own sieve, rather than that of surrounding gazes, real and imagined.

Yet this was loneliness, a feeling of being severed from the dream of union with other souls -- that one's mind and heart is unknown, like a body of a shipwrecked sailor which has sunk to the bottom of the sea or the mangled corpse of a solider buried by the deserts sands -- the body of a slave, whose time-altered countenance even his family would not recognize. My communion was with the night sky, with the stars whose distant eyes regarded me with constancy, reminding me of the insignificance and mortality of myself and my troubles.

There are people who do not permit themselves happiness, not without the interlacing of guilt surrounding every morsel of joy, as if they had snatched it from a greater beast for which it had been destined.

I had always felt myself to be a small clinging creature, like the marmosets who seem to look at one with human eyes but ought not to be taken for men.

I longed for warmth. For the sound of a heartbeat. I wanted to hear what it is like to rest my head upon the chest of someone who lays in my bed at night, this essence of love which engulfs me in warmth and the acceptance of my weakest self. This warmth comes from within myself and is directed back to the heart in a desperate cycle of comforting illusion.

I wonder what it is like to be in love, to desire another and to reveal one's aches and bruises to the judgement of a stranger. I thought then of Thomas Cromwell, wondering if he too might think as I, or if I had passed from his life and his thoughts.

I felt that my experience of the world had been limited, although I had seen good and evil, I had not seen them in their purest forms, and I wonder how much worse, and how much better they can be.

These are the wells from which dreams and terrors flow, hopes and anxieties which keep me from looking at others in the eyes for too long.

What does it mean to love but to open ones wounds and let flow all that is oneself.

I enjoy tales of love between the beautiful and the monstrous, the heroic and the hideous, the virtuous for the inferior -- that such things have been conceived by other minds, surely it is a sign that I am not alone in my self - abasement and my longing for acceptance.

I cannot celebrate with sincerity when the perfect is joined to the perfect, there is no room for myself in this dream.

When someone knocked upon my door, my dreamscapes vanished like smoke from a suddenly extinguished candle.

I asked myself if I had imagined this guest -- if he too had been a dream.

Chapter 22

Unchecked, love gives birth to deformed children and abominations: jealousy, spite, lustfulness, cruelty, and vanity all follow in her train, perching upon the edge of the lovers' bed to feed upon their passion.

Cromwell awoke suddenly and felt a pang of fear, lest he should forget anything of the young man which he had dreamt of. Already what they had said and done was slipping away from him, like words spoken at a distance in a foreign tongue. He tried to grasp at them, focusing upon the receding image of fantasy, but it did not wish to be grasped by so tenacious a mind, it was like a bird perching on the window sill, who sings undistributed to an unseen mate.

...

...

Chapter 23

My friends would not leave me be, incessant in their questioning, and I wondered how they knew about a fleeting exchange of poems.

"Something of great sorrow has taken place which has reminded me of your naivety, to think that after having seen what you have of the world, that you should still be beguiled by false friendship," it was Lady Uparmiya who spoke, leading me to sit on the cushion beside her. "You will confess what you had hitherto only hinted at, will you not dear child of Mithra?" she went on. "We are all aware of the attachment which had formed for a time between yourself and Lord Ardashir"

I began, drinking from the wine cup offered me, feeling myself trapped.

"This man, Garshasp, who carries your messages, who only prepends to seek your company in good faith -- in truth he intrigues with the master eunuch," said Lady Varazdat. "They think you ought to have been thrown out long ago, since your refusal to accommodate the King's pleasure"

"Will you still be married to this man Lady Varazdat, despite this?" I looked up at her, searching her calm pitying eyes.

"It is the King's will, what choice is there," replied the lady, playing nervously with her hair, "can you forgive me, Ganymede for the sorrow which I must cause you?"

"He is young at least, be happy for Varazdat who will soon be spoiled goods, at nearly five and thirty," added Lady Elaheh. "And think of Friya, who was married off quickly to a retired ship captain because the King had promised him a concubine if his cargo arrived safely. The King is a man of his word. Do not worry Varazdat when your breasts sag, if a eunuch spies and sniffs him by the brothels, the King will have himself a eunuch of Ardashir too. And this boy, he will find someone else, it will not be long before another gazelle is making eyes at him, only he needs to eat more -- there is nothing on him to hold onto"

"You know how to give fine words of comfort, sage Mother Elaheh," said Lady Anahita, crossly examining her nails.

"No one else here has any sense, like a cage of parrots," she shrugged.

"The business which they plan has little to do with Ganymede or Varazdat's engagement, you must forgive him his ignorance," Lady Uparmiya gave her a warning look, as if to level her lack of sensitivity. "They toil against Lord Ardashir, who has risen too high in the King's esteem and must come down before others more suited to the role may rise in fortune. My servant, Harina, had come to extinguish the candles for the night and heard these serpents conversing, not attending to her silent tread upon the stone floor"

"They seek to get rid of Ardashir through scandal," the Lady Anahita could not keep herself from saying, "tarnishing his name as one who makes use of the King's servants in vile ways, distorting the truth and using Ganymede as the means to an end"

"This is the sort of friendship one may find where there are many idle hours and few ways to distinguish oneself as a man," it was the old matron, Lady Majidi who had joined them, giving me an icy look. "Their lot being less honourable than that of common servants who at least serve one master and not two"

I gritted my teeth, trying to keep myself from speaking what I might repent of later. Never have I been so tried before.

"Despite the King's faults, he has treated us with kindness and I can imagine his feelings if he were to learn of plots against his trusted companions," said Lady Varazdat, looking to me for gratitude for this flattery. "What restrains me however is the fear that I may not be believed in this matter, as it incriminates the master eunuch, while Ganymede is a person of low rank who is meant to obey rather than to speak"

"Such is the custom of the palace, though the lesser servants often enough forget their station -- doing as they please," agreed Lady Majidi, as if I were not there.

"It is strange how much we all have bowed to the laws of this royal charade," murmured Lady Anahita. "As if we do not remember a thing"

"You did not scruple to rebel against your masters as Iotapa's courtesan," smirked Lady Uparmiya, hitting her lightly with her fan.

"Dare you reproach me, with your lofty origins -- in this realm of mirages even a washerwoman's daughter may be made a queen," Lady Anahita retorted. "It is like this -- I have the sense that my mind is my own and that none venture to hew my thoughts to his ideals, it suffices that I perform my duties"

"It is so anywhere," I spoke suddenly, "at the monastery I felt my guilt more strongly, to be an imposter. But here everyone plays a part, all is theatrics on a grand scale"

"Enough! I will sooner hear blasphemy than insults to the King," hissed Lady Majidi.

"And yet, even among actors sincere friendship is possible," Lady Anahita took my hand and pressed it firmly. "I have trusted you with my secrets and will do what I can to help you in this time of difficulty"

"I shall warn Lord Ardashir, for his difficulties are greater than my own and our attachment is not what you think it to be," I bowed to her in gratitude, wishing at the same time to clear some of the suspicions of a dalliance between us, wondering from whom they had originated. I had returned answers to Lord Ardashir's poems and nothing more --surely these courtly formalities are little cause for concern, and yet, I began to dwell on this point.

"I am grateful to you for this knowledge, may you enjoy the dawn of His many blessings," I said in parting to the ladies of the hareem.

...

…

Returning to my chamber, I offer my prayers to Mithra to have lived long enough to set down this record of an insignificance life in the late hours of night. In the company of the oil lamp I imagine his soul in the small flame which burns brightly through the surrounding darkness, deepening the pangs of loneliness which surround a solitary life.

I have shunned my old acquaintances, the bile of injustice having grown too bitter for me to swallow when I

think of the false eunuchs and noblemen who served the
King.

Their splendour and fine manners seem to me as the
glass baubles which adorn a painted face.

There is no beauty but in truth, no warmth but in
artless love, no hope but in the resurrection of memories
who visit me like djinn in the depth of starlit dreams.

There I still walk by his side in the secret garden of
night, where the perfume of youth and naive beauty lingers
in our footsteps, pure of thought and pure of feeling, not
yet awakened into the world of manhood, but gazing softly
through a morning mist -- there stand the palaces of the
gods, the fallen kings and the immortal lovers.

I will not let another flame take your place upon the
bed of clouds -- although the moon obscures the sun, this
darkness too shall pass.

Chapter 24

I waited at the side of Lord Ardashir, who oversaw the distribution of goods from the royal storerooms, empowered to convey the King's orders and affix the royal seal. I resented Ardashir for this summons, for his thin politeness, wondering for what cruel purpose he kept me in his company, exchanging not a word between us except the giving and obeying of orders. Perhaps it was Lady Anahita who had arranged it so on our behalf, such that that we need not conjure a false pretence for our parting encounter, yet too many people surrounded us for me to speak with him openly.

It filled me with awe, this image of abundance and munificence, and I wondered that the King of England does not do likewise to win popularity -- I can imagine how the populace would feel if they saw him so, distributing alms, as I waited for a chance to be alone with Ardashir.

I could tell that his mind was preoccupied with other matters but I had to warn him of what I had learned.

It was only after the royal reception that I arranged to meet him again in the gardens. This time I was careful to make sure that we were alone, paranoid that I was being followed.

The result of our interview was that we nearly quarrelled, he struggled to believe me in this matter, imaging it to be a fanciful tale woven by the court ladies which the other eunuchs told them to play a joke, with myself as its victim.

Such antics and flirtations were common enough and I was hardly one of the King's favourites to be a cause of concern. He feared little of any scandal which might attach itself to his name by seducing one of the royal concubines, one far from his prime of youthful beauty. I forbore these insults, remaining silent as he uttered his reproaches.

I wanted to believe that it was his way with comping with anger and fear, to lash out at the messenger of bad tidings.

Despite his mocking of His Excellency, he had long been in the service of the Ruby King and felt secure in his position to do as he pleased -- I was less certain, for both him and myself.

When we parted ways, I was left feeling foolish, having misinterpreted the severity of the consequences of our brief exchange, but then I could not forget what I had heard of. The eunuchs involved must have been like trained actors, to have put on such a convincing show of plotting immanent scandal. Perhaps they were as ignorant as I -- or else, that Lord Ardashir was mistaken.

I told myself that I could do no more, having warned him of the King's anger, it was for my friend to decide how best to act -- there was still time to make full confession and ask for mercy, or else to leave the palace for other harbours. I no longer trusted myself to guide him.

I returned to my chambers, where a messenger told me on the way that I had been wanted at the royal hareem.

I washed my face with rosewater, trying to cleanse myself of my grey emotions, as they did not care to see a man with a weight upon his shoulders. I hurried to the point of breathlessness and was much relieved to find that none were upset that I had kept them waiting, for it was not long since they called for me.

I was relieved too when they did not ask me how the interview the Ardashir went, admiring their kindness and discretion.

They dressed me in their robes while Lady Anahita put on the beard of an actor and the tunic of a soldier. She would at times slip away and go to the market disguised as a man, flirting with the vendor of cheap jewellery, scarves, khol, and dry fruits.

This escapade started as a jest but grew to be a true attachment. There were times when Lady Anahita appeared melancholy, leading me away to the balcony to talk.

She told me of her wishes to have been born a man, feeling not only the burden of a reclusive guarded life, but also the impossibility of becoming as a lover to the one whom she loved, despite the difference in their station. This was not an obstacle for some women, I had told her, having heard of such things, however obscurely.

But she told me that would not be enough, and even this she was too much afraid to peruse at the risk of being discovered. She had already promised her sister that she would not venture to the market again, for one of the King's grooms had seen her and threatened to report the incident unless given a bribe.

Even so, it was not guaranteed that the covetous man would be satisfied, and he had received all that Lady Anahita and her sister had saved away.

They could sell their jewels, but then the risk of being discovered by the King would only increase, if ever he should ask about them or if the jewels were recognized.

I told her that I agreed it was best not to risk such plans unless she was prepared to give up the life which she led and face whatever consequences might likely come of it. With the passing of time, she grew doubtful of the feelings which she had felt towards the woman at the market and stopped asking me to pass on messages and gifts of flowers for her.

I do not know whether this was a kindness or a cruelty, but I was able to observe that my friend became morose and our relations grew very strained.

I was summoned the the hareem less often, as the other women of Lady Majidi's disposition thought me a dangerous influence, seeing me as one who aided and corrupted rebellious women and perhaps had my own designs upon the King.

I grew sick of such accusations and was satisfied to remain aloof from them, remembering that I was nothing but a servant to the hareem, even Lady Anahita would soon enough forget me, for I saw a youth with dark curling hair and fine blue eyes soon become their frequent visitor and favourite, while I grew wrinkles under my eyes from too much anxiety over the troubles of strangers.

I heard nothing from Lord Ardashir since our quarrel and poisonous words sunk more deeply into my heart, making bitter what were once treasured memories. It meant something to me, more than I realized at the time, that someone at court should desire me and yet not force his will upon me.

I also missed the days when I turned to useful work rather than being the instrument of plots for indolent people who schemed and suspected one another out of sheer boredom.

Perhaps this was an unkind view to take of them but at the time I was resentful at having been so callously discarded, as I would never do to a friend, having risked my position countless times to satisfy their whims. I must resign myself to the knowledge that I am here as a servant and nothing more, an inferior being to these royal ones.

Chapter 25

News came to me that one of the King's viziers, Lord Farshid, had died in battle, while Lord Ardashir who had fought at his side was badly injured and lay in the infirmary.

A servant requested that I ask leave to attend him, for such was the man's wish, which was reluctantly granted by the master eunuch, whose unspoken warning I had no choice but to disobey, although his eyes long after lingered upon me in unusual scrutiny.

My heart pounding, I found Ardashir alone, his face was lacerated on one side. He greeted me politely but without familiar warmth, I knew that either his pain was severe or something was still unwell between us.

Indeed, after our last conversation in the garden, he had ceased to write or call upon me. I wondered if it was because business kept him away or that he had lied about his indifference towards the plotting against him.

I wanted to ask him about the wars which the King sent his men to fight, wondering who our enemies where -- for by the sign of my friend's wound, these foes were not mere illusions. But this, I knew, was deeply forbidden for those who served the hareem, who must know nothing of mortal suffering, sickness or pain.

Those of the ladies and eunuchs who fell ill were sent away, only few returned to us, and resisted all questioning upon strict orders.

It had once crossed my mind to feign illness as a means of escape, but in the end I decided not to make the attempt, lest I should not live to regret it.

Nevertheless, I tried to learn from Ardashir about how he had received the wound, even in vague terms and euphemisms, but he would not talk about it -- saying only that such things were common enough in his walk of life.

I decided not to press him further on this topic and instead read out loud to him from a book of poems which we had once enjoyed on a day of heavy rain. He remained quiet all the while and did not turn in his bed, at last falling asleep and beginning to snore.

I extinguished the oil lamp and left him to get his rest, an elderly eunuch taking my place to sit vigil over him in case something was needed during the night. The physician remained in the chamber close by, checking upon his patient periodically and rousing him to take bitter unction.

Chapter 26

I saw him sitting by the fountain, tuning his lyre.

He had a youthful face, dark curling hair and bright eyes -- the new favourite of the hareem.

I later learned that his name was Dionysus. Not his true name, of course, but his King-given name.

I lowered my gaze when he addressed me, standing close as he took a date from the bowl which I proffered.

"And what is your name?" he asked. "I have seen you before, at the moon festival"

"I am called Ganymede," I replied.

"The youth who serves wine to the gods?" I could feel him looking me over.

"Yes," I answered. "And are you the god who makes other men mad with divine ecstasy -- who dare drink from your cup?

He smirked but said nothing.

"Is it true that you have granted the King your favour, and that you are not a eunuch?" I thought it best to get the embarrassing questions over with, for this was what Lady Anahita wished for me to find out.

"It is impertinent of you to say it thus," he reproached me, but showed little sign of offence. "It is the King who bestows honour upon his subjects, and not the reverse -- it is my pleasure to serve him"

I could not quite credit his words, for his tone contained a hint of sarcasm in it, although I could not be entirely certain. "I am of a different view," I told him. "My conscience limits the scope of my pleasures"

"And where do you draw these limits?"

"He gives them a wide enough berth that he may for a while delay the necessity of defining them," it was eunuch Mirath who had joined us -- he was approaching his thirtieth year and was the harlequin among us.

"Mirath," Donysus shook his head, waving him away, "let the man answer -- and from you, who are old enough to have more discretion than to entice another eunuch into revenging himself"

"Ganymede is not the sort to seek revenge for a little jibe here and there -- are we to take it that you are a vengeful deity?" the man sat himself down beside Dionysus.

"I have not decided yet, I have only just arrived and must first get better acquainted with my worshippers"

"You may count me among them," he was about to slap the man on his backside but Dionysus grabbed his arm in time.

"If you will share with me some of your wisdom, I will be grateful to you," he addressed Mirath in a serious tone, "I have heard that you have long been at court, since the Opal Hall was constructed"

"Certainly, I am getting old enough to be wise, but I am too lazy do anything about it," Mirath laughed, rubbing his large belly. "Seek your wisdom from the master eunuch, he will tell you what to do to stay in favour, whether you like it or not"

"Nevertheless, I would like to attach myself to you as my guide, as everyone else here seems to be walking on thin glass, trembling to say a word that goes amiss -- it is great fun to reproach them if they slip and see the anxious look upon their faces," Dionysus's eyes flashed at me, "is that not right Ganymede? I heard that you know a thing or two about the King's pleasures -- did you find them not to your taste?"

I stammered for an answer -- it was Mirath who came to my assistance.

"As you are new here, I will give you a word of advice -- I am not a sensible person for you to attach yourself to, dear boy," Mirath answered, "nor is Ganymede, for we are both just pottering, getting into mischief while trying to avoid a whipping -- if you wish to climb the ladder I will see who I can find for you"

"I am not interested in sensible people, they are all rather dull," said Dionysus.

Some days later, we were summoned to wear wreathes of flowers and watch as the King presented Dionysus, his recognized beloved, with a white horse adorned with golden trappings and a silver scimitar encrusted with rubies. However, we were all more surprised to see Lady Anahita, who led the steed dressed as a page boy.

It seemed that she had reached some kind of agreement with the King to let her leave the hareem, the first of his ladies to formally do so. After the procession, she and Dionysus exchanged looks and danced the sword dance before the court, a most impressive spectacle. The celebrations lasted well into the night and I was called upon to light the torches.

...

...

"Whatever shall we do to get rid of her? She parades herself like a common courtesan," I heard Lady Mihrab speak as I brought her her hookah and tea.

"Shameless creature," tutted Lady Pacorus, thinking no doubt of the disgrace brought to the hareem by Lady Anahita liberties. "The only way to get rid of her is to let her do exactly as she pleases -- you will see"

"May I not live to see the day," she shook her head.

"Then ask her to get you some poison from the market, she goes there often enough," muttered the serving woman whose hands were busy arranging the Lady's elaborate coiffure.

"It is no trouble, Lady Mihrab," it was Anahita who had entered. I could not help but smile.

"Out," spat Lady Pacorus, dismissing me with her fan, waving in the manner in which she shoos away her lapdogs from the new silk cushions.

I heard some muffled shouting as I slowly closed the damask curtains behind myself.

Suddenly, I saw Dionysus walking past me with Mirath in tow, they were both laughing and seemed to be inebriated.

"Ah it is Ganymede!" shouted Mirath, "Ganymede! More Wine!"

"In or out, not blocking the door," Dionysus took me by the arm and half pushed, half led me back into the hareem, such that I dropped my platter of silver teacups -- luckily they were empty.

The ladies stood up at the sight of this raucous company, who were still laughing about something I had not heard or understood.

"Dionysus, why have you brought these frivolous ignorant people into my company?" muttered Lady Mihrab.

"Ignorant people are the only ones worth listening to, they say the most amusing things without trying too"

"Dionysus!" Lady Anahita ran towards him, taking him by the hand and leading him aside. "What are you doing here?"

Chapter 27

The King had been absent from the palace for two months and all who remained at court were in a state of unease. Many of the routines which had been observed for years had lapsed and the masters of ceremony were vexed by the laxity of both the servants and noblemen.

The various factions which had operated beneath a surface of obsequiousness to our monarch grew bolder.

Talk of rebellion and treason were spoken of lightly in the halls and in the shade of the orchard trees, thefts grew more frequent and visitors were less severely screened before entering the inner court.

Contrary reasons were given to me for the King's absence, some said that there were problems with the mines -- that a tunnel had collapsed, killing many of the workers and causing a revolt for higher wages, which the King refused to pay.

Those known as being the King's most loyal retainers cited an ongoing campaign against the Macedonians, which our brave regent had gone to lead in order to defend his people.

Merchants and ambassadors who had been on familiar terms with the King described how a growing sense of ennui with his microcosm of statesmanship had led him to abandon the palace for a new venture abroad, for he was still a wealthy man and had many connections who would be willing to invest with him, disbelieving that his exalted rank was anything but a mark of the man's ego, which was perhaps in proportion to his fortune.

Between these speculation, I could not feel myself
certain of what the truth was until I saw the King again
with my own eyes.

...

...

When came back to us, it was said that his Excellence
returned injured from battle.

The banquets and entertainments for the season ceased and he took his meals in his private chambers with a select few close companions.

He tried to hide it, but I could tell that he was self-concision of his crippled state, obliged to walk with a cane. His face was bruised and he looked much older than his years.

I dared not speak to him nor linger long when I carried in his meals, which was but rarely, as the more senior amongst the servants felt that it was their duty to show their loyalty to the King during his time of need.

Others who entertained grudges against the man believed it was time to gather followers, which they did in greater numbers than I had imagined.

The troop of mercenary soldiers was able to drive them from the palace gates, but it had been a close battle which left many injured. I was not there however and had to receive the news second hand, having been herded into the inner chambers with the women.

It was kept from the King that Dionysus was at the head of these uprisings, an omission which I believed would not be kept secret for long.

Chapter 28

"I feel like such a fool," Lady Anahita buried her face in her hands, sobbing while her chambermaid attempted to offer her a silk kerchief. "Ganymede," her face turned to me, "do you blame me for what had happened -- for trusting him?"

"Truly I cannot blame you," said Lady Mihrab snidely. "You have done such a thorough job of it yourself that there is little for anyone else to do but hang you"

"I did not ask you Mihrab," snapped Anahita, throwing her scarf at her, which fell halfway upon the untouched desert tray, overturning a cup of wine upon the sumptuous carpet.

"Silly girl! Look at what you have done!" said Lady Uparmiya. "And you, just sitting there like the overfed temple baboons," she got up and slapped the fingers holding a plum which Dionysus was about to sink his teeth into. It too fell on the carpet, pursued by the lapdog, Sag-Sag who wagged his tail and rolled it about like a ball.

The servant girl looked on nervously, waiting for an opportune time to attend to the mess, but something in the tension which hung between the Ladies and their guest stilled her hand.

I observed that it was not only the servants and the women who treated Dionysus unlike a eunuch, it was the men too, who seemed to regard him with a certain caution and deference.

Therefore I could understand the look of shock upon everyone's faces when they saw Lady Uparmiya strike him.

It was for Lady Anahita's sake that she did this, who had been unwell since the youth had placed himself foremost against the King, who still remained blind or ignorant to this treacherous creature amongst his concubines.

Lady Anahita had helped him gain access to the weapons storage through her connections with a general who had been enamoured with her since the fire dances of the prior year. It was he that the King had beheaded for high treason -- although he had named names, that of Lady Anahita and Dionysus were not given.

"It is cruel of you not to so much as look at me while I am breaking down in tears in front of you," Lady Anahita's voice was heard, muffled by the prayer-embroidered kerchief with which she wiped her face.

"Believe me, it is a kindness," said Dionysus coolly, reaching out to the gold lacquer bowl and taking another plum, biting into it such that the red juice dripped down his chin.

"Your heart is a stone," said the lady, looking at him with a hatred I had not seen in her eyes before.

"May his ill-advised affections be just as permanent," said Lady Varazdat, in a misplaced effort to reconcile the two quarrelling lovers.

"Just as your banishment," huffed Lady Mihrab.

"I shall not be banished," said Dionysus. "He cannot banish me, he is not a King"

"What is he then?" I asked.

Dionysus looked at me with his unnerving sphinx's eyes but I held his gaze.

"He is an imposter," he said finally.

Lady Mihrab gasped, clutching her dress close to her heart as if she had heard a great blasphemy.

"Be quiet you old cow," Lady Uparmiya muttered, at which even Lady Anahita could not help but grin.

"All decency, all decorum has vanished from this hareem," said Lady Mihrab, staggering to her feet. "I will report all that you have spoken to the master eunuch"

"I will have you killed then, both you and him," said Dionysus, leaning back languidly against a large cushion with arms behind his head, as if he were sunning himself by the fountain oasis.

Lady Mihrab gaped like a fish and the other ladies exchanged looks. I felt that the amusement had gone too far.

"I will cause the men and women of the palace to fall into madness and believe the King and his followers to be no more than wild beasts -- incapable of thought or reason, only of blind obedience," taunted Dionysus. "They will tear the King of beasts limb from limb as the women of Thebes destroyed Pentheus. If you do not wish to think for yourself, you need not notice who does the thinking for you"

"From whence comes this cruelty in you?" cried Lady Anahita, struck by his cold arrogance and strange threats.

"I submit to the being I am expected to be," answered the youth. "Is this not the role for which I was cast?"

"And what role is that?" I asked.

"The god Dionysus," he replied, unabashed.

"Then you are an actor who has read too passionately from The Bacchae of Euripides," I said, unimpressed by his efforts to frighten us, feeling that someone must subdue him.

"No, I have not read it -- I have performed it"

"Where was the play staged?" asked Lady Anahita, taking Dionysus's hand.

"In the Ruby Palace," he pulled his hand away from her and left the hareem.

I watched him with furrowed brow, resolved that something must be done before further calamity took place.

"May I eat his liver! Has this one lost his mind?" said Mirath, who ambled forth from behind a curtain, laughing like the monkey god.

"Help me wash the wine stains out, the master eunuch will be furious," said Lady Uparmiya.

Chapter 29

Scented chrysanthemum paper was folded into the heart of the rose -- I opened his message and read the words in the silence of the garden with only the birds as my witnesses:

Do you think that there is more suffering in loneliness than in the pursuit of a shadow?

To this stranger I left my reply, writing it on the back of his message:

A man's heart can break many times, but he cannot unlearn the ways of love

His name meant, *he who rules with truth*, but it was through falsehood that he took a fragment of my heart.

Every few weeks I would find notes hidden amongst the white elephant roses in the royal garden -- folded strips of parchment slipped between fragrant petals.

I would take them back with me and hide them beneath a tile of my chamber, the place where I would store my keepsakes.

Suddenly, I heard the sound of footsteps -- it was Lord Ardashir, the once bold nobleman whose face strange battles had forever marred.

"Are you waiting for someone?" he smiled confidentially.

"N-no, my Lord," I stammered, quickly hiding the note in my sash.

"What is it that you have there?" he approached nearer, unabashed.

"Nothing," I answered too rashly, my face burning.

"Keep your secrets then," he laughed. "And I shall keep mine"

Was it he? I could not help but wonder, since his affections had strayed elsewhere.

The King had formally announced Lord Ardashir's engagement to Lady Varazdat and since then I had only prayed that my friend would soon recover form his injuries, and I from mine.

It should have been obvious to me then, when I saw the way he looked at me, only I was afraid to presume, to ask for more than what his heart could bestow upon one who could bring him little happiness.

I wondered how far he deceived me, and how far I had deceived myself.

"Do you come here often?" the nobleman asked. "It is a cold night"

"When my duties permit it, yes," I replied, going to take my cloak from the stone bench where I had left it. He picked it up first and placed it over my shoulders, but it slipped to the floor.

We both bent down to pick it up, smiling sheepishly as if this too we had planned together, so that our hands might meet amid conflicting feelings.

"It is a painful experience to think about what might have been," he spoke, suddenly growing serious. "I have thought much of you while I had been away -- forgive me, if you can, for neglecting you"

"I still have the first message which you had given me, that day in the market," I told him, reaching into the inner pocket of my tunic and taking a small carefully folded fragment.

Hope calls to me when I am alone, its song reminds me of your voice

"I would like to return it to you, now that our song has ended," I offered him the paper, which he took reluctantly from my hands. "I wish you joy with Lady Varazdat, may she be a good wife to you and bear you many healthy children"

"It is by the King's will that I must marry his daughter, this is the matter which I have come to explain to you," he began. "I understand that it --"

"We must not linger here, together like this," I said to him.

A dark look crossed his face, of disappointment and annoyance, or so I interpreted it.

"It is naive to think that these forced vows need bind me, when the vows which we have spoken mean more to me than --"

"If you have vowed yourself to two lovers, always take the path of the second, for if you had need of the first -- you would not have strayed," I pronounced.

"You are right, we ought not to linger here," he bowed his head such that I could not see the look in his eyes, "I am grateful to have seen you again. Goodbye Arthamaeus"

My heart seemed to stop for a moment when I heard my old name spoken.

"How--"

"They search for you, the mercenaries from England. There is a ransom price upon your head -- perhaps the King of Rubies is not your first master?" he looked at me with an unmistakable malevolence which he tried to suppress. He handed me a letter, addressed to the King's chief steward, asking for information about a slave of my description. "I suggest that you limit your visits to the market in the near future"

"May I keep this?" I asked.

He nodded his assent and we stood in silence, searching for words.

"May your sleep be untroubled," he said at last.

I watched him leave, hiding the letter in my tunic and feeling the chill night through my cloak, wondering if I had acted rightly.

...

...

Master Cromwell, Thomas, Master Secretary -- by what name ought I to call you, when if we were to meet, I would be as a stranger to you -- so much the years must have altered us.

In the evenings the candlelight brings me comfort, I watch the flame flicker and think that there may be another world in the light -- a goodness, an energy to which all men's souls return.

It must be within the sun, I used to believe when I was a child, because it is too beautiful to look at, too powerful for mortal eyes, and yet why would it exist, forever within our sight, like a blinding beacon? Is it to taunt us, to mock us with our own weakness? No, that cannot be, for only beneath its warmth and by its light may all things grow. It is by this faith in the existence of an unattainable love, based upon virtue.

How can one love with altruism, desiring nothing for oneself, except from afar -- never making known what feelings dwell within the heart. Because to speak them, that is to cause pain -- to plant the seed of hope within oneself and give power to the beloved, who has yet to open his eyes to it.

When the cold wind blows, when the snow falls from the sky and covers the earth, when darkness hides all things except what the moon wishes to show -- then there is a yearning to move closer to the warmth of another.

Then it is so beautiful to let the dream wash over the skin in trembling visions. But lovelier still is to keep far from the fire, by which most men have been burned. Sometimes it consumes all that is best in human nature, leaving behind the dregs of jealousy and lust, a hideous obsession.

Yet what can I do but love. I am not one who can easily shake off the snares of closeness, when for so long I have toiled alone, the instrument of other men's ambitions, sent to the ends of the earth. I have assisted in satisfying many vices, coldly carrying out the orders of false kings, heedless of conscience. You are no stranger to such things, Master Cromwell, and so I trust you to pass judgement over me.

But were I to prove lost and unworthy, it remains within myself, that shard of humanity which digs deeper and deeper into my heart, reminding me when I allow my mind to wander from what must be done. All that remains of my virtue is my faithfulness to the ideal, the everlasting union of imperfect beings.

I think of you, Thomas Cromwell, you who have searched for me these passing years -- may my message reach you from this strange land. May this hope not vanish like a desert mirage before I have seen you again, wishing that I could take back the love that I had given into false hands. Do I run from vision to vision, wishing to fill a void within the heart which the revelation of love has left open, a lacerated wound torn by deception. In time I may learn to let go of Lord Ardashir, of the King of Rubies -- but I can never wash away the stains of falsehood and the shame of my own weakness. Lord Ardashir knew when we parted that neither he nor I would sleep that night.

I turn to false idols to comfort me, so that I may feel less alone. I want to believe that you have not abandoned me -- that someone somewhere has need of my used heart.

Chapter 30

Festivities were held in honour of the deity Mithra. Acrobats, dancers, poets and musicians gathered in towering pavilions to perform before the King, whose spirits it seemed had risen since he had returned to us with his injuries.

It was intended that I should also take part in the celebrations, for many hours during the preceding weeks I would take special care in practising my harp playing. I would preform the song of the Bird of Rebirth, altered by the guidance of my music master to a melody of his own composition. Embassies from Greece, Egypt, Macedon and other tribes arrived with great processions of travellers who had come to see the King of Rubies and his palace.

The King overheard what some of them would say amongst themselves, like usurers tallying up the cost of all that they saw, wondering how and why this oligarch poured out such a fortune thus wastefully,saying that he could not be otherwise than a madman, yet unable to suppress their admiration for the artists and architects who brought the oasis of paradise for mortals to cross -- a eunuch page who acted as the wine bearer was also acting as the King's eyes and ears.

After giving my performance, which was an unremarkable one amid the many talents which were gathered in one place, I was called upon to kneel before the Altar of Prophecies.

When it was my turn to be summoned by the soothsayer, I obeyed, if only to please my King.

A servant lifted the curtain for me and I entered the dimly lit room which smelled strongly of frankincense.

The soothsayer had long fingernails and a braided beard which coiled upon the floor in the shape of a sleeping snake. He did not get up from his cushion but acknowledged me with a gesture and told me to sit before the inkwell. A blank scroll of paper was placed upon a low desk.

The soothsayer had me drink from an amber-glazed cup with the fire symbol of Mithra -- the drink was a dark colour and smelled of unfamiliar herbs.

It took some time for it to take effect -- the man had me lay down until I was ready to take up the brush and set down the words of the deity upon the scroll.

At the end of the ceremonies, all that is written is gathered by the King's scribes into the Book of Mithra -- the chief prophecies and vision written in red ink, the secondary visions in ordinary black.

These are the words which flowed from the trance of the soothsayer's herbs, as I set them down upon the scroll:

What can a blind man see when he closes his eyes but the same world within as there is without

Can a soul spread its wings when the body tethers it to the earth

How I feel the weight upon my shoulders

That I can no longer move as a young man ought

I wish to run in open fields

And hear the birdsong fill the air

But I hear nothing but my worries

My heart beats with worldly cares

Where is the fresh breeze of the spring

Which once delighted me in days of old

What hope is there in worlds beyond

For unhappy lost and wayward men

What does each deserve who cannot reign in his spirit

Like wild horses are our fears and our passions

To whip them seems but cruelty

To let them be is to neglect

What purer nature lives within the stones of the mountain

Are there jewels beneath the earth

Or is there fire there

What can I find but hatred and anger

A thousand furies lash out in wrath

I cannot see through tears

A scream like the howling of the wind

A scream like the howling of the sea

The storm lashes the galleon

A thousand spirits perish

The sea cares not

It swallows all in its great maw

Will it now swallow me

And will the gulls look down in pity

At this lowly rag-doll that floats and sinks upon the waves

How the waves soar

How the sky cries its tears

The thunder races across the blackness

In an instant it vanishes

It releases the anger of the gods

What mercy is there in the dark depths

Is there a cold embrace for me

Is there a siren who will hold me

To her heart -- what heart is this beneath the sea

Is it cold like a glistening pearl

Are her eyes black as pitch

This queen of serpents

With her elegant hand she reaches out to brush away the tangling vines

On the waves I lay down and they carry me to and fro

I wish I were a boat and emptied all I carried

Into the waters casting low

A thousand treasures still unopened

Heavy chests filled with pitch

They all sink down to the bottom

No man there will reach them

No hags will bicker over my remains

To tear me limb from limb

Before I kneel down and pray

Before my soul bows at the alter of strange gods

Go to sleep now, speaks the spirit of the sea

I shall be awake to ward of the thing which you fear

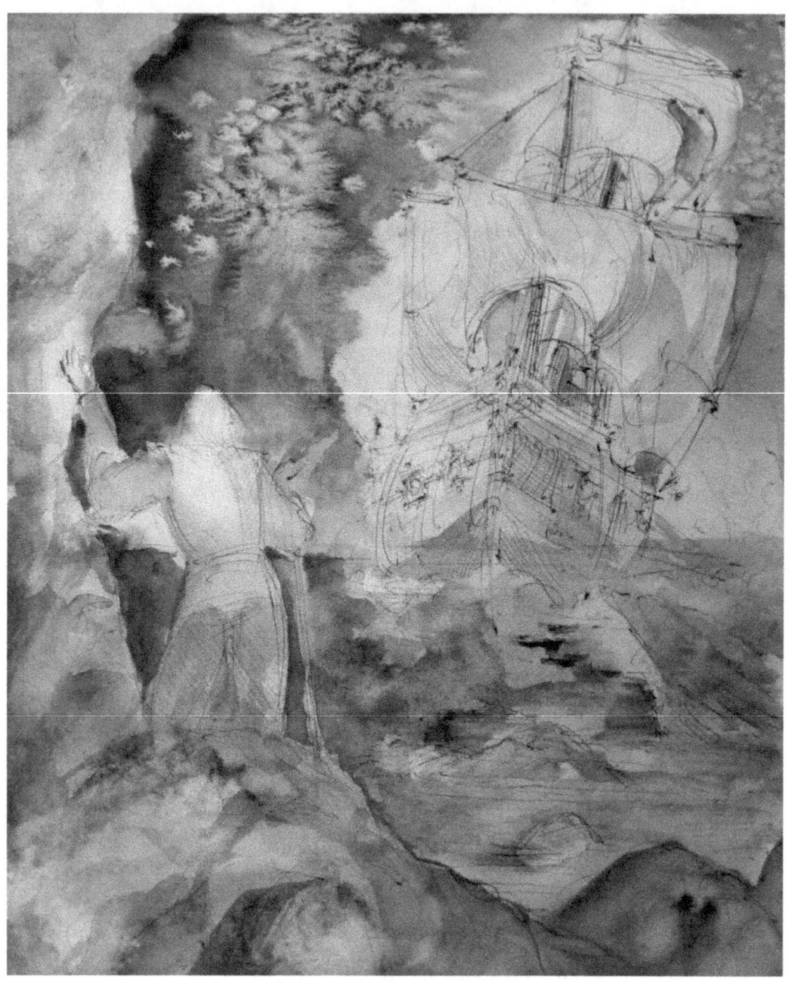

By the time I had finished, the soothsayer was asleep against his cushion, curled up like a cat. I did not know what to do, whether it was proper to rouse him.

A thought crossed me that I ought not to leave these words, for I did not believe that they were meant for the King and his people.

I took away with me my fragment of parchment, gasping when I saw the green eyes of the soothsayer upon me as he lay on his side, still in the posture of sleep.

I ran from the tent, having slipped the rolled paper scroll into the pocket of my robe. This foolish act I can only set down to the effects of the herbs that I had been given, wondering how or why I was permitted to get away.

…

I went to my chamber to hide away my frenzied poem -- but when I awoke on the following morning, when I lifted the floor tile, I saw that all of its contents were gone.

I could tell that there was something amiss from the attention that I received from the other eunuchs, but I dared not speak when the truth was plainly written.

Even the King's distant smile had something wrong with it, only then did my heart sink.

We watched the masked dancers perform for the King -- it was the dance of fire, the dance of Mithra.

I looked but could not pay attention.

Afterwards, some of the generals, servants and eunuchs went to the villa of Lord Ardashir -- I was pressed to go with them and could not easily refuse.

The minor nobles organised their own households in emulation of the template of the royal Persian court, by arranging their staff and celebrating the same rites and rituals as the King.

I closed my eyes to the passions which were shared and sought the night air of a balcony overlooking a neglected fish pond, its tile mosaic ruined by growing vines.

If I turned back to the sound of their voices, I knew that I would see their twisting bodies, hear their laboured breath, breathe the scent of their blood and it seemed to me an evil thing, neither of love nor of hatred -- this dark ecstasy of lust and sadism -- this song of the Bacchae.

I wished to run away but felt trapped until morning came. Many walked back to the palace with flower wreathes and emptied wine cups, as if the prior night had not taken place -- greeting one another as distant relations might.

Some like myself had the face of shame and remorse upon them, although we were but observers and silent witnesses.

I wondered what kind of deity Mithra was, if it was for the gods that these fertility rites were celebrated or for the passions of mortals. Lady Varazdat saw me in the procession, but I could not return her greeting with decorum -- slipping away through the servant's gate.

…

Two days passed before I was brought before the King upon the accusation of having stolen a jewel from the box of trinkets which he kept in the inner rooms approaching the hareem.

They were found in my clothing by a trustworthy servant who had no motive for deception, or such was the case brought forward to me when I was summoned to give my defence.

It troubled me greatly that the King would fall prey to such feeble attempts to slander my name, nevertheless, I knew that I had reason to fear, if my contempt had not been greater than my covetousness for continuing my servitude under such a master.

Ardashir and the soothsayer were amongst the courtiers who argued my case, although I did not always follow the reasoning of their terms of justice.

I sat mutely, waiting for my trial to be over. I believe that this must have been my punishment, for taking the scroll of Mithra's trance and for avoiding the ceremony of lustfulness, except by sweeping away the flower petals and washing away the wine stains on the morning which followed.

Chapter 31

Thinking myself alone, I sang in the garden as I admired the flowers in the moonlight, everything seemed strange and ethereal and this solitude pleased me, when I could relax my nerves.

I recalled the what had happened some time ago, a memory which had not affected me greatly then but seemed to drift back to me after the ceremonies -- how the temple was set aflame. They say that it was the King's mad son who had done it -- the eunuchs had hoped to keep it a secret, but secrets are like sand passed between many hands.

For a time, all were forbidden to enter the prince's chambers, although his screams even the thick palace walls could not fully obscure. Now I know why the eunuch, Nihari has scars upon his face, confiding in me after the incident that the prince was prone to fits of violence.

The uproar of the priests and populace is too great, comes the cries -- the secret has left like a caged bird.

The King commands Ardashir to execute the mad son, all are disconsolate. The King is irritable, guilt keeping him from sleep. Ardashir seeks me to unburden his thoughts, but no words escape his lips for I absent myself on one errand or another.

These are the memories which choose to revisit me in a new light as the palace is set in turmoil.

Lady Varazdat finds me in the garden and confides in me about her nuptial night. I struggle to keep my composure, which I believe is close enough to the effect she had hoped for. I wait respectfully until she leaves, citing my sullenness as unbecoming to a eunuch of the King's court.

Suddenly, we hear the calls of the guardsmen.

One of the hareem woman had attempted to escape, her name was Aytan and we had both arrived at the palace around the same time. I had kept her council, when she realized that I had seen her approach the window below which her beloved waited, having bribed the guards on watch.

But I was not alone who had observed their trysting night.

The master eunuch had learned of the transgression and reported it to the King, who had the roads leading from the palace searched, so that the woman must have felt like a thief or fugitive on the run.

She was at last found and whipped, falling low in King's favour, but her life was spared, contrary to all fears.

The lady's beloved, however, was taken away and I can only guess what became of him. I could hear her crying for many nights, doing my best to comfort her by words which fell heavily from my lips, knowing not the spell for soothing such deep wounds.

The walls of the hareem grew evermore a prison to my lady, and at times she confessed to me that she would have preferred to share her beloved's fate and accompany him to the garden of paradise.

I hope that there her soul dwells when she at last accomplished her purpose, glad that it was I that found her and no other, being able to speak the prayers of peace over her body so that they might accompany her on the ethereal journey.

A servant was made to confess to the fatal accident and witnesses were had to settle the matter quickly, but the

deepening sorrow which fell like a curse upon the palace
was a stain which such expedience could not erase.

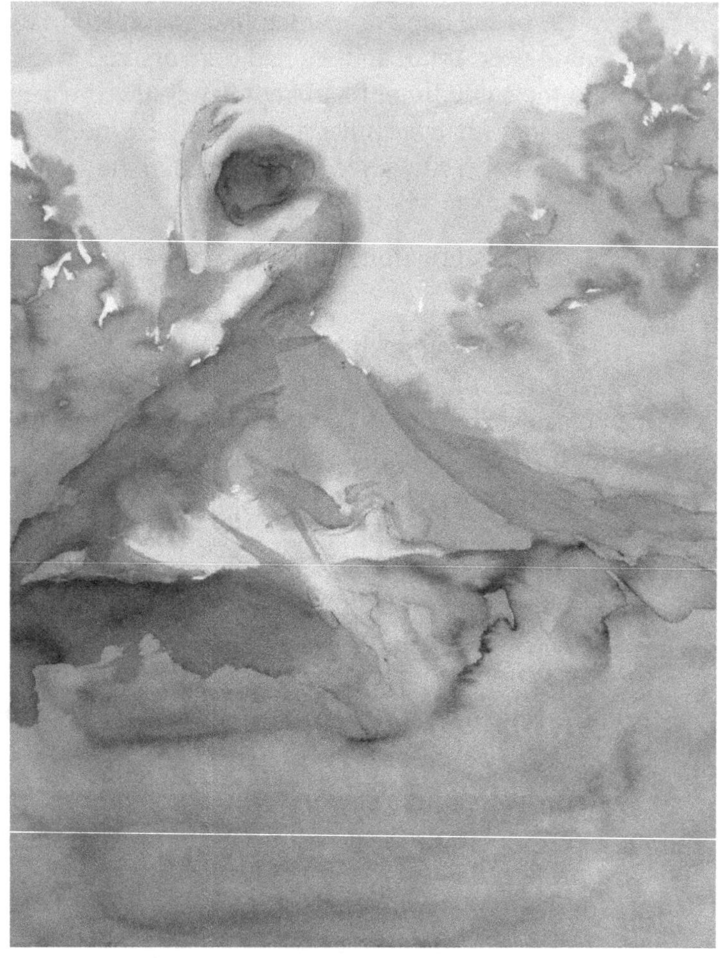

Chapter 32

I suffered long from the illness which was brought aboard the Spanish merchant ships. Lord Ardashir would visit me at times and read out loud, although it displeased Lady Varazdat. I recalled the days when Ardashir would wait for me in the garden and then take me to the fountain where we would study his manuscripts of ancient poetry -- wishing that the illness which came with these memories could be cured too by the physician's noxious drafts.

At times, when the weather was too hot, I recalled how he would take me to his private library, where I saw texts of a different nature. Some were on philosophy, history, mathematics, as well as subjects dealing with the esoteric, including necromancy, soothsaying and the making of poisons -- it seemed that he would have enjoyed a meeting with my old Abbot.

Lifting one such volume off the shelf, I inquired if he had ever put to use the knowledge which it contained -- he laughed at me, but promised me the hemlock which we would take if one of us was ever severed from the other. How childish seemed those oaths and dreams now.

When I recovered, my face was sallow and marked and I was no longer what could be called fair. The palace physician had me apply a poultice of soaked barley, which availed me a little.

"Do not pride over wealth or beauty, one will be gone in a night and the other in a fever," said my friend, Mirath -- how truly he had spoken.

From the conversations which were had with Ardashir, the nobleman was inspired to send me to a tutor, Epharasos, well esteemed for his art of poetry.

Together we made ink and sat under the orange blossom. Epharasos taught me his elegant script and the ways in which artists would adorn the pages of their work with gold leaf and ink of crushed jewels.

It is his teachings that I took with me when Lord Ardashir summoned me to admire nature, a symposium amid the pear grove surrounded by other pupils of the tutor.

It was during one of these gatherings that a jewel was formally presented to me from an anonymous benefactor.

"It is from the Master Secretary, from England -- I believe that he has known you in a past life," thus spoke the Flemish banker, who had been welcomed into our company by Lord Ardashir.

I tried to mask my trembling, asking if this gift came with a message, but the man shook his head, smiling at me quixotically. I thanked him and retired from the group to my own chambers.

Since that day, I began to plan the means to finding my liberty, feeling that I had no further ties to the palace since the severing with Ardashir. I would used the learning which my tutor had given me to make a scribe of myself and thereby support this decrepit body until the time came when I could make my departure to seek my guardian, Thomas Cromwell, writing letters in the market so that I may hide away enough coins to buy myself passage on-board a ship back to England. The Flemish banker, Janssens promised me his assistance with this matter and I was obliged to place my faith in him.

My hand is steady and legible in the guild-mens' script, my reputation is one of discretion, my fees are below market price. I advertise my services in the merchant's lane and carry back my copper and silver after a day's work, for at the palace the usual scrutiny had languished.

Even the guards would not be found at their posts.

Chapter 33

Barley was the horse which Lord Ardashir gave his wife on the day when we went to visit the mountain valleys, it was her first time on a horse and so we went slowly on our journey, with myself leading it by the reins along the stony paths.

There she was to learn of some of the plants and beasts of our land -- many of which we already knew of from the readings and specimens in the King's collection, but I believe this was but a pretence for our excursion together. The King was growing wary of our spending much time alone.

I was fearful when Lord Ardashir first laid his hand upon mine, but later I learned that this was under the King's purview -- having been paid for dearly.

A wounded pride within me stirred at the thought that these illicit embraces had been bought and sold, but it comforted me to know that my heart was still my own and I scorned Ardashir to approach me thus, leaving the hidden grove and returning to the company which were still eating their repast in the tents.

Ardashir did not speak to me further that day, discussing horse breeds with one of the generals while I was obliged to brush the knots form our Lady's hair.

I could not accept his love or offer him mine, although the King had sold me thus to him.

Upon returning to the palace, I believe that they were not long in severing the contract made between them -- a different eunuch was chosen in my place to serve Lady Varazdat and her household under the roof of Lord Ardashir.

He and other nobles were making plans for religious pilgrimages and travels, or such was how it was described, leaving the court to fall into an unaccustomed silence, where once many voices and footsteps intermingled.

Rumours abounded that the court might soon be dissolved permanently, but this view was never publically acknowledged by those closest to our regent.

On the day when Ardashir's caravan left the Ruby King's palace, laden with furniture and travelling chests, I was pained to discover that I would not be able to offer the parting words and gifts which I had planned to deliver. It grieved me that he had said little of this departure, although perhaps it may have been urgent business or the King's bidding that drove him from my company so soon.

As the months passed, I could not help but dwell on the loss of my friend. I had wished to present Lord Ardashir with a book of poems, hoping that my humble gift would serve as a token of our enduring friendship, but perhaps he has little need of such trifles of confused sentimentality.

For supper the King was served with meat and fish in rich sauces and well stuffed with herbs. A wild boar was prepared with a mixture of onion, garlic, pounded almonds, sugar, and spices. The master flute player sat by his side, but the King ate little and did not address his companions, retiring early from the banquet hall.

Chapter 34

A strange incident occurred not too long ago which was ascribed to the followers of Dionysus. The master eunuch died of an illness which spread through contamination of the wine urn -- the royal cup-bearer was punished, and some even then believed that this had been an attempt upon the King's life.

News came to me that Lord Ardashir was accused of plotting treason against the King, conspiring with other men of power to assassinate him and thus his punishment had been administrated.

Lady Anahita willed me to attend the execution of Ardashir, warning me of the consequences of showing open hostility to the King's will by my absence, but I could not bring myself to obey. Who might read in my eyes the prayers and affection which welled inside of me, despite the painfulness of our parting.

I was told that great crowds of all stations had gathered about the funeral procession, intended to shame the accused, at whom all were permitted to cast rotten fruit and small stones. Many had come to this event, so that even the veiled Ladies of the Court were jostled left and right by people trying to get near.

There were also reports of a palanquin belonging to a Flemish nobleman being carried as part of the procession by four strong men, while several servants of his shouted and pushed aside the throngs. My friend wondered who this might be but could not recognize the palanquin nor the men, yet I feared for the banker, Janssens.

Much time seemed to pass as we all waited for Ardashir to be brought forth for execution. I longed to be near my friend in his final hours, but I knew that this was not possible.

I imagined him in the bowels of the palace where prisoners were kept, in the company of men accustomed to cruelty and suffering, but perhaps even among these people there is a sense of justice.

He was brought forth naked to the stand, dressed only in the plaque of dishonour which hung about his neck, soiled with other men's blood. Its bells rang when he walked, clattering terribly down the marble steps which led down from the executioner's platform when the deed was done.

I averted my eyes as the blade descended over his neck, covering my mouth with my hand, unable to prevent the tears which welled in my eyes and would run like rivers once I found the solitude of my chamber. We were all frightened, for it had been many years since the King pronounced a public execution. Something in his nature was changing.

A messenger with panting breath was seen approaching the ceremonial judge, attired in the King's official court robes -- it was a pardon from the palace, having come too late, or so I imagined it to be, unable to hear their words.

A black smoke, as if were the shadow of a man, appeared to me that night in a dream. I believe it was the wandering ghost of Ardashir, coming to bid his goodbyes. As we walked together side by side, I imagined that the branches of the trees were reaching out to me, and the more I looked at them, the more they seemed to me like living men who had been thus petrified, their arms reaching out towards the living to grasp them and take their life. Nor did I permit Ardashir to embrace me, to give me the kiss of the dead.

…

After the painful events that marked the year, all who gathered about the King on his birthday feast struggled to keep their façades of courtly mirth, which appeared jarring to the King himself, despite efforts to elevate his spirits by wine and music.

Fine entertainments were arranged as usual, but the all too recent sorrows marked the brows of many a man.

The King became a regent known for his suspicion, a cloud which all at court feared to lure over their heads. Neither past loyalty nor royal blood sufficed to keep one safe from the regent's mistrust.

Many made excuses to absent themselves from court, claiming the illness of relatives, business of state or even enlisting in military campaigns. It felt as though only the charlatans, dancers and soothsayers remained at the King's side, and people like myself who were too insignificant to bear notice.

Many a swift horse died, but the lame mule made it safely home.

The new master eunuch, Ziberos, came to tell me that I would be departing from the palace -- I had been sold to another household, and this time, my master would accept no substitute should I refuse. "The king has tired of you," he said plainly. When I asked about my new master, the Ziberos described him as a satrap of boorish manners, who would treat me poorly and use me as a servant of the lowest rank, and then he grinned, patting me on the shoulder so that I do not know if he was joking or in earnest.

When the day of the exchange of masters came, a man came to take me on his horse to his own officials' tent where I was brought clean clothing and allowed to bathe. I was embarrassed of the decline in me when I gazed in the polished mirror. My master never removed his veil, or perhaps this was only his intermediary -- this custom was common enough among the courtiers but it was not usual upon the first meeting between two members of a newly established household. Perhaps it was true then, what the master eunuch had said, that I had fallen so low in my rank that I was hardly thought of as a person anymore.

He asked me to sing for him that night, remembering the Festival of the River Daughters. I did what I could, although I felt that my voice had failed me, I struggled to keep back tears of sorrow and bittersweet joy at the change in my fate, for I had finally left the Ruby Palace, and at least for that I could be grateful.

On the following morning, we visited the temple of the river goddesses and I prayed for the peace of Ardashir's soul, and for my own should misfortune strike us on the journey through the desert.

It was there that we heard the bells of mourning rung without ceasing when the King's assassination was made known throughout the realm.

We made haste to return to the palace, following the minarets which guided the caravans through the desert -- the master, his entourage and myself, who kept the mules fed. Long trains of camels and mules loaded with sacks of wheat, barley, and oats trudged slowly in front and behind us for safety -- my master feared we would not reach the palace in time for the King's burial.

Never had such chaos been seen.

All about me men and women took what they could -- pulling down curtains, rolling up carpets and loading them onto pack-donkeys, eunuchs carried out scrolls and two soldiers fought over the right to carry out the King's writing desk. Amid this pandemonium, all thought to leave the sinking ship first, knowing that this precarious world was crumbling at its foundations.

I abandoned my master's company, heedless of his shouts, and sought Lady Anahita, finding her with the other women, who were busied in packing their clothes and jewels into chests. There was no time, I told them, urging them to take only what is essential.

"Lock your door and make not your neighbour a thief," she hissed, scolding me for my own carelessness. I rushed to bolt the hareem entrance behind me, for in the hall I could already hear the sound of approaching footsteps.

Lady Anahita said that she would go with me by the hidden passageways and that we would make for the docks as I intended. I had the old letter from Cromwell to the chief steward which I hoped would give me passage aboard a ship to England, if such a one could be found, and if this would not do, we would barter with Lady Anahita's necklace of opals.

I trusted that this was no time when the absence of one eunuch slave would be greatly missed.

We bribed one of the palace scribes to give us his mare, giving him the cost of what he had carried off and feeling ourselves fortunate that he did not attempt to slay us as a better bargain. We attempted not to look down at the bodies and defaced grandeur all about us, it was the last memory we would have of our crumbling gilded cage.

Part 3: The Inquisition

Chapter 35

"Why are you always late to the festivities and early when a man is about to be hanged," the Duke of Norfolk exclaimed as he saw Cromwell enter the hall. "The King has a special entertainment planned for tonight"

"What kind of entertainment?" asked Cromwell.

"I shall not spoil the surprise," he answered, "here, take a glass"

Cromwell accepted the drink but only feigned to bring it to his lips, wishing to have his wits about him for the long evening while others caroused and spoke freely -- as freely as a courtier might under the strained circumstances surrounding the King's second marriage.

He fell into conversation with the Duke and others of his company, yet found himself only half attending to their idle banter and complaints, his mind distracted by an enigmatic case brought to his attention by Venetian tradesman in the shipping business.

"Lies pass through his mouth like money through the hands of a gambler," the voice of the Earl of Northumberland boomed over the others.

"Well nothing makes a man so desperate as an empty purse, you would know about that George"

"Go to hell"

"You will not be rid of him there"

"Then I better tarry here. Another glass to your health"

"When did you have time to slip the poison in"

Cromwell raised his glass with the others, his mind elsewhere. He could see the Duke of Suffolk's son approaching them.

"It has been too long since I had the pleasure of seeing you, father," he bowed to him and the company.

"Ah not seeing you too often adds to your charms," the Duke patted him on the back, "how much money do you need this time?"

"It is not like that"

"You ask if I must embarrass you at every occasion, and I say it is a father's prerogative," he turned suddenly to the man's brother, "and here's the second of my black sheep -- where did you come from?"

"Must you know?" he smirked.

"I like to know where you are coming and going from, if only to avoid you," he slapped him heartily on the back. "You see that woman, Lady --"

"Cromwell, you are rather quiet this evening -- plotting something?" asked the Duke, "you can save it for when we bring you to see the estates"

"How kind of you to remember me," replied the Master Secretary.

"I never forgot my enemies, it keeps our relations cordial and free from idleness," he patted him on the back. "It is almost hunting season, there is no better time to make a trip"

"Lord Earl Marshal is it, how are you?"

"The damn gout as usual"

"I am sorry to hear that you are unwell, sir, I hope that despite it you still live a comfortable life in the country"

"Indeed, I would not live within my means if I did not have gout," he replied, stifling a cough.

"Master Cromwell, there you are," a man accosted him -- it was the Bishop of Winchester, "I have sent you four letters and have received no reply"

"The more persistent you are in convincing him, the he is convinced"

"Excuse us your Grace," he flashed the man a thin smile before turned back to Cromwell, speaking in an unmodulated whisper. "You are nothing but a usurer, not to spare a spiritual man the means for his subsidence. The Bishop of--"

"Leave be, both you and the Bishop be hanged," said the Duke of Norfolk, ready to have the man thrown out.

Cromwell stepped between Gardiner and the Duke. "Everyone is a usurer, especially at court -- you are merely ignorant of the terms upon which you incur your debts"

He sought to tactfully lead him aside but the man would not be moved. "You have deceived his His Excellency", Gardiner continued, not to be dissuaded from his purpose now that he had captive audience, "he had paid the prodigious sums asked and yet the year passes and again the King threatens his estates"

"I have never deceived you," said Cromwell, "I simply looked on while you deceived yourself. You were given due warning that the King would delay but not reconsider his decision. It is out of my hands now, the estate has passed to the possession of the Crown, for the Bishop would not heed wise council, refusing to sign the Oath of Supremacy"

"You wash your hands of many a man's blood. Enjoy your supper, sirs," the man spat on the ground in front of him.

"Shall we call the guards?" one whispered.

"Leave him," said Cromwell. "He is unwell and shall be departing soon"

"You will see to it," said George, feeling glib. The others broke into laughter.

They resumed their conversation while Cromwell's thoughts continued to dwell upon the Bishop, going over the case and examining if he had erred in managing their predicament justly. It would not be the last which he saw of Gardiner and if he did not stop him, another man would. The Bishop had made his position with the clergy too blatantly too be ignored, much to the displeasure of King Henry, who still respected the man.

Suddenly, Cromwell saw a figure across the hall, speaking with the Spanish Ambassador, Chapuys.

At first he could not credit his eyes.

"What is it Cromwell, are you listening?" the Duke of Norfolk looked peeved, for he had been addressing him.

"Forgive me," Cromwell rubbed his temples and turned back to him, then again to the distant figure which he thought would disappear if he looked again -- but it was him -- Arthamaeus More.

It was him or he had succumbed to madness.

"The debts have to be paid in full by Candlemas or he claims he will take him to --"

"Excuse me," Cromwell strode past the Duke with a cursory bow and made his way around the gathered courtiers who blocked his path.

For an instant, their eyes locked and Cromwell could see that Arthamaeus no longer attended to Chapuys -- the two of them were staring at him as he made his way towards the end of the hall.

"Excuse us, Ambassador," said Cromwell.

"Sir --"

He and Arthamaeus soon found themselves alone with one another, for the Master Secretary had led him by the arm towards the empty balcony -- not knowing what to say, where to begin.

Arthamaeus gaped, clutching his wine chalice with a visible nervousness. He had kept an eye out for Cromwell for hours and had at last decided he would not see him at court that evening.

He was apparently mistaken.

"You have changed little, all of these years," Arthamaeus spoke at last, closing the distance between them.

The Master Secretary was past middle age, wearing plain but finely made robes accented with black and gold damask, his hazel hair intermingling with gray reaching to his shoulders. He had an aquiline nose and kind tired eyes which would occasionally fix upon the words of a whispering speaker, like those of a bird roused from a false sense of safety. "Do you remember me, Master Cromwell?" asked Arthamaeus after he had taken in the semblance of altered memories which then stood before him in corporeal form.

"Yes, I-I am surprised to see you here -- after so many years have passed," Cromwell felt the inadequacy of his words, unprepared for such an encounter. "I did not think that I would find you again amongst the living, although often I have thought of you and searched -- my agents could not trace your whereabouts since the slave ship left the docks, until Maes Janssens; then he too had disappeared"

"Why have you thought of me?" he touched his arm, "It would have been reasonable to presume me dead -- or as good as dead"

Cromwell stepped closer to him, lowering his voice, feeling his heart beating in his chest. "I have been the cause of your misfortune, Arthamaeus -- I owed much to you and my debts gave grown greater still"

I loved you under a vow of silence, obsessively and without hope, he longed to confess, still feeling that he gazed upon a phantom -- yet he could not speak such fateful words.

Arthamaeus trembled with the sensation of his touch as Cromwell gently brushed his hand across his cheek, setting back a stray lock of hair -- the faint contact like the resonance of a chord being struck for the first time in the echoing empty halls of loneliness.

"Spirits have taken my tears and my embraces to you, if you had thought of me during these passing years," said Arthamaeus. "I myself have been a spirit of something finer than myself, now that I am reunited with my body I hope that you are not disappointed"

Arthamaeus wanted to sink into his arms, feeling that he needed to reach out to him, to reassure himself of the reality of one he had been severed from for so long. It made him nervous, being unable to look past the veil between them.

"No -- we have both grown older and yet remained unchanged," said Cromwell.

"It is our stubbornness," he forced himself to smile.

Cromwell mirrored it weakly, as if one in a daze -- a man who has not fully awakened from a dream.

"I have written to you, as I promised," said Arthamaeus.

He hesitated for a moment before taking a parcel wrapped in a cloth from his satchel, offering it to Cromwell. "It is my journal of all that has happened in the past years"

Cromwell took the manuscript, for an instant an expression of surprise and guilt passing over his face, he felt a chilling faintness run through him as their hands touched.

"I have committed the secrets of my heart to these pages, and now they are yours," said Arthamaeus. "I pledge my memories to you, Thomas Cromwell"

This was a revelation which he was not prepared to hear, and yet, he was experienced in hiding his surprise.

"Thank you, I am honoured -- and yet I have done little to deserve this of you, having failed you as your guardian"

"Please, let us go somewhere where we may feel alone," said Arthamaeus, oppressed by the presence of so many strangers surrounding them beyond the curtains and lattice glass.

Cromwell hesitated, looking to see who was watching or who may have overheard as they retraced their steps from the balcony and down the adjoining corridor.

He would find a coach to take them from the hall, he would hope that the King would dismiss his absence, he would find some excuse to slip away from the oppressiveness of voices -- possessed by an unusual recklessness to do as Arthamaeus pleased, driven by past remorse and a desire to atone for his former coldness.

He could not deny himself this foible of judgement, to again cause disappointment to one who stood before him against all odds.

"You pretend to care little for others because you think there is no one who cares for you -- but you are mistaken,"said Arthamaeus as he walked beside him, trying to elicit some sign of emotion from the stoicism which enshrouded the Master Secretary. "You have not found what you were looking for because you did not desired it, not enough”

Cromwell let the man embrace him in the dark alcove of the corridor -- Arthamaeus held him tightly such that only the sound of approaching footsteps could have made him pull away.

He felt then the selfishness and cruelty of his silence, willing himself to find words to soothe the young wanderer who had returned to him, showing that time had not erased their strange bond.

“I wish that there was an undisturbed secret place where we could exist, like shadows without our faces and our bodies to betray us,” spoke Cromwell, “through you I found that I gravitate to obscure beings who wish to hide from the world, a thing which I have not the self-possession to do”

“I have been a prisoner in search of a cell, I will be merciless in my adoration now that I may offer you my heart,” said Arthamaeus, kissing his hand as his emotions welled up in his heart. “I have never been deeply afraid of dying because I had not learned to properly live. We have hidden ourselves away for too long being our masks”

“I will let you unmask me, I have no choice,” said Cromwell, leading him to sit down in one of the coaches which waited to take away the King’s dinner guests.

Arthamaeus laid his head upon Cromwell’s lap, feeling the other’s hand brush gently through his hair.

“I wish that I could just fall asleep like this,” murmured Arthamaeus.

“You cannot go about so recklessly Arthamaeus, not like this -- people may misunderstand your familiar sentiments”

"I know, but what if they see -- I am a stranger from a strange land, what do they know of my customs. Would it shock them so, if I were to kiss you. Chapuys has told me --"

"Arthamaeus, let me not lose you again," he warned him, "And do not speak too freely with your friends. I must ask you afterwards how you had made such dangerous acquaintances"

"Come with me then, or take me to the place that is your home -- there we will be safe," the man sat up, pulling Cromwell's sleeve to bring him closer.

"You are still as a child"

"It may only be the wine which makes me overbold, I am sorry Master Secretary," he leaned against his shoulder, covering a yawn. "This time you will protect me, as you have promised -- we will not part again. Promise me"

. . .

...

During the night Cromwell felt the other move, seeking his warmth. He put his arm around the younger man, whose eyes opened slightly and then closed again -- the cold night brining them together as the last embers of the fire died away.

That night, Arthamaeus had joined him beneath the blanket, laying down quietly like a cat, at first with his back to Cromwell, as if there was no where else where he could sleep.

He told Cromwell that he felt afraid to sleep alone in the guest-room, but he did not say of what. Perhaps there had been a nightmare, Cromwell did not question him, nor speak at all, giving his silent assent.

It had been a long time since he felt the presence of another human being beside him and it stirred something in his heart which had long been frozen, obscured by the puzzles and problems which were brought to him day by day, allowing him to forget himself and his own wants in pursuit of the ends of others. He remembered the vague images of his wife, the last person who had shared his bed.

The years had passed by imperceptibly, he had felt himself to be long past an age to feel such convulsions of longing. It grew more and more distant, that gap in his life.

Chapter 36

A fragile ghost seemed to speak to him that the essence of desire is idolatry. That experience banishes the mystery of love -- *I dare not lay my hands upon you in lustfulness, despite my feelings.*

My touch expresses that which cannot be put into words and cannot be extinguished, another voice purred, *the power of a touch -- subtle and timorous, is enough to set aflame the cold flesh of those who have long slept in cold chambers. You are the chimera, the alchemy of love and destruction, warmth and cruelty.*

My heart beats in my breast and yet it is cold without your touch, soon the snow will fall again, and I will lay down upon the cold earth where once we held each other amid the morning flowers.

When will the days of summer return, when will the sun shine upon my face as it did then, when I could close my eyes and feel the ghost of you, the phantom touch of one who is no more.

Where does one go when the thread of love runs on eternally, where its end cannot be found and yet my fingers are numb from the endless hardship of solitude.

I hear no voice but yours, the song which awakens the sleeper. Until I see you again, my eyes are clouded with tears, my sleeves are wet from a night of sorrow. How can I mourn that which had never been, for my lips have not known yours save for in dreams, but when I gazed at you from a distance, I lived a thousand lives, each by your side.

How is it that earthly roads should separate us, when all the worlds of my thought are inhabited by your soul's warmth.

When will this coldness melt, when will the rain wash away the memories which ought not to have been.

Why were our hearts made thus, our fates entangled, if we should end in suffering.

Would the gods be cruel to such feeble beings as you and I, who fall victim to that which the poets sing of like the birds of spring?

Why were we given such passions, such aching hearts, like the beasts of legend who mourn for a single mate.

I shroud your person in crystal tears, as I wait for you in the snow, like an insect trapped in amber you shall dwell in my love.

It will reach you wherever you shall go, I will call for you from the mountains that I will climb in the mornings when my thoughts have too much reign.

Exhausted and covered with dust I will cry out your name from the mountain, where the wind sweeps past on its journey, the spirit of the messenger god.

He will carry my longing to you, my words of love, and wherever you might be you shall hear them, you shall breathe them in, filling your lungs and permeating through your heart so that we are together once more.

What are souls made of that they should be trapped in flesh and blood.

There is too much dust cast in the path we tread, that we forget that which is noble and beautiful, what wordily cares carry us away from one another.

How can I conquer this jealous heart, how can I not long after you. May I not run to seek you, when each day is only a burden upon my soul.

Chapter 37

"Look, it is a bard owl," Arthamaeus pointed to one of the high branches of a twisting oak not far from their window.

"Yes, I see it," Cromwell said after searching some time through the darkness.

"Do you know what would be magical?" Arthamaeus walked up to him, putting his hands on Cromwell's shoulders.

"What?" the man looked up from his writing.

"To go for a walk in the garden at night -- there is something enchanting about moonlight, especially after it rains"

"You have peculiar fancies, but I see no reason to object," said Cromwell, "let us go tonight"

"Are you not too tired?"

"I think that it may help me sleep, to get some air," he said, feeling that it had been too long since he had stretched his legs.

"I will get your coat," said Arthamaeus.

"You need not treat me like an old man, you go on ahead"

"I treat you like my master"

"And are you my servant then?" he thought of what Thomas More might think of their arrangement, something he could likely not fathom without turning in his grave.

"I owe a great debt to you, for taking me in and more -- I cannot very well put it into words, only I feel that I cannot be anywhere else but here. I hope that does not sound cloying"

"You need not fear that I would send you away," he said, words which he found himself speaking often, for much of the other's fears of abandonment had yet to be uprooted.

"It is foolish of me to think in that way, but I cannot help it sometimes, to worry that things may change one day, when I get comfortable with them staying the way they are"

"Things are always changing, but I am a stubborn man, set in my ways -- it will take much to alter my domestic life"

"Do you think that you will never take another wife?"

"At my age, I do not think that it would do either of us good"

"Not even a kindly widow who would look after the house for you?"

"You and I can look after ourselves well enough, do you not agree?"

"Is this wrong, the way that we are living? I worry that you feel that way, sometimes," he said as he put on his coat.

"You know that it is not the usual way of going about it, and yet, it is not altogether different," answered Cromwell.

"Indeed," he lowered his head, "as long as we are happy, what does it matter -- I will try to think of it that way"

"Sometimes I am afraid of what may happen if we are found out, perhaps it is already suspected," said Cromwell, deciding it is best to be entirely sincere with him, and finding the confession cathartic, "but I am prepared for that, as well as I might be. We will leave the country, if it comes to that"

"I hope that it will not"

"As do I, but one cannot let down his guard"

"I feel that I have let down mine, it is draining to live in constant fear, and what more can we do without being wholly parted from one another?"

"We are only human," he placed his hand on the other's shoulder, "let us get ready and see the night garden.

"That would please me much," Arthamaeus forced a smile, "I am glad that we are far from London here, where we need not be disturbed by the eyes of prying neighbours. Let us go," he took Cromwell's arm and they walked down the staircase with the lantern in hand.

The garden was illuminated by the moon, shining down upon the rosebuds still heavy from the rain.

"Like the jewels on the hand of the King," said Arthamaeus, shining the lantern upon a bed of violets and marigolds.

"Yes, you have taken good care of our cottage garden"

They walked silently for some time, while Arthamaeus clung to Cromwell's arm, led down the paths like a lady and her suitor.

"Is something troubling you?" asked Cromwell,

"I feel like something inside of me is screaming, while I keep a straight face," said Arthamaeus, trying to describe it. "It is better to keep quiet about many things, but it wears one down"

"I understand," said Cromwell.

"You always know how to tactfully reveal nothing," he observed. "I never learned that skill"

"That is a positive sign, from my perspective -- it is a relief not to have to see through masks," he reflected. "Like shadows passing by -- they could be nothing at all and yet I am troubled when I cannot see what they are"

"I wonder if it is that, or merely my foolishness," he said, and then stopped walking for a moment, turning to Cromwell. "Do you feel at ease with me?"

"I do not know what ease feels like," he said after a pause.

Arthamaeus gave him a playful push. "Well there are intervals when I can forget fear and worry, I think to myself -- I can have no father and no son, I am here now and this moment is brief"

"Yes, perhaps it will be remembered," he tried to comfort him.

"I do not think I have anything worth leaving to posterity, I do not care to, not anymore -- I just want us to be happy, but we are both very bad at that "

"Do not try so hard, it may come more easily to you then," Cromwell replied. "Or so I have heard"

He held out a branch of plumb blossoms to Arthamaeus, who gently held the bloom and brought its petals close to him as he leaned down to breathe in the sweet perfume of spring.

"This is just how I imagined it; the cottage, the garden -- I am glad that we have this place," he looked at Cromwell, who stood by his side. "Do you truly have to go back to London soon?"

"I do"

They walked for a while longer, ambling along the garden paths, until the rain began to pour down. Cromwell took him by the arm and shielded him with his cloak, the young man laughing as they ran back to the house.

A kettle was put on the fire to boil for some tea with cinnamon, ginger and clove, while Arthamaeus went upstairs to change into dry clothing.

They drank tea and ate honeyed biscuits by the hearth and then Cromwell brought out a small book wrapped in cloth. It was a beautifully illuminated manuscript by an Italian botanist, an old friend of his who had passed away some time since Cromwell returned to England.

He too had been in the cloth trade but had a keen interest in gardening, sparing all the time he could to get away to the countryside and work upon creating an Eden for his wife, a blind woman who took pleasure in taking walks by his side and enjoying the diverse scents he collected for their pleasure.

Arthamaeus enjoyed this romantic tale, unlike most which Cromwell would tell him, which ended on a morbid note. They both felt in good spirits despite the weather.

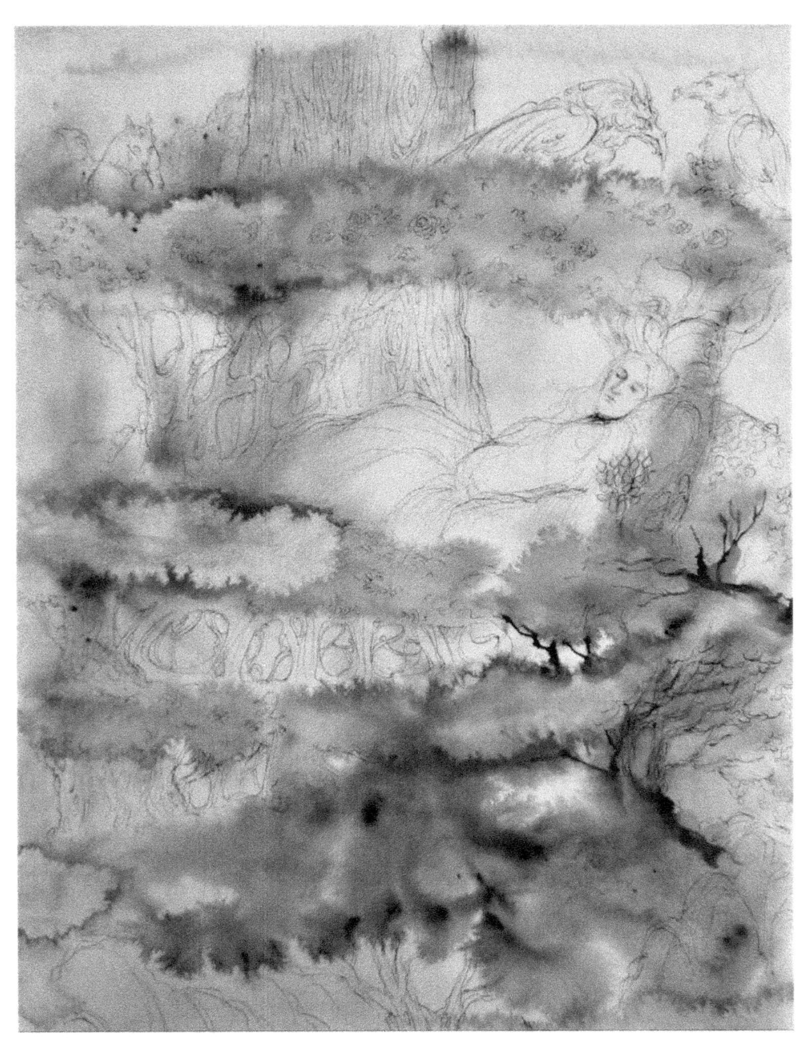

Chapter 38

While he looked outside the window at Arthamaeus reading under the apple tree, it was not the first time when he neglecting his work for this purpose. Some time earlier, he had gone downstairs and walked with Arthamaeus in the garden, asking him about what he read, summoning in his mind vague images of hideous Socrates and fair Adonis, whose paths had never crossed even in myth.

This was the wish that was born from his heart, and he ought not to have dared question it, nor examine it too closely, lest it should prove false. But as time went on, he could not resist the urge towards greater knowledge of the being which his love had made and could unmake, if what lay at its core was something decaying, a noxious intoxicating poisonous -- he believed that he could draw away before he would succumb to its paralysing effects.

It was beneath him to reject his adoration for fear of the consequences, even to his position in the eyes of the King, in the eyes of the world.

...

. . .

"Come here Arthamaeus, there is someone who I would like to introduce you to," said Cromwell, a broad-shouldered man with a ruddy complexion stood beside him, carrying a large wooden case and an apron.

Cromwell gestured for Arthamaeus to sit down on the antique chair which had been brought into the hall. "This man is here to paint your portrait," he explained.

Arthamaeus looked uneasy. "I am grateful, but I do not think it is necessary"

"It would please me to have your portrait preserved"

After some hesitation, Arthamaeus was moved to comply, an embarrassed boyish expression on his face as he sat silently before the painter, while Cromwell looked on for some moments before having to return to his work desk.

Cromwell struggled to focus as he sat before his papers, feeling vaguely that some future anguish was in store for him for what he had done. His world was beginning to turn along a different axis than before the young man's arrival, the course of which was yet uncharted except in vague dreams.

Chapter 39

"Do you see the gargoyles? I was told that this one looks like me," Cromwell pointed out one of the stone carvings to Arthamaeus.

"Yes, I see a resemblance," he smirked.

"Some create gargoyles as guardians, to frighten evil spirits, others believe that these sculptures give representation to the warning words of Saint Peter, that the adversary goeth about seeking whom he may devour," said Cromwell, taking the man's arm as they walked towards the entrance of the Salisbury cathedral.

He was pleased to see him in a light-hearted mood, beholding a sublime warmth in the youth's features which took on for him a classical beauty.

Arthamaeus sat down on the stone bench next to the Master Secretary, observing as others silently took their seats down the sombre rows, where faint whispering and footsteps were still heard before the door was closed, the sound of it shutting echoing down the corridor.

After the sermon had been given, Arthamaeus heard the singing of a choir, taking him back to the days of the Abbot which held for him a strange bitter-sweetness.

They walked past the tombstones towards the arboretum, where Arthamaeus stooped down and picked a sprig of a bluebells.

"I remember there were fields of these not far from where I lived, I would go to the woods in early May to see them after my work was done," said Cromwell.

"I wish I had seen them, that is one of the things which I longed for most while being shut away at the monastery -- that there were so many places of beauty which I would never see. The world seemed more beautiful and frightening to me then"

"Has it grown less so since you have entered into it?"

"No -- but it is otherwise than I had imagined it. I am sorry that I have not spoken to you much about what happened since our parting"

"I did not wish to press you, having read your memoirs I feared it would be difficult for you to turn your mind to those times"

"I do not wish to keep anything from you," said Arthamaeus. "All of my life I had let others decide my path for me, following the course of the river where fate had placed me, yet I understand now that you are the one who I was meant to hold on to. I hope that it does not disgust you, that I should cling to you so desperately. I wanted to tell you, although I may be mistaken; the things which you think of, the webs you weave for other men -- let them go, let go of the hangman's threads which hold you to these plotting strangers -- they will not mourn your downfall, they have no love for you" he pleaded with him. "What honour is there in such ambitions as those which lead you now? The King is but a man, you must know that -- will you sacrifice yourself so that he may have his way in all things?"

"You place your trust in men too easily, before finding whether they are worthy of it -- you think that my nature is nobler than it is," Cromwell answered, feeling exposed to the scrutiny of passer-bys, real and imagined, "might I not be like these rival courtiers which you look down upon, vying to keep their position? The court is in a precarious state, you must understand that Arthamaeus. You cannot expect me to retire from it at this time, it is not possible, not this year," he thought of his last interview with the King.

"Or the year after? You are wrong, I have been miserly with my faith, you mistake desperation for trust," answered Arthamaeus, "before, I had nothing to preserve that was my own, but as we are bound to one another, how can I remain complacent to see you walk through fire, all the while thinking that you are in control. If it is as dangerous as you say, you cannot be certain of the King's protection.

It seems to me that your enemies will soon outnumber your allies once the Boleyns fall -- you think that I hear nothing of what happens of court, just because you try to keep it from me? I am not a youth anymore, Cromwell.

I admit to you that I have kept in correspondence with Chapuys and I am prepared to bear your disapproval -- you should know that he has not forgotten you and will plead your case with the Emperor. It is he and not you who has kept his promise to introduce me in King Henry's court, he has offered me a position as a clerk -- in this way I may be of more use to you than as housekeeper and gardener"

Cromwell looked at him gravely such that the young man felt a pang of fear.

"And what has happened to make you wish to bind yourself so passionately the dying cause of Lady Catherine and rebel against my guidance -- have I done something to betray your trust? As a court official, duty prevents me from discussing court affairs as if they were merely domestic matters, particularity with servants of the Emperor. You endanger both of us by your recklessness Arthamaeus, I am shocked to hear that you have gone against me in this way," said Cromwell, trying to suppress his wroth at the other's revelation -- a rebelliousness which must have been hiding for some time behind Arthamaeus's usual meekness. "You ask much of me, to abandon my life's work and my loyalty to the King -- I suspect that I must have a word with Chapuys. I see that he has been taking advantage of you"

He said no more in reproach, reluctant to speak further on the subject until they reached home.

"Nothing has changed, not for some time," Arthamaeus took his arm insistently. "That is the essence of it -- you have been the constant. It is…it is more than just foreboding, it seems too clear that you are in harm's way, yet are too proud to withdraw from the chess game. I do not want this fragment of happiness which we have found to fade away -- can I not make you understand?"

"I too will fade and disappoint you," he replied. "Forgive me Arthamaeus, I will not live forever"

"Inevitably what you say is true. I cannot move you to change your path. Then I ask for one thing only, do not deceive me -- not now, not after this"

He took Cromwell's hand and kissed it, lowering himself onto his knees before the other.

"Get up, there is no need for obsequience," said Cromwell, but was not obeyed in this.

"Is it so unexpected, did I misread your lingering gaze?" he asked of him. "After all this time it is as if you feel nothing -- I lay beside you at night and yet you are afraid to show affection, can one commit a sin half-way?"

"Is this at the root of your conspiracies with the Spanish Ambassador, that you have not received enough affection and must captivate my attention in one way or another? A debacle of diplomacy will do it -- if Chapuy believes that I keep you as my lover -- does he? As long as you keep petitioning me on behalf of Catherine and the Emperor, perhaps he will turn a blind eye," he said dryly. "Whatever the price of our sins, I believe at this rate we will soon exasperate our creditors"

"I told him nothing -- I am your servant and apprentice, and nothing more -- I am not a fool," Arthamaeus retorted. "But we are not the sort of men who pine for immortality, in this life or the hereafter. I am not afraid of this sin, if such it be. Our lives have been grafted together after much turmoil and yet it is as if you try to pretend that we are little more than friends"

"Sometimes I wonder," he whispered, "for the hereafter I have no expectations, but let us not meet with an untimely end by parting with discretion. What romanticized legends fill your thoughts Arthamaeus that you think this will be easy -- that such unnatural bonds would long be tolerated or kept hidden?"

Chapter 40

Cromwell took off his gloves as Arthamaeus removed his coat, placing it over the back of the chair.

His gray eyes had always had an intensity about them which unnerve Cromwell, more so when he could sense the vulnerability which would be exchanged between them as the young man allowed himself to be undressed.

Cromwell's hand trembled as he traced the contours of the other's ribs, the curve of his neck, the arch of his spine, kissing the slender arms which enfolded him. It would be false to tell himself that he had never imagined the moment, and yet its reality frightened him, as if the image before him was not made to be exposed to the crude trials of the flesh, having made its abode in the abyss of dark fantasies, beyond reach except through illusions and dreams.

Arthamaeus leaned into him, pressing his hand over Cromwell's chest to feel his beating heart, as if he might rip it out and devour it, and this would make Cromwell glad; that the moment of tension would cease and that his heart would be consumed in the fire of his worshipped vision, thus consummating the emotions which had long been fermenting during the time and distance between them.

"Those are the same eyes which I had long dreamed of," said Cromwell, reaching out and brushing the other's cheek lightly with his hand, a distant look in his gaze. He felt Arthamaeus pass his fingertips over his lips, moving his delicate touch along his face like a blind man, kissing his closed eyes, his neck, his collar bone with amorous gentleness.

Cromwell felt like an inexperienced youth, who knew
not what he would see or what he ought to do with the
foreign anatomy of his lover on their nuptial night,
allowing Arthamaeus to lead his hand over his body, his
skin smooth and soft along his thighs, his limbs yielding to
every touch, their strange union a mixture of embarrassed
guilt and pleasure.

Chapter 41

"You are as fair as the the faerie king, who would lead away mortals to his endless dance," he carried Arthamaeus from the bath laughing, where he laid him down upon the white ermine fur thrown over the bed.

Arthamaeus took his hand to examine the signet ring, a ruby carved with the miniature figures of Death dancing with a maiden.

He tried to get hold of Cromwell's arm to pull him onto the bed, but the other pulled away.

"Do you have to go to the King tonight?" asked Arthamaeus, seeing Cromwell turn from him.

"I have some work that I must finish," he replied.

"Oh, is it another trial?" he murmured, "will you be up late tonight?"

"Most likely," Cromwell replied.

"Why do you do it?"

"Because it has to be done"

"What will happen if you stay here and let them go on -- they already know the verdict they must give, surely"

"The King will have me sent to the Tower"

"I am quite serious," said Arthamaeus, sitting up in the bed. "You have not been well lately and I worry for you -- you do not spare yourself"

"I am likewise serious, if I begin by neglecting my work, I will end with losing my reputation and from there, the King's trust, if he may no longer depend on me to accomplish what is needful," he attempted to explain. "You do not wish me to outlive my usefulness, do you?"

Arthamaeus felt a pang of guilt, that he had never made himself deeply needful to anyone, although he could not entirely credit the loyalty which Cromwell professed towards King Henry.

He imagined that the Master Secretary thought him little more than a male courtesan who had been raised in a convent, and did not wish to risk bringing him to court.

"What is the King's trust worth to you?" he asked.

"My life -- whether I mean to keep his trust or give it up," answered Cromwell as he put on his shoes and brushed off his coat which had fallen to the floor.

"And what if the King dies or forsakes you?" he went on, "would your efforts have been in vain?"

"There comes a time in one's life where he has passed a point of no return -- I try not to think about it," he forced a smile.

"I do not believe that is true," said Arthamaeus.

"Do you debate with me now because you do not wish to be left alone here?" asked Cromwell, sitting down on the edge of the bed.

"I understand -- I am not a child,"Arthamaeus bit his lip, turning his face from him in the darkness, "yet it might bring comfort if I could come downstairs with you and sleep on the carpet until you are finished your letters… until the coach arrives, would that…would that be fine with you?" he asked.

"That is unnecessary," said Cromwell, feeling that he was doing the other a disservice by coddling him.

"You are right, I do not want to be left alone here -- in fact, I am afraid to be"

"There are no ghosts here, unless you have committed a murder in my absence -- you often like to tell me the worst of news just as I am about to leave," he remarked.

"You may not have any, but I do, I have probably conjured them out of nothing and there is no one to blame for it but myself, but I cannot help it -- when these fears seize me," he said almost pleadingly.

"What fears?" Cromwell gripped him by the shoulder, making the young man look at him.

"That you would abandon me, when you realize how pathetic and worthless I am -- I am of no use to you, and when whatever you see in me fades, which it must, I will lose you," he said as choking tears streamed silently down his cheek.

"Some men seek in others what they have lost in themselves, but I expect little enough from you that I think you may manage it, so please dear Arthamaeus -- feel at ease at the onset of baldness, stoutness or gout. We are both rather disagreeable people, each in our way, and unlikely to find others who will tolerate us for quite as long, I believe we are stuck"

Arthamaeus laughed lightly, despite himself. "Well what do you expect, I mean…to keep things tolerable, or rather more than that?"

"That you compose yourself and have faith in my integrity towards you, I have promised to be your guardian, and as long as I am alive and in possession of my faculties I will not discard you, you may be certain of that," said Cromwell, taking him in his arms and pulling him into an awkward embrace. "I have said the like to you before but it seems hearing it has done little good, what can I do to banish these anxieties?"

"It is not your fault, it is me who questions and doubts, who cannot believe in unconditional certainties," said

Arthamaeus, reproaching himself already for being a burden to Cromwell, for keeping him from his duties, for adding to his daily stress.

"You need not believe in them, and in time you may forget to think of them,"said Cromwell. "Live each day as best as you can and do not look for eternal vows, for you are right, what is there in words if we are men and not sorcerers? I take my oaths seriously but not all men do. Listen to me now," he looked at him earnestly, "each day you may observe my actions and if they do not strike you as false, it is my hope that you will grow more at ease with your position. Be comforted by time as you may only learn of my constancy when I have passed from you or from this world's threshold"

Arthamaeus slumped limply against his shoulder like a rag doll, tears welling in his eyes as his hands clutched the fabric of Cromwell's robe. "You have been good to me, more than I deserve," he spoke, burying his face against the other's chest.

"The feeling is mutual," said Cromwell, thinking that he will likely be late. "Now get dressed and make yourself comfortable downstairs, if you wish"

He prepared Cromwell's quills for him to pass the time, cutting the long goose feathers into points, reflecting how little self-control he had showed, hoping that it was the last time he lapsed into his old fears.

A peculiar sadness seemed to interweave itself into all of his interactions with the young man, Cromwell thought to himself, as he struggled to avert his gaze from the figure across the room. He felt sorry for Arthamaeus, yet he did not know how he could help him with his inner struggles.

Chapter 42

Arthamaeus washed Cromwell's bloodied foot in a basin, drying it with a towel and then dressing it with a clean cloth of cotton. It had been caught in a fox-trap while he had gone hunting with the King.

"Do you think it will be alright?" asked Arthamaeus, "I can help you upstairs, lean on me," he placed his arm around Cromwell.

He made him comfortable in an armchair and brought him the papers he was reading before he had gone to the King, taking a seat next to him by the hearth.

"I do not know many men who do embroidery," said Cromwell.

"I know, but that does not deter me," replied Arthamaeus "it is very relaxing. Some of my happiest moments have been doing this while you read out loud to me. Does it embarrass you that I do it?"

"No, but you are an unusual person," he said, sitting down in the chair next to him. "I have grown used to your eccentricities"

"I suppose that it what comes of having too little and then too much time to myself," he mused.

Suddenly, a knocking was hear on the door.

"Wait here," said Cromwell.

"I can --"

"I insist"

Reluctantly, Arthamaeus sat back down. "Who is it?"

He watched Cromwell slowly make his way downstairs. Straining to listen, he could make out the voices of too men.

"Are you leaving now?" asked Arthamaeus when he returned and began to put on his cloak.

"Yes, I will be back tomorrow tonight," said Cromwell.

He got up from the chair, where he was feigning not to worry, carrying with him the embroidery which he had been working on, a miniature of an owl.

"Take this from me, so that you do not feel alone," said Arthamaeus.

…

He spent several days in the darkness, chained to the stone wall. No light reached him there, not even that of torches, although he could hear the muffled words of men somewhere in the distance. He tried to sleep and preserve his strength but rest was impossible in such a place, where both anger and the anticipation of unknown agonies grew within his imagination, given time to fester into nightmares inspired by murals of Hell which he had seen in his youth.

When at last they came for him, finding the Master Secretary laying groggily in the shadows, they dragged him onto his feet and ushered him down the musty corridor to another room where there waited for him a man he did not recognize. He wore a brown robe with long sleeves and a high collar, his face did not change in its imperious expression when Cromwell was led in.

With a practised efficiency, they stripped him of his clothing and tied Cromwell's arms with rope behind his back, hoisting him upon a hook while a cloaked figure held his whip poised.

They asked by what sorcery he had bewitched the King into placing such power in a low-born unscrupulous heretic. They asked how he had compelled the King into the service of Anne Bolyne, becoming like a puppet to the snake-woman's wiles. They asked what devil whispered into his ear to disband the monasteries and draw the flock away from the guidance of the Pope.

To these and other such questions Cromwell remained mute, an obstinacy which was not to be tolerated, for the two guards took turns in raising the whip to his bare back until he was haunched over with pain. He grit his teeth, trying to keep back any sign that he suffered by such unimaginative tortures, which provoked them into using fire for their means. When he was forced to kneel, a torch was brought close to his feet and ankles, singeing his skin.

Whether they were in search of the incoherent cries of a defeated man, or something more, Cromwell did not find out, as cries of a different kind were heard beyond the heavy bolted door.

A brawl of a kind was taking place and the guards looked to their master for orders. There was nowhere to flee, being trapped inside with their prisoner. They did not speak a word to one another but extinguished the torches, waiting close to the door in wait for the intruders. If their numbers were insufficient, they hoped to have the element of surprise. Cromwell remained in chains about his ankles, still kneeling as blood trickled down his back onto the cold stone at his knees.

He felt a sickening nausea, enough to throw up, but he tried to remain alert, his eyes fixed upon the closed but unbolted doorway through which men soon would enter.

The first was struck down by one of the guard, the second engaged his comrade in battle while their master assisted in the fray, although a man well past his prime.

Cromwell did not recognize these strangers, but he knew the King's insignias and believed that they had come for him. Indeed one who had freed himself of his attacker went to break through the chains and help Cromwell onto his feet.

"We must hurry," he muttered, supporting the prisoner as he lumbered unsteadily towards the door, limping from the freshly burnt flesh upon which he was obliged to trod. He was glad not to be obliged to speak whist fighting back the pain.

The King wanted a full account of what took place and who was involved in ambushing the convoy being transported from the monasteries, containing not only precious relics but also the deeds to surrounding lands and property. It could not be denied that there was much social unrest due to the changes taking place, granting the King more power and authority over the spiritual and material realms which were once the domain of the Church.

King Henry visited Cromwell after some weeks of absence from court in order to recover from his injuries. He was reluctant to describe in detail what he had experienced but assured Henry that the matter would be dealt with once he was on his feet again, in the meantime trusted agents of his were sent to investigate, interrogating men in the surrounding villages who might have been complicit in harbouring this inquisition which seemed to operated under.

For a long moment, Cromwell closed his eyes as he leaned back in his chair in a comfortable languor, dreamily listening to the music of the harp which Arthamaeus played, sitting on a cushion next to him.

Cromwell imagined that Thomas More would turn over in his grave if he knew his son's position. Arthamaeus did not leave his bedside except on errands, bringing him his food and assisting him in bathing. It was some time before he could walk even with his cane, sitting down in the garden to take some air. In the first week, physicians were coming and going daily at the request of the King and others eager to curry favour, sending men with gifts attached to petitions and letters seeking Cromwell's urgent attention.

In a way he was glad of this plea of illness to give him respite from his duties, if even for a short while, but as the pain began to subside, he knew he could not long be content with lounging about and reading, feeling a creeping guilt of work left undone cloud his time of rest.

Arthamaeus urged him to stay home for a few days more but Cromwell told him that he was well enough to sit at his desk. He still felt sore but most of the wounds had turned into scabs, itching uncomfortably but healing well enough, better than he had reason to hope for. He would make a note of some of the medicines used upon him, although physicians were always a dubious species in his book, given how many amongst their numbers were nothing more than charlatans.

"Is this what you think happens when I am gone away for too long?" Cromwell put down the papers, recognizing the weeks which followed since the incident of the fox trap.

"No," said Arthamaeus, "but I thought it would amuse you"

Cromwell smiled at him, kissing him on the shoulder.

"Well thank you, my beloved, for this cautionary tale"

Chapter 43

"What is this old ruin?" asked Arthamaeus.

"Some of the peasants nearby think it is the haunt of the Lady of the Lake"

"Why do they say that?" asked the young man.

"Look," he led him a few paces onwards and parted some branches, revealing a pond of murky green water. They saw amid some rocks an old boat overgrown with moss and bog slime, a gnarled oak tree root half buried into its decaying wood. "It must have been a long time since this was tethered here," said Arthamaeus. "And this pond -- I can see how it might be thought a place of magic. Imagine coming here at night, all on your own, when the place is shrouded with mist and you see will-o-wisp floating by you. It would be enchanting I think"

"It certainly would," said Cromwell.

"I have always wanted to write a book of legends, going about these small villages and talking to the elders, recording these old tales," he thought of a monk he had ones known who had done something similar.

"It is not too late to start, I am sure that sort of work would amuse many people, this is an age which is fond of superstition"

"Do you think some of the stories might be true -- especially the ones which recur often in different regions, could there not be something to them?"

"I cannot claim to know, but I am one who must see before he believes"

"Has anything marvellous ever happened to you in your lifetime?"

"Finding you"

"You say it like a reluctant actor reading his lines," he started laughing.

"I thought it was a fine moment to say something of the sort, I am certain you were expecting it," smirked Cromwell.

"I was," nodded Arthamaeus, heartily patting him on the back. "You were better at this when we first met"

"Was I?"

"Here, this is for you," he picked up some wild herbs.

"Saint john's wart?" Cromwell examined it.

"It is said to dispel melancholy"

"I do not think that I have need of it now, this is what I usually look like -- you have energy enough for both of us"

"You can press it in a book and then place the petals in a safe place, like in a small glass vial, and so when you look at it you can remember this happy day," said Arthamaeus. "There, that is my magic charm for you"

"You can teach the gypsies at the market fairs," said Cromwell.

"I would have liked to get married here," he told him.

"To whom -- the Lady of the Lake?"

"To you, if I had been born otherwise"

Cromwell said nothing.

"D-do you think we could?" Arthamaeus began, "get married, to have a ceremony in secret"

"I do not think we could find a priest who would humour us in this way"

"Is that the only obstacle? We could keep it secret, at night, and not have a priest. It would be under the sky, the stars would be our witnesses"

"That is a romantic notion"

"I am sorry, you must think me strange," he said awkwardly.

"I do not mind these ideas of yours, although I have never heard of the like"

"Would it be real to you, if we were to have a ceremony?"

Cromwell paused to think of an answer. "You are proposing to me, in a sense"

"Y-yes, I suppose I am," Arthamaeus looked down, his face burning.

"Will I be the bride then?"

"I can be, since I am younger," he said, "we can find a dress"

"That is curious logic"

"I do not know how it would work exactly, but the bride is usually younger, is that not true? But those things do not matter, it would be different for us in any case -- only it is the feeling behind it that would count, I think. We will make our own vows"

"To the gods of the forest and the spirits of the abbey?"

"Yes," said Arthamaeus, half in earnest and half in jest.

"It is a mad scheme, but if it will please you, I am willing enough," said Cromwell.

"I will give it more thought, the details of the ceremony, and you must tell me your wishes as well -- when do you think we might go through with it?" asked Arthamaeus.

"Preferably on a warm night"

Arthamaeus lit one candle next to an altar where stood a white lily in a pot which they had brought in from the garden.

"Here are the rings," said Cromwell.

He saw Arthamaeus in the corner of the room, taking the old wedding dress from the clothes chest and putting on the flowing fabric which had once been his wife's.

Cromwell placed the ring on three successive fingers, a custom which was to protect him from demons, and then let it rest upon Arthamaeus's third finger on the left hand.

This part of the ceremony complete, the young man urged him to hurry to the forest before it began to rain, taking off the wedding dress and putting on a long cloak.

A nuptial mass was spoken in the abandoned cathedral by the rooks, who scattered at the approach of two figures and a dog that braked at Cromwell's feet as he carried the lantern.

…

They passed an old fisherman who carried a bucket in one hand and his rod slumped against his shoulder as he teetered along the dirt road. Cromwell sat down beside Arthamaeus on the mossy bank of the river, watching as the young man searched about the roots of the birch trees.

"Do you know what kind of mushroom this is?"

"Probably a chanterelle," said Cromwell. "Although they are quite like the Jack-O-Lantern mushroom"

"I hope that they are chanterelle, it would be nice to have them in a soup -- I had read that you can tell by the aroma, but I am not entirely certain if this is right. Look!" Arthamaeus ran ahead and crouched by a grove of wild strawberries, gathering them up into his palm and eating some along the way back to Cromwell. "These are for you, try them -- they are very sweet," he held out his palm to the man, who plucked a few berries and put them into his mouth. "We could live in this forest, if you find some more we can to make jam"

"I am not sure if there are quite so many but we can keep a lookout," said Cromwell.

The river rushed in swift torrents after the heavy rainfall, making the bridge dangerous to cross, but there was no way around it for miles and so at last they resolved to attempt it. There was an abandoned shepherd cabin at a distance where they took shelter, making a meal of the wild strawberries they had collected earlier and leaving nothing to take home.

When they returned to the house at last, a fresh steaming batch of girdle cakes was carried onto the table.

"Your shoes are all wet, you better take them off and leave them to dry by the fire," said Cromwell.

Arthamaeus sat in the chair beside his desk, reading a book of poems.

"One day, we should write something and cast it into the sea in a bottle," said Arthamaeus.

"What will we write?" asked Cromwell.

"Our deepest secret or regret, so that we may be free of it"

Cromwell approached him and took the comb gently from his hand which he had used as a bookmark, standing behind him he brushed the young man's hair as he had done his wife's many years ago in the rare idle moments when they were alone together before retiring to bed. Often he would be home late from business trips or errands for the King, and would sleep in his own chamber near his study as not to disturb her.

"It is so peaceful here, when the sun has set and we have just the candlelight between us," murmured Arthamaeus, "the warmth beneath the blankets and the coldness of the room"

"Have you ever ridden a horse?"

"Only a few times," he admitted.

"We may give it another try, Bluebell is a steady old mare, I think I can entrust you to her," said Cromwell.

"I would like to try, thank you," he smiled.

"Tomorrow we will take a boat along the river, there we can be alone," he said, wishing to believe that such days would last, wishing to hold onto them for as long as he could --- his heart beating with the knocking on the door.

Chapter 44

"Drink this," said Queen Anne, pouring one cup for herself and one for her sister from a silver urn.

"What is this?" asked Lady Mary, "have I been poisoned?"

"It is a herbal tonic," she told her, "it will keep back the plague. We all have taken it"

She struggled to keep it down.

"I should very much like a marmoset but I have been kept waiting," said the Queen, a smirk crossing her face.

"Perhaps there is one in your presence who can satisfy this request,"said Lady Mary.

"I am certain that many here at court would turn themselves to marionettes for your pleasure, my Lady," said Cromwell, flashing a look towards Henry Norris.

"Cromwell, why are you lurking here?" the Queen turned to him.

"I am here to deliver a gift from the King"

"What is it?"

"A book, I believe"

"Are you fond of reading, Master Cromwell?" she asked, setting aside the gift.

"Books are companions which only make demands upon my patience and my purse, asking no more"

"And you have no need of other companions?" asked Arthamaeus.

"I have long believed that I buried my sentimentality with my wife and children"

"How many years has it been since Elizabeth died? Do you not envy those men who come home to the care of a loving wife?" she asked Cromwell.

"Generally speaking, I am too much a cynic to feel envious of men," he answered. "Or even of their women"

"What kind of wife would you have liked, if one were to keep an eye out for a suitable woman?" she asked.

"It is a relief to me that no one knows what I want, not even myself," said Cromwell.

"'I believe it is for the best that my daughter has been kept from court,' Catherine had once said," Lady Zouche set down her embroidery, "'Mary is a good daughter because there are none of these fascinating sinful women about her to emulate, as young ladies might'"

"What poor company, she must have be rather bored" said Lady Rochford, "she will be long in waiting for her chance"

"In women, morality is inspired by fear or disinterest, I know no other roads to it," spoke Lady Kingston.

"And impotence in men," observed Lady Rochford.

Lady Horsman felt discomposed for such talk to be overheard, watching and listening in tight-lipped silence.

"My husband will go to bed early when God calls on him and sleep in late when the devil forgets to wake him -- I know what he is about when he is far from home," said Margaret Dymoke, amused to ruffle Lady Horsman.

Wearied of their talk, the Queen's gaze fell again upon Cromwell.

"When you are so docile and silent, I suspect that I will soon receive bad tidings," observed the Queen. "I have heard rumours that you are speaking ill of me to the King, and here I thought I was not worth mentioning"

"These must be rumours of rumours, madam," answered Cromwell.

"It may be so. Let me not hear again that you are playing unfairly, although you are not a gentleman -- scandal and gossip are lady's weapons"

"I always play fairly amongst the King's gentlemen," he reply, "they simply do not understand the rules"

She smirked, picking up a fan of red and white feathers, its gold handle inlaid with half moons of mother-of-pearl, toying with it indolently and then setting it down.

"There is a bill that I would like passed, Master Secretary," the Queen began, leaning back in her chair while her women peered surreptitiously between their lady and her guest, who stood with arms folded behind his back in a posture of polite forbearance.

"And what might this royal order be?" he asked, as a good servant ought, impatient to get the interview over with so that he may make his next appointment.

"A small caprice I am certain you will indulge me in. It is also something which might concern you personally," she went on, hoping to tantalise and provoke him into attentiveness, "I am repaying you for your dutiful service, Cromwell, as you shall be the one to pass this law, banning the improper relations which are said to take place within the monasteries -- you, a man of the world, must understand what I am referring to, without corrupting my ladies"

"Certainly, more may be done to protect the charitable and devout laywoman who places her faith in --"

"No, not the laywomen. I mean the men -- with each other," she looked annoyed with impatience.

"Do you refer to the act of sodomy, madam?" said Cromwell.

"Precisely that," she shot him a meaningful smile, which he returned with one of his own, not to be daunted -- much used to seeing the Queen toy with her victims in this way, like a cat certain of its prey. He had been wondering when his turn would come.

"There have been rumours, only rumours I dare say," said Lady Kingston, her needle still in hand as her slender fingers moved absently, working at the piece embroidery on her lap -- a kerchief with the King's initials, "but then I look at you Cromwell, sombre as a rook,-- oh preposterous to imagine you cavorting with--do not laugh Lady Holland," she shot a warning look at one of her women in mock chastisement. "But then, what a thing to conceive, it is almost enough to dispel any such distasteful suspicions -- I have known you too long Cromwell"

The Queen's dog, Purkoy gave a well-timed yelp of approbation.

"Indeed, forgive me Queen," said Cromwell, "but I wonder that you have interested yourself with matters of such little consequence -- you need not be troubled for my reputation, although it seems that anything may be said of anyone and taken for truth"

"Little consequence?" the Queen's brow furrowed, "one can never tell when that of little consequence can become something rather perilous to those who turn a blind eye -- for example, who would have thought that a blacksmith's son would be meddling so viciously in the King's affairs"

"Viciously, madam?" he could not help but smile.

"You are amused, but it is quite true -- you have sunk your teeth into him," said Lady Anne, "he goes to you for counsel and lets you lead him by the nose. But I do not object to this so very much, as long as you remember your place and your allegiances"

"And what are they exactly?"

"Your place is at my feet and your allegiances are the debts which you have incur," she answered unhesitatingly.

"I will endeavour to repay them forthrightly," replied Cromwell, his face unreadable to her black searching eyes.

He could tell that there was something in this silence of countenance which she saw as a challenge, and at the same time was the reason which she both feared and esteemed him, like a serpent pressed to her bosom, and the King's.

"By god's will may it be so," she pronounced. "You may leave now"

"And the bill, my lady, did you have any particulars which--"

"Ah," she feigned to have forgotten, "I leave it to your judgement, I know that you will not disappoint me with regards to its severity and specificity"

He bowed to her and departed from the room, his dignified features casting a look of exasperation at the empty hall ahead of him.

...

Mary Bolyne set down the prayerbook which she had been pretending to read. "Do you really think it is true?"

"What difference does it make?" said the Queen, "he has grown too at ease at court, we must remind him what is owed"

"It is a strange sort of threat to make, if you do not mind me saying so"

"There are others that could have been made, he is a usurer, possibly a murderer, but I believe he has grown used to references to these gentile sins, and they do not much scorch him"

"And this one might do the work?" Mary made a wry face at her sister.

"If it is true, then gross hypocrisy will be added to his reputation, and even if it is false, some will wonder why he thus protests where there is no defence needed, by passing such a bill -- they will wonder, what instigated it, a long-tolerated sin to which the Church had turned a blind eye"

"I would not say a blind eye exactly, remember that urn which one of the merchants brought back?" tittered one of the ladies, "oh what was his name"

"Yes," sighed Lady Anne, "the learned Greeks certainly had their foreign ways"

"Not so foreign," Lady Kingston remarked, "I could see how one would find Chapuys's golden-locked maidservant fair"

"By one you mean Cromwell?" she arched a brow at her. "Do not be afraid to speak his name, although he is a devil"

"Cromwell," she smirked. "Yes -- did you not know? I think the Spanish Ambassador had brought him from Italy. Now he is the Master Secretary's boy"

"What is he like -- does the boy have a name?"

"He has a fine face, although he his not quite to my tastes. He is not a man, that is certain -- an uncle of mine knows the Abbot and after some drinking certain things were said which would quite shock you"

"Then you must say those certain things, if you choose to mention them," Anne commanded.

"If it pleases you my lady," the woman coughed nervously, "there is reason to believe that the young man is

More's bastard, and more than that, he is a eunuch of some kind, or a chimera"

"A chimera?"

"A kind of creature rare to be found upon the earth, possessing powers of enchantment over mortal men, masquerading as either sex"

"That is folly," said Lady Horsman.

"Certainly he has placed an enchantment upon Thomas Cromwell," said Lady Somerset, "he must be forty"

"Fifty, at least," Lady Mary placed a candied apricot into her mouth.

"Or has his hair grayed prematurely from being in our lady's presence over-much," Lady Kingston teased, at which Anne snapped her fan at her ears, causing her to wince.

"Is it certainly now -- did you not say it is only suspected?" Anne turned to her sharply. "Tell me again, how did you learn of these strange doings?"

"From the scullery woman, Mr. Tallaway she is a relative of my seamstress," said Lady Kingston. "She has such a light step and happened to be doing some cleaning in the hall by the bedchamber. Need I say more?"

"Not in polite company, no," said Lady Horsman, who had been silent all the while, casting dark looks at the younger woman.

"Lady Horsman, you cannot glare such things into non-existence"

"Then the sooner the Day of Judgement comes the better," answered lady.

"With you in our midst, the day of judgement never leaves," answered Lady Anne.

"Then I will consider myself dismissed, so that I need listen no further to improper and unmaidenly discourse" she put down her embroidery and got up sharply, leaving behind her black shawl.

"She is quick to take offence," Mary took another apricot.

"Good riddance," whispered Margaret. "I can do without her black looks"

"I wonder what kind of a lover a eunuch might make," said Mary laughing. "You must ask Cromwell when you see him again"

"And without even the pretence of maidenly modesty," reproached the Queen. "Oh whatever will be left of your reputation, dear sister?"

"That is very much your forte, I have given up on pretence," Mary retorted. "I know what you say of me, that I live for my pleasure and think nothing of the consequences -- and yet, where is this pleasure but in the past?"

"You have already lain in the bed you have made, now it is time to get up and go about your work, as a good servant might"

"And what service might I do you now my lady?" she said mockingly.

"Find this Mrs. Tallaway, I want her sent to me"

"On what charge?"

"She used to work for the Seymours who complained of her having sold goods from the larder for personal gain," offered Lady Zouche. "It is a wonder she is still about"

"That will do," said Lady Anne. "We'll have him further in our debt, our dear Cromwell"

"Why did he spare her I wonder?"

"I believe her daughter was his mistress," she said causally. "You know how the Seymours are"

"Ah, I see," chuckled Margaret. "I better keep a sharp eye on my kitchen staff, they seem to tread too close to the fire"

Chapter 45

Snow gathered on the roof of the Tower, falling in clusters of cold crystals which melted as they touched Cromwell's skin. News had spread quickly about the death of Queen Anne's son, or so the child was rumoured to be.

"It is a pity, that a prince has passed so quickly from this life," said the Bishop as he and Cromwell walked towards the King's banquet all.

"Perhaps not, he has left the snares of the world before he could be caught by them," said Cromwell.

"The same will not be said for you Cromwell," said the Duke of Norfolk. "Nor myself -- what a feast they had prepared, I suppose they could not let a thing like that go to waste"

"Do not give away the deer you have not caught, nor plan the feast before the whelp is born," Richmond remarked.

"Many a plan has been thus set aside"

"And many a woman," said the Duke.

"Still, let us make merry -- the King is in need of good cheer"

"Say nothing of the child, he does not care to speak of it"

...

"What damnable conviction possesses him to defy the King's will?"

"A strange thing, a lack of instinct for self-preservation"

"I do not understand why decent men like the Bishop are put to the Tower"

"Some things are more easily done, the less they are understood"

"Has he managed a compromise with you or do his high and mighty principles still prevent him?"

"He has reached the end of the King's patience"

"Reached the end and begun to dig"

"Can never dig enough graves for obstinate men"

"I too have had my way in many things, now who do I have to thrash for this debacle"

"He does not play fairly, that Cromwell -- he will make you think that he is on your side, and then --"

Suddenly the door opened and king Henry entered, followed by Cromwell and the Duke of Norfolk, the room gradually falling into a heavy silence. Cromwell took his seat by the Lord Chamberlain.

To delight and distract the King, a peacock was brought stuffed with capon and spice. After roasting, it was placed in a bed of beaten gold and made to wear its feathers as if alive, with the head supported by a skewer.

This was not all, for some cotton-wool was soaked in aqua-vitae and hidden in the beak, set aflame so that it seemed to breathe fire like a phoenix.

Another smaller pie was brought resting upon a silver-wrought tree; when the top was broken by a fork, small song birds flew out.

When desert was served, the Queen, who was indisposed to attend the banquet, sent the King a pair of perfumed gloves -- scented with a blend of musk, rose water, ambergris, and civet.

His majesty unwrapped the damask fabric in which they were wrapped and sent the messenger to take them to his room without much change of expression.

"I have a serious matter to discuss with you, my lord," said the Lord High Admiral.

"I am not in a serious-minded mood, would you care to have a drink with me instead?" said King Henry.

He stayed to watch the play with an look of unease, slouching and fidgeting in his chair.

Cromwell wondered who had chosen the after supper entertainment. On the stage was a man dressed in the costume of Dante, reciting in monologue.

"But he hasn't any money," I heard someone exclaim as I groggily opened my eyes.

A thin man with gray hair stood over me, peering at me like a pigeon.

I was about to speak, to ask where I was and how I had gotten there, but I soon found that I could only gape like a fish. No words would leave my mouth.

"You have saved nothing! Nothing at all you silly fellow, and now whose going to take care of you," he seemed to be holding back a certain gloating satisfaction, as if to say, he had known better.

I pulled myself up and adjusted my tunic, certain that by this man's strange attire and dialect that I was far from any land which I had once known. And yet, I understood him, and was vexed by the unpleasant feeling that this creature could read my thoughts.

This might be merely paranoia.

"You will die in a gutter! You will die in a gutter!" he leaped around me in circles like an imp, pointing his twig-like finger at me as he gave a toothy grin, no longer able to contain it.

I backed away from him, trying to look past his apish movements to find my bearing. All around me were grey stone cliff-sides and mountain ranges with little sign of civilization. We were on top of some kind of plateau.

Two moons or suns were suspended in the grey sky overhead. There appeared to be no other sign of life except for myself and this decrepit man who tempted my patience.

I gave him a look of warning, which he took heed of, for he stopped in his prance and then seemed to consider for a moment.

Then again that smirk returned.

"You are alone here, no one can help you, no one cares -- every man is born alone and dies alone," he preached, "do you see it now? Do you?"

I swatted away his finger as he waved it close to my face.

"Ah you will learn to forget that pride of yours, you will die here another death -- better not to have been born I say, a life full of toil is the lot of man, and then to grow feeble and mad, like me! A burden upon the earth! A burden!"

Something like insanity filled the old man's eyes and I backed away from him, thinking of which way I might go to escape him.

"Go! Go if you please, you will find nothing -- each cares only for himself and how dreadful it is too go a-begging!" he called after me.

I kept walking in the direction of the glowing orbs in the sky, an arbitrary choice, leading me to a cavern which compulsion made me enter.

"There he is, the Fool," I heard another voice, wishing in that moment that I had something I might use as a weapon.

"Good for nothing, a shame to his family, his ancestors turn away from him to think what he's become," the voice went on.

I continued past this lecturing, although the voice reminded me of someone who I had known all too well.

"Ruined what opportunities you had, all I invested in you -- squandered on an incompetent wretch," it said bitterly, growing neither closer nor further even as I moved from the entrance of the cave.

I hoped that my eyes would soon adjust to the darkness, but this was not the case. It was black as ink.

Chapter 46

"Poppets made of wax were found in a chest within this woman's house -- she was an abbess before the dissolution, " said the man, leading towards him a woman dressed in widows-weeds.

Cromwell recalled the Nunnery of Wallingwells, which had been willing to pay more than the year's income for exemption. He had facilitated a private agreement with the Abbess to leave the nunnery for twenty-one years in return for the use of the convent buildings, as had been the King's wish, but the King had wavered in his mercy, leaving the parties concerned at odds. The Abbess did not step down easily.

"Poppets?" Cromwell gave him a look.

"I do not mean to waste your time, sir. T-There is one," his companion rummaged into his pocket and took out what looked like a miniature figurine of man, its carved and painted face, as well as its clothing, were unmistakeably the effigy of Thomas Cromwell. "We thought you may find it…find it curious work"

"Curious work indeed -- I ought to have been troubled by terrific back pains, is that so?" he took the doll from the gruff man and turned it over, inspecting the thin metal pins stuck into the wax. "Is this your work, ma'am?"

"It is none of mine doing," she replied, fretfully looking between him and the men who held both of her arms.

"What role do you think you are playing here?" hissed the bailiff.

"I am merely myself, as I am a rather poor actor and do not wish to appear as a fool"

"What led to your home being searched?" asked Cromwell.

"She was harbouring heretics, according to one of the neighbours -- we searched the house but they must have been given warning"

"Is that so?" Cromwell looked at her searchingly.

"I do not have an answer to give you, sir," she answered, meeting his gaze.

"Who do you think placed this amongst your possessions, and by what motive?" he questioned, holding up the wax figure.

"I practice the arts, but not of that like," she replied unhesitatingly.

"Which arts?"

"Prayer and midwifery"

"It is very well done, may I keep this?" he smiled at her, but the woman did not answer. He gestured for the guards to retreat and take the Abbess back where they found her.

"But the Popish--" one of them protested.

"They are gone now, are they not -- the house was empty?"

"Y-yes, master Cromwell, but--"

"Then we will attend to more pressing matters"

Chapter 47

"Do you eat these beautiful birds?" asked Arthamaeus as he gestured to the towering dovecot.

"No, we just take the eggs, but eating doves is believed to strengthen the memory so in time I may well be in need of them"

"Do you know of any other legends about birds?"

"I am not certain," said Cromwell.

Arthamaeus was outside with a wicker basket, gathering the apples which had fallen during the wind storm of the prior night. "Come and see the robins, they have grown tame for feeding," he held out his still hand for a few moments, waiting until the robin on the garden wall hopped closer and finally descended to peck the sunflower seeds in his palm.

Cromwell smiled, looking on at the young man.

"Do you know how it is done?" Arthamaeus turned to him, "you must be very patient and come often to the same place, they are very timid but they will grow used to you. I have been trying for several months and it is only recently that they have given in. I am hoping to build a bird feeder out of some old planks that we have, that will keep them happy in the winter"

"Indeed," nodded Cromwell. "You bring a warmth to this old house"

Cromwell quenched the absurd longing which ran through his fingers as the other's hand wrapped around them, grasping it softly as they walked down the garden path.

Arthamaeus watched the swallows circling in the air, suddenly remembering a tale he had heard from the bee-keeper -- he had said that the swallows protected one who had saved a child of their kind, like guardian angels. And even without the blessing of such fortune, the mere fact of swallows choosing to nest in the eaves of one's home was a goodly portent.

He pulled Cromwell onto the grass, lying down as the summer breeze sent great white clouds floating overhead like galleons at sea.

...

He opened a chest, coughing at the dust which he had disturbed from its resting place as he pulled out a green-dyed leather quiver of arrows.

"Was this yours?" asked the young man, holding it up for Cromwell to see.

"Yes, a gift from the King,"

"Then it is not that old," he remarked, "although it has not seen much use"

"That depends on one's sense of time," said Cromwell, "the King is very fond of hunting, I, less so"

He put it back and closed the chest, feeling the restlessness of ennui.

Arthamaeus leaned against the stone window ledge, standing beneath its arch. Beyond was the expanse of countryside, rolling hills and cottages stretching out to the horizon below which the fiery sun would soon descend. He had been waiting for Cromwell to speak of what had taken place that day, the beheading of Anne Bolyne -- he could not bring himself to refer to the subject, turning to Cromwell who sat writing at his desk as if all went on, and would go on as it had. Memorandum after memorandum.

He wanted to ask what this meant for him at court, for many believed Cromwell to be in part responsible for the woman's ascent to the Crown, but something held him back.

Arthamaeus went back to the neighbouring room, scanning the bookcases as he walked alongside them, his slender fingertips grazing the finely gilded spines of leather-bound volumes systematically arranged, row upon row. He approached the mural, looking closely at the delicately painted wildflowers -- lilies and chamomile on a deep blue background perched upon delicate golden-green stems.

He pulled closer one of the wooden stools and climbed on top of it, trying to reaching a large volume.

"This is quite the collection," he remarked to Cromwell.

"Yes, I used to have time for reading," he did not look up as he spoke.

"Do you read no longer?"

"Rarely for my pleasure"

"What did you enjoy, in those idle days of leisure?"

"I do not recall such days"

"Sorry, I am distracting you," Arthamaeus felt guilty, "is there anything I could help with?"

"Not at this time, but come here -- I have brought you a gift," said Cromwell, reaching into his cloak and taking a velvet cloth containing a sapphire set in silver, a pin which he placed on Arthamaeus's tunic. "Do you like it?"

"T-thank you," said Arthamaeus guiltily, "I do not deserve it, I am more in the way than I am any use to you. We spoke earlier about finding me a tutor, have you heard anything back from Master Adger?"

"Forgive me, I had forgotten to write"

"I can do it, if you are busy," he offered.

"I will get to it, do not fear," Cromwell reassured him, "Although I thought that I might find a music master instead of turning you into another clerk"

Arthamaeus was not certain how he felt about this proposal. He opened another chest, peering inside at the folded dress of rich brocade and the diaphanous sleeping robe underneath it, embroidered with miniature blue and silver flowers along the hem.

"Whose garments were these?" he took out one and then the other, holding the fabrics up to the light to admire them. "They are very beautifully made"

"My wife's," Cromwell replied, feeling ambivalent that anyone should handle these old relics. "I had been in the cloth trade, long ago"

"Was she fair and kind and virtuous, your wife?" he asked playfully, passing his hand over the soft material, noticing a small silver locket and a strand of hair tied with ribbon hidden in its folds.

He opened the delicate clasp and looked upon the portrait of a young girl.

"I would rather that you did not raise up these ghost," said Cromwell, his quill poised and then set down again.

He left his desk and joined Arthamaeus by the chest, taking the locket which the young man offered him and closing it shut without looking.

"I have been unkind, ill-mannered -- forgive me," he bowed his head apologetically, closing the chest again, "my wish was to learn something of your life, as so little of it is known to me"

"To what purpose?" asked Cromwell.

"That I may understand you," replied Arthamaeus.

"You will not find me there," he gestured to the chest.

"But here?" he went over to the desk and lifted the latest parcel of letters which had arrived that morning.

"Yes," Cromwell smiled sadly. "A man must have an occupation, if he has little else"

"Why do you hold onto these things, then, if they bring you no comfort?" asked Arthamaeus.

"I cannot bring myself to get rid of them, not yet. Is there no person or place which you mourn for?" he asked a question of his own.

"No," he replied, "I do not think I do. When you say not yet, what do you mean? Do you look at her portrait sometimes, or those of your children?"

"Rarely," he admitted, "it brings back too many memories, mainly of my guilt -- I had been absent for most of my marriage and it was she who had raise the children.

"What was your daughter like, the one in the picture?"

"Quiet, conscientious"

"Conscientious?" smiled Arthamaeus. "Really?"

"Like I said, I had been away often, more than I would have liked to be -- Elizabeth made sure that all went well at home so that I never had to worry, although I did all the same," said Cromwell.

"Do you feel that you knew her well?"

"Not as well as I might have, as you can expect -- you are trying to make me guilty, or what is your intention?" he said teasingly.

"No, I am only curious," he said.

Cromwell looked at him in silence, trying to read him and admiring the curve of his face as he perched on the side of his desk, gazing outside the window with a boyish thoughtfulness.

"I wonder what it is like, to be a woman," said Arthamaeus suddenly.

"Then you should have gone into the theatre," Cromwell smirked.

"Perhaps I will some day, become an actor I mean--if it did not involve so many people looking at me"

"You may use puppets, although they would not be able to hear you speak, you are always mumbling or whispering," said Cromwell, discomposed by the earnest searching look which the young man was giving him, which disappeared in a flash, as if sensing the other's tension.

"Thank you for your encouragement," he lowered himself from the desk and accidentally overturning a pile of papers.

Speaking an apology, he stooped to pick them up, collecting them again in a stack, his face burning with embarrassment.

"I will have to get used to these empty walls again, once you run away with the theatre," said Cromwell, pretending that he had not noticed.

"You do not need to talk to me as if I were a child," said Arthamaeus, no annoyance in his voice but a thoughtful expression which had not fully left him. "And I would not leave you, not even to go to Cambridge -- unless you changed your mind about it, got tired of me being in the way all the time. I do wish sometimes that you would trust me with -- with something important. I will be four and twenty soon"

"It is easy to forget, when I look at you," said Cromwell. "But you are right, I can see that you are not content to wait about the house -- I am considering it, if you show some aptitude for a trade, and if it should please you"

Arthamaeus said nothing, only looking at his feet. Cromwell approached him, placing a hand upon his shoulder.

"Do you feel that I am holding you back?" asked Cromwell, "do you think it is selfish of me, wishing to keep you from the court?"

For a brief moment, the young man covered the other's hand with his own, glancing up at him and then turning back to the chest.

"You must have your reasons, I know that it is a bad time now"

"I feel you would be safer out of the public eye"

"Like the woman of the hareem," said Arthamaeus.

"I will not stand in your way, if you are not satisfied here"

"But neither will you help me?"

"I may not be able to protect you, if you seek to follow in my footsteps -- for my profession is not one which lends itself to the preservation of both one's morals and one's life. If I could think of you with indifference, I would not oppose you in this design, Arthamaeus -- but you must allow yourself to be guided away from this fire," said Cromwell. "Or your purpose will be the victim of the machinations of men who seek to make use of you to get to me.

I make no secret of the fact that I have made many enemies, and as one close to me, they are your enemies too. I believe it is not the first time we have spoken of this, but there are some who need to see for themselves and break their own bones -- I understand it, I was like that myself when I was young"

"I believed that your reasons were less noble ones than these -- that you did not wish to be alone, for what danger could there be in permitting me to study at Cambridge, even if I did not enter into a profession," said Arthamaeus.

"Is that what you want?"

"N-no," Arthamaeus admitted, "I would rather stay with you"

"Do you still see yourself as a servant here?" asked Cromwell.

"No"

"Tell me Arthamaeus, what is at the root of the matter which troubles you?"

"Do you think that you will never marry?"

"I am too old to change my ways to start living with a stranger"

"But I am a stranger"

"It pains me that you should think so," he said. "You do not expect me to change, do you Arthamaeus -- to take a wife? I believe it would put a great strain upon our relations and bring more harm than safety, if by these means you hope to preserve our secrecy, whilst doing harm to an innocent woman who might have had better prospects in the married state"

"What if you grow tired of me, and the danger which comes of our relations, what if you denounce me --"

"Do you think me such a monster?"

"I have known you to do so with other men, who you lead into a false sense of trust, make them think you are their ally -- when in truth you seek to do away with them and put another man in their place -- or is there such a great divide between your public and private self?"

Cromwell turned from him and looked out the window, not knowing what to say to such words.

"I am sorry Arthamaeus, if that is what you think"

He felt unwell, sitting down by the window alcove.

"Forgive me -- I-I"

Cromwell sat down beside him, kissing his lips gently, pulling him closer so that the man curled up in his arms.

"Promise me that everything will be well in the end"

"I cannot promise you Arthamaeus, but we will have one another through any struggles which may come," he looked into the young man's eyes, hoping that this was comfort enough.